Reader reviews for *A Letter for Hoot*

"A fascinating read! I felt like I was right there with the main characters, walking alongside and solving the case right there with them. Holly writes very well and this novel is sure to captivate your attention. I couldn't put it down— I finished the whole thing in an afternoon. A great read!"

– Chris, reader

"Vivid descriptions and a dynamic plot make it tough to put down! Part Hardy Boys, part Encyclopedia Brown. Spofford engaged my imagination on two very distinct levels: the naivety of youth in summer and the somewhat paranoid melancholy of an adult who has watched a few too many murder mysteries. I'd highly recommend to readers of all ages."

– William, reader

Reader reviews for *Hot Ice, Cold Blood*

"Gripping from page one! This book is a fantastic sequel to *A Letter for Hoot*. I could not put it down! Holly's excellent description of situations puts you right at the scene! A must read for suspense lovers!"

– Amazon customer review

"An engaging new novel and spine-tingling thriller! I once read that over 3,000 books are released to the public each day. Given that statistic, it is a daunting and brave task to put oneself out there as a new author. Lucky for all of us, Holly Spofford made the decision to share her gift when she published *A Letter for Hoot* and *Hot Ice, Cold Blood*. In each of her novels, Holly's ability to develop interesting characters is a reader's pleasure to behold, all the while leaving you on the edge of your seat as to the outcome of the story. Likewise, Holly's attention to the little details of each story rank right up there with one of my favorite authors, John Grisham."

– William, reader

Reader reviews for *The Even Game*

"Holly Spofford's final installment of her crime and murder trilogy takes the reader on a trip through the mind of a cunning and ruthless killer so bent on revenge that she eventually loses all rationality. Where this leads makes a thrilling finale to a gripping and interesting look into the mental process of obsession and how it controls and dominates the mind it infects. A thrilling end to this new writer's first masterpiece."

– Ed, reader

"To say that this book is gripping is an understatement! Holly has an incredible way with words that draws a clear picture in your mind and pulls you right into it. If this were a movie, I would be peeking through my fingers!"

– Cheryl, reader

Other books by Holly Spofford

A Letter for Hoot
Hot Ice, Cold Blood

THE EVEN GAME

HOLLY SPOFFORD

Edited by Kristen Corrects, Inc.
Typesetting by Kingsman Editing Services
Cover art design by Shezaad Sudar

First edition published 2022
ISBN: 978-0-9994143-2-3

HollySpofford.com

For Daisy and Nick
I'll miss you

CHAPTER 1

Rubi Lee sprinted away from the screaming sirens, away from the carnage in the garage. She struggled to think clearly. Behind her, red and blue swirling lights dotted the night sky. No way was she going to do time—again.

Branches scratched and tore at her party dress. Her bare arms and legs pumped in unison. Falling snowflakes blinded her. She propelled herself over the frozen ground, not feeling the cold. Violent, bloody images from the garage rolled through her mind like fat storm clouds. *Don't think about the garage! Don't think about it!* Rubi Lee forced the horrid images out of her scrambled brain.

Through Margaux Ford Park she ran to the south gate. Breathless, she stopped and was relieved to see it—the white van—where earlier, she and her now-dead brother Zeke had left it. *Don't think about him! Stop!* She knew the police would put an APB out on her and the vehicle. The sirens sounded closer and closer. *I gotta get my stuff from the van!* Twenty yards stood between her and where her phone and backpack waited. Headlights eclipsed the entrance to the park.

Sucking in as much air as her nicotine-ravaged lungs allowed, Rubi Lee raced to the van. She threw open the passenger's side door and fumbled for her backpack. The slam of car doors and voices cut through the night.

Flashlight beams cast bright streaks across the snow. The voices grew louder. She glanced through the driver's side window and saw, in the distance, two officers jogging toward the van. The crunch of snow under their boots echoed through the night. She grabbed her backpack and sprinted hard and fast in the opposite direction.

Rubi Lee ran until she thought her heart would erupt out of her chest. "Oh God!" She bent over and vomited. She stood up slowly and placed one pale hand on a tree to steady herself, then wiped her mouth and shook her head. *Breathe, just try to breathe.* Wet coughs wracked her body.

Once the coughing subsided, she rooted inside the backpack and pulled out leggings, a sweatshirt, and sneakers. She pulled the sweatshirt over her dress, yanked up the leggings and kicked off her tattered, filthy flats. She shoved her cold feet into the sneakers and thrust the flats into her backpack. She found her phone, but kept it turned off to avoid being tracked. She rummaged in the side pocket of the backpack for her beloved, trusty knife. *Ah, here you are Timmy. Thank God.* The moonlight reflected off the blade. She smiled, dropped Timmy back into the pocket, and hustled out of the park to a road. There, she'd begin a long walk, away from the lights of Washington, DC.

Rubi Lee, frozen to the core, trudged down the deserted street through the snow. She had no choice. *I need a car. Walking is gonna kill me.* In the distance, a dimly lit sign for a motel stood out against the falling snow. She hustled up the darkened driveway and took refuge under a clump of trees. A rest was needed.

A few cars were parked in front of the doors of the no-tell-motel. From her hiding spot, she checked for video cameras. None were anywhere she could see. Rubi Lee attempted several doors, but all were locked. She waited outside the squat, decrepit motel when a car skidded to a sideway stop in the parking lot. *Oh shit! Hide!* The coarse bark of a snow-covered pine tree scraped her face when she pressed herself up against it. Peering around the tree, she calculated the car was roughly twenty yards to her left. Watching and shivering, she thought, *This could be my chance to get my hands on a car.*

The driver killed the lights and clumsily hefted himself out of the vehicle. He threw his bearded head back, taking one last swig of beer, and threw the bottle into the darkness. She sized him up and smiled. *Short, skinny, and drunk—the best kind*, she thought as she watched him stumble toward the light of a room. He favored his left side and fought to keep his footing in the snow. He held his keys up to the light before finding the one to his room. Like a lion stalking prey, she padded closer to him. He bobbed back and forth and struggled to insert the key into the door. Fifteen feet stood between her and the man. Rubi Lee clenched her teeth against the cold and closed in.

"Got it!" He unlocked the door and returned the keys to his pocket.

He was barely inside when Rubi Lee charged him. Caught off guard, he fell hard when she shoved him and landed face down, yelping, on the filthy shag rug. She jumped on his back, straddled him, and pinned his arms with her knees. He struggled under her, but she overpowered him.

"Get offa me!" he slurred.

Rubi Lee wrenched his head up by his stringy,

unwashed hair. She whipped out her knife and laid the sharp blade against his throat. "You make *one* move, and you're dead," she whispered into his hairy ear. "Understand?"

His foul breath came out in spurts. "Oh God! Don't—"

"Shut up!"

The cold tip pricked his neck. "Please," he whimpered.

"Where are your keys?"

"Um, in my . . . ah . . . my pocket, the . . . the . . . jacket pocket."

"Good boy." She slid her hand into his pocket. She jingled the keys and tossed them on the bed.

He begged for his life. "Please, please don't hurt me. I gave you my keys. I won't tell no one about this."

Rubi Lee sighed. "I know you won't. You won't have the chance." And in one quick movement, he became her first victim.

She stepped outside, but the blast of cold stopped her. *Clothes*, she thought, but knew her chances of finding anything were slim. She looked around the room for things to take. She grabbed a pillow off the bed and headed into the bathroom. Off went the damp sweatshirt and clammy party dress, which she stuffed into the pillowcase. Towel wrapped around her, she grabbed a washcloth and used it to pull open the top drawer of the crooked dresser. Nothing. The second drawer held what she wanted: a sweater and a hat. *Bingo*. She changed quickly, careful to touch nothing. She used her elbow to flick off the light switch.

Pillow, wash cloth, and towel in hand, she slipped through the door and jogged toward the car. She opened the door to the still-warm vehicle. An aroma of beer and tobacco wafted into her face. "Time to get the fuck outta here." She started the engine.

* * *

As she drove away from the motel, Rubi Lee checked the fuel gauge. *Good, a full tank. I can go for a couple hours.* The snow had relented but cars crawled along. She itched to punch the gas and escape. Speeding was out of the question, given the snowy interstate and the fact that she just murdered someone. Having grown up in Louisiana and Texas, driving in the snow was something she never experienced. She glanced to her left and noticed the bright red blinking of hazard lights on other vehicles. *Guess I should put them on too—wherever the hell they are.* She punched the dashboard until she heard the rapid *click click click.*

Nerves on high alert, she stared into the blackness through the windshield. The rhythmic swooshing of the windshield wipers eventually helped calm her raw nerves. *Breathe evenly. You're far enough away from that hotel. And you left no clues you were there. Be calm*, she thought. Her death grip on the steering wheel loosened. The muscles in her neck and shoulders soon unwound themselves from painful knots. Rubi Lee nestled into the car seat and drove. Something crept across her face, something she had not felt in a long time—a smile.

BANG! A rock spewed from a salt truck grazed off the windshield, ruining her feeling of tranquil safety. "What the hell?" she screamed. "Fucking truck!" Rubi Lee jacked up the volume of the radio and focused on the lyrics of the song playing. Something about freedom and how the clothes do not make the man. The beat and vocals were catchy, like many songs from the early '90s. The heat pumping through the floor vents felt glorious on her frozen feet.

Images of her Uncle Victor lying in his wife's arms, blood pouring from his chest, crept into her head. These images were pushed aside by a more unbearable vision: her beloved brother, Zeke, lying bloodied and dead on the cold cement floor of the garage. Her handsome, loyal, younger brother was dead.

Zeke is dead. Victor is dead. And I'm on the run, driving some dead guy's car in the middle of a fucking snowstorm. And all because of one person, Rubi Lee thought. She used her sleeve to wipe her runny nose and damp eyes. One. One whom Rubi Lee would hunt down and avenge her brother's death.

I'm coming for you, Daisy fucking Taylor. Just you wait. I don't care where you are. I'll find you and your family. You'll feel pain like I do.

Her heart began to race, and her mind tingled with thoughts of revenge.

Stop, Rubi. You need to focus on driving, she told herself. Her hands shook and her head hurt.

"Christ do I need a drink," she mumbled. Ahead, she saw the white, black, and yellow MARYLAND WELCOMES YOU sign. A few miles in, she pulled off to take care of her fix.

CHAPTER 2

Inside the dingy Last Call Tavern, Rubi Lee bought a pack of cigarettes from a vending machine. Dust-covered heat lamps coughed out insufficient warmth. Wisps of heat drifted down and mingled with the cigarette smoke expunged from the handful of early-morning regulars. The group of men was dressed in plaid flannel shirts, jeans, and heavy boots. Hats of all kinds sat atop their heads. Bottles clanked and hoots rang out when someone one-upped their pal with a joke filthier than any of the others.

Rubi Lee perched on the backless barstool. From behind, she resembled a middle school boy, her petite frame swallowed up in a bulky sweater. A wool hat was clamped over her short, black hair. Her dark eyes roamed the cold, derelict bar. *A shithole like this won't have cameras*, she thought, seeing none. Discolored wood paneling hung off the walls in patches like banana peels. A behemoth old-school cash register sat opposite the bar. Its drawer gaped open like the mouth of a toothless old man. She eyeballed the cash, surprised at the amount it held. *Plenty to hold me over*, she thought.

The bartender sauntered over to her. "What can I get ya?" His watery eyes ran up and down Rubi Lee. From under the bar, he pulled out a bowl of pretzels.

She inhaled deeply and blew a stream of cigarette

smoke into his face. "Shot of Yukon." Rubi Lee helped herself to some pretzels.

He appraised her again. "Be right back."

"Make it a double!" She took her knife from her pocket and placed it on the bar top underneath a napkin.

He returned, placing the shot glass in front of her. "Ya know, for a little thing, you drink like a man."

Rubi Lee snorted, "And I can hold it like a man." She glared at him and threw back the shot. She closed her eyes and savored the warm amber liquid sliding down her throat into her empty stomach.

"'Nother?" the bartender asked.

"Yeah," she answered and glanced again at the cash register. Rubi Lee figured there was a couple hundred dollars in it. *I gotta get my hands on that.*

"Here ya go." The bartender placed the shot glass down and turned to his friends. "Hey fellas, watch this hot little lady throw back her second double of Yukon!"

As if she was some type of side show freak.

All eyes turned to Rubi Lee. With lightning speed, she pulled her knife from under the napkin and seized the unsuspecting bartender by his shirt. Rubi Lee yanked him toward her. "*What* did you call me?" She tapped his jowly face with the blade. A small cut made him squeal. The bar fell silent. A trickle of blood dripped off the shiny blade.

Eyes bulging, the bartender sputtered and coughed. "I ah, I . . . "

"Call me that again, or *any* other name, and I will stab you through the face, cut off your tiny balls, and stuff them down your throat. Got it?"

He shook like a leaf in her formidable grip. She knew

he understood. She shoved him backward before she sat back down. She threw back her shot. "Get me another." He quickly obliged and left her alone. The show over, the men shrugged and resumed their storytelling. After thirty minutes, the pack of inebriates straggled out. Rubi Lee watched the bartender stand in the door and wave to his friends. Eyes on his back, she slid from her perch and ducked under the side of the bar.

"Come to Momma!" She scooped out most of the cash but left one bill in each drawer for good measure. Doing that instead of completely cleaning out the cash register might give the illusion that the bartender wasn't robbed.

Inside the car, she stuffed the cash in the glove compartment and drove off.

* * *

The early-morning sky was a symphony of bright colors. Rubi Lee felt as if she had been awake for a week. Up ahead, a large sign for a gas station beckoned her to pull off the road and follow its neon letters like a moth to a lamp. She knew she needed sleep more than food. Insomnia ruled her life for years, but exhaustion washed over her. *I'll sleep later. Time for coffee, though.* She pulled into the large, packed lot.

Her bladder felt like a swollen balloon. Fresh air, a bathroom, and caffeine were what she needed.

She tugged on her hat and headed to the front doors. She stole a quick glance up at the flashing lights above the door and saw a camera. *Crap. I've got to keep moving.* She kept her head down and moved on. The last thing she needed was to be identified on a security camera.

Outside, Rubi Lee slurped the coffee. Even though it was weak, its heat cleared her foggy head. Her heart stopped in her chest when she saw a police cruiser crawl into the lot and pull up only ten feet away. A young female officer got out.

Quick, get in the car! In one hand, Rubi Lee held the coffee and bag of donuts. In her haste, she dropped the keys on the cold ground. "Shit!"

"Everything okay?" the officer asked. "Looks like you need an extra hand."

Rubi Lee managed a frozen smile. "I'm good, just dropped my keys." Her heart battered her rib cage. Face turned away, Rubi Lee retrieved the keys off the cold asphalt.

"You sure?"

"Yes ma'am." Rubi Lee felt her looking at her. "I'm a klutz." She forced a laugh.

"Okay. Hope your day gets better. I know mine will after a cup of coffee. You take care." The officer tipped her hat and walked off.

"Thanks again." Back in the car, Rubi Lee pummeled the steering wheel and broke out in a cold sweat. "Fuck!" Her stomach twisted at the close encounter with the officer. As she pulled out, she had a difficult time pulling her eyes from the rearview mirror. The reality of her situation crashed into her like a wrecking ball. She lit a cigarette and drew in a long, smoky breath.

A few miles later, a calmness settled her as a solution wormed its way into her head. She inhaled deeply, a smile of contentment painted on her thin face. *Time to get rid of Rubi Lee Dixon.*

CHAPTER 3

Interstate 95 rolled on interminably as did the annoying, twangy country song playing on the radio. "This shit sucks," Rubi Lee said, changing the station and stuffing the last donut into her mouth. With the last swig of coffee sliding down her throat, Rubi Lee crossed into Pennsylvania. Even after four donuts, her stomach still felt empty, and her head throbbed. Only more caffeine and nicotine would eradicate her headache. "Thank God, a minimart," she said when she passed the large blue highway sign advertising a minimart and other stops.

Rubi Lee pulled into the lot and scanned the area for police. None. At one of the six pumps, Rubi Lee saw a woman about her age filling up her car. Something about the car made her look twice—the red scrawl of *Louisiana* at the top of the license plate. Louisiana, the state where she spent too many miserable years. A state to which she and Zeke vowed never to return, especially after they moved to DC where they worked for Uncle Victor. She and Zeke anticipated a productive and happy future. Until a few hours ago when all hopes and dreams of a future blew up in her face.

Rubi Lee watched the woman replace the nozzle and walk in to pay. She pulled on her hat and followed her inside.

The bell tinkled above the door when Rubi Lee entered. The enticing aroma of fresh coffee coupled with the smoky scent of hot dogs made her stomach holler. She poured twenty-four ounces of steaming coffee into a cup, and perused the aisles for beef jerky—*Zeke's favorite*, she thought. Into the basket she placed the beef jerky, sunflower seeds, and more donuts. Satisfied with her nutritional choices, she stood in line behind the woman from Louisiana. To her left was a stand which held bleach wipes. *These may be handy.* She plucked a package.

"Next!" the cheery cashier called.

"Morning. I filled up on number three. How far until Sullivan County?" asked the woman driving the car with Louisiana tags. She handed over a credit card.

The cashier returned the card. "No more than sixty minutes. Just head northeast up the interstate and you'll see signs. You're not from around here, are you?"

"I suppose my accent gave me away. I'm moving here from Louisiana for a new job," the woman replied.

For God's sakes, shut up! Rubi Lee thought, listening to the women. *If Zeke were here, he already would've eaten the bag of beef jerky waiting for this moron!*

"Well good for you. Sullivan County is real nice. It's quiet, beautiful and friendly. You'll like it there," the cashier said.

"I can't wait!" The woman turned and left.

"How're you doing this morning?" the cashier asked Rubi Lee.

"I'm fine. How much?"

"That'll be seventeen dollars and twelve cents."

Rubi Lee threw a twenty-dollar bill down and hustled

out to the car. She did not need to be remembered by some cashier. Two parking spots over, she saw the woman from Louisiana talking on the phone. Rubi Lee slid into the car and took in her appearance: short dark hair, petite build, very pale complexion.

It hit her like a wrecking ball. *I know how to get rid of Rubi Lee Dixon*, she thought and followed the woman out to the highway. She smiled and flicked her eyes skyward. "I don't know if you had anything to do with this, Zeke, but if ya did, thanks. I won't let you down, little brother."

An hour later, the woman exited at the Sullivan County sign. Rubi Lee followed her through the small, quaint town of Shunk until she turned left onto a tree-lined road called Pinetree Way. Rubi Lee parked a few yards away and waited. She glanced in the rearview mirror and saw the Louisiana car parked in a driveway of a ranch house. Each tidy house sat tucked away from the road, separated by thick pine trees and far away from prying eyes. *Good*, she thought before exiting the car. Coast clear, she got out and rooted in the trunk for the tire iron. She slid it up her sleeve and walked toward her new life.

* * *

Electricity jolted through Rubi Lee at the feel of the cold metal tire iron in her palm. Crouched behind a row of thick dwarf firs, she watched the unsuspecting woman pull boxes from the trunk of the car. *Stay cool*, she thought as the woman stood, arms loaded. Rubi Lee watched her struggle to stay balanced across the blacktop driveway. Silent as a whisper, Rubi Lee slithered from her hiding spot. Timing was everything. She watched the woman totter up the brick steps. Rubi Lee closed in.

The woman stopped suddenly and froze. "Great, where are my keys?" She patted the side pocket of her coat. Not finding them, she checked her pants pocket. "Ah." Dropping two small boxes on the brick step, she dug into her pocket and removed her keys.

Frozen in place and completely exposed in the driveway, Rubi Lee willed the woman, *Don't turn around!* Finally, the woman unlocked the front door. She dashed up the steps and slammed the woman on the back of the head. Boxes flew when she crumpled like a ragdoll. Rubi Lee smiled and dragged her unconscious victim farther into the house. On the living room floor, she dropped her like trash.

Rubi Lee took in the modest ranch-style turn-key house. *Not bad for my first home.* In the small kitchen sat a table with four chairs. She carried one into the living room where the unconscious woman lay. After years of carrying large containers of slaughtered chickens, the woman felt like a bag of feathers when Rubi Lee hoisted her from the floor to drop her in the chair. With her trusty knife, Rubi Lee slashed a towel into strips for knots. Satisfied the woman could not escape, Rubi Lee hustled back outside to close the car doors.

Gradually, the woman roused and blinked her eyes. All she could see were the tops of her thighs, her feet, and the wooden floor. Confused and terrified, she slowly raised her head. Blinding pain shot from her neck to her eyes. Her stomach heaved. She could not move her arms or legs. Fear squeezed her pounding heart. She screamed as she pulled hard at the cloth restraints.

"Hello Tanya. I'm glad you're finally awake." Rubi Lee walked in the room.

The woman, Tanya Holston, snapped her head up and stared at her captor. "Who . . . who are you? What happened? How do you know my name?" She blinked, trying to make sense of her situation.

Rubi Lee walked over to Tanya. "Simple. I have this." She waved Tanya's Louisiana license in the air.

Tanya struggled to comprehend what in the hell was happening. "I don't understand. I've never seen you before. Why am I tied up?"

"I'll show you." Rubi Lee gripped the back of the chair Tanya was tied to and spun it around. "*This.*" She pointed to a table.

Tanya looked down at the small table in front of her. On it were her wallet, her phone, car keys, an ID badge, and a laptop. Last in line was Rubi Lee's trusty knife. Tanya's eyes lingered on it. "Oh God. What . . . what do you want with me?"

Rubi Lee picked up the knife and cleaned her fingernails with it. "Nothing *with* you, but something *from* you," Rubi Lee responded and pulled up a chair opposite of Tanya.

Claws of terror clutched and tore at Tanya's insides. "What do you mean?"

"You are going to give me the usernames and passwords to your phone and your fancy new laptop." Rubi Lee picked up the computer and admired it. "This is nice."

Tanya tried to muster up an ounce of bravado. "I won't until you untie me."

Rubi Lee sliced Tanya with her eyes. She stood. From the table she picked up the knife and brandished it in front of Tanya's face. She leaned forward and hissed, "We can do this the hard way or the easy way. Your choice."

Tanya swallowed hard. She knew crazy when she saw it. "Oh God, please don't . . . don't hurt me." Tears rolled down her cheeks. "I'll . . . I'll tell you."

"Good girl," Rubi Lee said. "PINS and social security number too."

Tanya divulged all her usernames and passwords to everything, including bank accounts. Rubi Lee took it all down in her own phone.

"I gave you everything. Please untie me," Tanya begged.

"I will when I know everything you said is legit," Rubi Lee answered.

Rubi Lee tested all the usernames and passwords. The *click click click* of the keys ramped up Tanya's anxiety. *Please let them all work!* she thought, watching Rubi Lee's elfin hands dance over the keyboard. Everything worked.

"See, that wasn't so hard, was it?"

"Why do you want all my information?" Tanya stuttered.

Tapping her fingers against her chin, she turned and looked into the face of her terrified captive. "One word. *Revenge.*"

"Revenge? What do you mean?"

Rubi Lee flicked her gaze at Tanya and laughed. "Yes, revenge. And now that I have all your information, I can start to plot my revenge on the bitch who took everything from me."

Tanya felt sick. "I don't understand. I don't even *know* you!"

"No, you don't. But if it matters, my name *was* Rubi Lee. But I no longer exist because now, I am . . ." Rubi Lee held up Tanya's license to her face. "Tanya Holston. Startling resemblance, don't ya think?"

Tanya stared at Rubi Lee. "*Was*? But *I'm* Tanya . . ." Dread swept through her.

"You *were*. But not anymore." Rubi Lee pulled the tire iron from her back pocket and swung it one last time.

CHAPTER 4

Rubi Lee prioritized her mental to-do list. First was to get rid of Tanya's body and quickly. She sat in front of the laptop and read that Sullivan County was known for hunting, as well as for its plentiful woods and streams.

I'll just stick her deep in the woods, let the animals do their work. She cast her eyes outside and saw the sun was beginning its descent behind the tree-lined horizon. She sighed. "Zeke, I wish you were here to help me," Rubi Lee mumbled. "But you're not because of *her.*" She blinked away the tears. Pain was something she abhorred. Pain meant weakness. Pain meant fear. She looked over her shoulder at the dead woman. "Okay Tanya, let's go."

* * *

For once, Rubi Lee was grateful for her insomnia. She spent the rest of the night unpacking Tanya's belongings and learning about Sullivan County. By seven in the morning, stomach acid roiled and burned in her gut. *When did I last eat anything?* She wandered into the kitchen and spotted the box of granola bars she tossed on the counter earlier.

"Gross! Who eats shit like this?" Eventually she choked it down. A trip to the store was inevitable if she was going to avoid perishing from malnutrition. Rubi Lee googled grocery stores nearby and discovered three were within ten miles, plus Fisher's Farmers' Market. Before shopping, she needed to attend to a task she finally could complete.

"Let's see where you are, you bitch," Rubi Lee mumbled as she googled Daisy Kathryn Taylor.

* * *

Outside Fisher's Market, Rubi Lee tugged on the handle of a rickety, rusty shopping cart. It did not budge. She pulled harder and cursed under her breath. "Come *on!*" She kicked the stationary cart. "Shit!"

"Excuse me. Do you need some help?"

Rubi Lee spun around ready to blast the poor soul who offered help. Her heart leapt into her throat when she saw who spoke. Behind her stood a short, squat man dressed in a police uniform. His broad forehead was barely covered by the brim of his police hat. A crooked smile exposed short, stunted teeth. Close-set, cheery blue eyes sat in a full face. Based on a hint of lines around his mouth and eyes, and a lack of any gray hair, Rubi Lee guessed his age to be mid-thirties.

"Ah, sure," she replied. *Holy shit! A cop!* She gave the officer a wide berth.

"Allow me." He stepped in front of her, jiggled the handle, and the cart sprung free from its conga line. "Here ya go, ma'am." He stepped away and let Rubi Lee take the cart.

"Thanks."

"You shop here often? I love this place. They got all the

things I like and it ain't expensive."

"No, no I don't. I'm new here." Rubi Lee started to walk into the store. *Leave me the hell alone*, she wished and picked up her pace.

He matched her step for step. "You are? Welcome then! I'm Deputy Chuck Willis, but everyone calls me Bump."

She wondered if she heard correctly. "*Bump*? What the hell kinda name is that?" A sardonic smile crossed her face.

"A good one! Earned my nickname when I was little. I was always falling and bumping my head—probably cause the doctor dropped me when I came out. LOL, right?" He grinned at her.

Bump? she thought. "Total LOL!"

"Yea. Sometimes I gotta read things a couple of times to get it. And I sometimes get real *bad* headaches. But Sheriff makes things easy for me. I work in the office."

"Sheriff's office?" Rubi Lee's wheels started rolling.

"Yes ma'am. I help with cases, paperwork, phone calls, and whatever else he needs. I don't really like it too much 'cause it's boring. I wish I could just fish and hunt all day."

Rubi Lee's ears pricked up when Bump mentioned cases. Her thoughts turned to the recent dumping of Tanya's body. *If they find her, that means a new case for the cops.* Rubi Lee cast her rodent eyes on Bump. *I may need a new friend.* She turned and smiled sweetly at him. "Thanks again, Bump. You're very kind."

"Thank you, ma'am." His round cheeks flushed.

"Oh, please. Call me Tanya. I'm too young for ma'am." She laughed and scrutinized him. *I'm gonna wrap this moron around my finger so easily.* "Well Bump, I need to get some shopping done."

"Okay, Tanya. Hope to see you around town." He tipped his hat.

Rubi Lee turned back to him. "Without seeming too forward, maybe you could show me around? Since I'm new?"

Bump reddened. "I'd, ah, like that. We have really pretty scenery and woods here."

"That sounds good. And maybe a drink after sightseeing?"

"Sure. I'd like that too."

"I'm headed out of town for a bit. If you text me, I'll call you when I'm home and we can meet?"

Bump began to sweat. "Okay, that ah, that sounds great."

Rubi Lee gave him her number and in a split second, she had her source.

Ding! Rubi Lee checked her phone. "Got it. Thanks Bump." She held his eyes for an extra beat. Turning back to the store, she made sure to swish her tight, yoga pant-clad ass from side to side. She felt his eyes take her in. *That was too easy*, she thought and entered the store.

* * *

Bump stared at his phone; a giddy smile spread across his face. *Did she really ask me out on a date? Yes! Yes, she did!* "Woohoo! It must be my lucky day!" he practically shouted as he watched Rubi Lee disappear into the grocery store. With a bounce in his step, he returned to his car and replayed their conversation in his mind. "Man, I hope the next few days go by real quick!"

In the patrol car, he lowered all four windows and cranked up the music on his phone. Bump sang along with the song pouring from the tiny speaker. Lyrics about walking on sunshine aligned perfectly with his bright mood. He smiled at life. The cloudless, extra deep blue sky stretched for miles ahead; the diversely colored front doors of Shunk's business district shone in the bright sun. Mature maple trees lined both sides of the street. Bump admired the newly paved road bisected with fresh yellow paint. At the traffic circle, he waved to the elderly couple sitting on the iron bench in the middle of the circle. "Today is a good day," he said aloud. "I have to tell Dad."

At the station, Bump parked and opened the crowded glove compartment. Inside, he rummaged for the picture of his father he faithfully took everywhere.

"Hey Dad. I met a girl! She's named Tanya and we're gonna go out on a date soon. I really wish you were here to give me some tips on dating." Bump tried to laugh. "I know you'll be watching over me and rootin' me on."

Bump ran a chubby finger down the once-white border of the picture and smiled at his father. *I sure do miss you*, he thought. His mouth curved down and his lips quivered. A lump formed in his throat as he gazed down at his dark-haired, grinning father sitting atop a tractor. Bump was suddenly transported back as the ten-year-old boy reliving the night, twenty-three years earlier, his young life was shattered.

It poured rain that night. He was shaken from a deep slumber by an insistent rapping on the front door of his childhood home in Lycoming, Pennsylvania. He'd opened his eyes when the squeak of the metal door traveled up the stairs. Low whispering gave way to a raw, guttural wail from his mother. It jolted him from bed. Flinging off the flimsy sheets, he bolted to the top of the stairs to see two police officers standing at the base of the steps.

His heart skipped through his pajama top. "Mom! What's going on?" Bump yelled down the steps. He gripped the handrail so tightly he did not feel the ache in his small hands. Goosebumps dotted his skinny arms.

His mother turned her crinkled, tear-stained face to the steps. Bump watched her lift her eyes to her only child. Clearing her throat, she told him, "It's your father. He was killed in a car accident tonight."

To Bump, it sounded as if she was reporting the news. His young brain struggled to digest what she said. Processing information his teachers taught was problematic for Bump.

This was different.

In a split second, his world stopped. Bump innately understood his life was irrevocably changed. His father. His hero. His cheerleader. And his best friend, was gone.

Four months after his father was killed, Joan, his mother, dropped him off at his paternal grandparents' house for his weekly sleepover. She never returned.

CHAPTER 5

As the months went by, Daisy was so happily entrenched in her job, she thought less and less about the night she and Nick were almost killed. The freezing, blood-soaked night in the garage at Margaux Ford Park seemed like a lifetime ago. However, she wrestled with the small part of her that felt remorse that two people, Victor Sykes and Zeke Dixon, were killed in cold blood. On the other hand, Rubi Lee and Zeke Dixon tried to kill her and Nick. She told Nick how she loathed them and what they did. He agreed with her and confessed he understood and shared her feelings.

Over coffee one morning, she asked Nick, "How do we handle, resolve, or come to terms with these two sets of feelings?"

"Daiz, I'm not sure. Obviously, there are professionals out there who can help. It's time."

Grasping his hand, she replied, "I'll call my doc later and see who she recommends."

"Good idea. I remember the police suggesting some counseling when we were ready. And now's the time."

Dr. Dana Specter, specializing in PTSD, came highly recommended from Daisy's doctor and practiced in an office not far from Nick and Daisy's house. Daisy scheduled an introductory meeting after work one evening.

"Good evening. I'm Dana Specter. It's so nice to meet you both."

Daisy was not used to being on eye level with most women. At five ten, she normally towered over other women. But Dr. Specter matched her inch for inch. Long, layered ash blond hair framed her oval face and fell over her crisp white shirt. Lavender-framed glasses sat on the bridge of a pert nose. Dr. Specter's melodious voice was like liquid velvet, making Daisy and Nick feel at ease.

"Please, sit." She extended a slender, sun-spotted hand at two dark green plush chairs. Daisy felt as if she was sitting on a puff of cream. "Can I offer you some coffee or water?" she asked.

"Water please," Daisy replied.

From a tucked-away refrigerator, Dr. Specter took three bottles. Daisy and Nick thanked her as she sank into a two-seater cream and green striped couch. Once settled, she began, "I'm glad you're here. I commend you for taking the initiative to seek counseling."

"Thank you for seeing us. The police suggested we seek therapy, and we knew we needed some help. We're very grateful for it," Nick said.

Dr. Specter's sympathetic, genial smile was comforting. "I'm glad." She sat back in the sofa. "Let me begin with a few items I tell my patients who experience a traumatic event like you did. Does that work?" Dr. Specter's eyes danced between Daisy and Nick. They said nothing but nodded their assent.

"Wonderful, thank you. You were the victims of a violent, terrifying crime. Part of my protocol, and that of the police, is for them and me to work together to effectively communicate about cases. Part of the communication process on the part of the police is sharing information with me after they have interviewed the victims. I believe you both were interviewed quite extensively."

"Yes, that's accurate," Nick replied. They were very thorough in their questioning, and we told them everything we could remember."

Daisy added, "It's been a few weeks since anyone has contacted us though. So, we're not sure what's going on."

Dr. Specter nodded and continued, "This may help. The purpose of the protocol is for me to learn about—and give context—to the event you experienced." She picked up her bottle and took a delicate sip. "I spoke with an Officer Barrett who was on the scene. We spoke in detail, and he informed me the investigation into that evening is ongoing."

Daisy and Nick exchanged a bewildered look. The word *ongoing* hung in the air.

Mind racing, Daisy cleared her throat and asked the question the crept into the room like an unwanted, dark entity.

"What do you mean by *ongoing*?"

"Truth be told, I asked the same thing. He would not elaborate, citing the 'sensitivity' of the case; given a United States Senator was involved." Her French-manicured nails sliced through the air with air quotes.

"We can only presume then, that since we have not heard from the police, that no news is good news," Nick finished.

"Like you said, Doctor, maybe the police are still

investigating Alex Boyd's office and can't share any more with you at this point—since she's the guilty senator," Daisy surmised.

Dr. Specter replied, "Anything is possible."

* * *

Over the course of a few weeks, Dr. Specter helped them to understand and navigate their feelings. Daisy was grateful she did not remember much of that night—other than fighting to the death with Rubi Lee. During one heart-wrenching session, Nick's unshakable façade crumbled as he recounted one part of that awful night.

"I . . . I was in the closet," he said through tears. "In the office. I was stuck, hiding behind . . . a heavy coat, a winter coat." Still as a rock, he sat and inhaled. "I wish I could forget that suffocating smell of *fucking* moth balls. God I *hate* that smell. It's a bad thing for me." He scowled and shook his head. Taking Daisy's hand, he continued. "The door opened and I was . . . staring . . . down the barrel . . . of a gun. I didn't know what to do. She aimed it at me. All I could think about was Daisy." He swallowed. "And how I'd never see her again."

"And look at you two now. Engaged since March, with an October wedding planned. It's not often I meet couples who have gone through what you two did. It's clear you both are exceedingly strong people who share a bond most of us will never know."

During their weeks in therapy, Daisy and Nick grew to understand that it was okay to lean on family and friends for help. The therapist reinforced the importance of keeping a consistent schedule and to slowly return to their life prior to the traumatic December evening.

"I also encourage you both to get into an exercise routine—nothing outrageous like marathon running. Your bodies will thank you when you release those wonderful endorphins. With that, I strongly suggest that you, Daisy, continue to work hard as a reporter and *you*"—the therapist pointed at Nick—"follow your dream of working with Mayor Basile. Politics need young, strong, fresh minds."

Daisy and Nick continued with several more sessions. On what would be their last meeting, Dr. Specter smiled at them as she commended them for their hard work.

"Listening to the two of you, I am so proud of your hard work. You both look and sound wonderful." She beamed at them. "Which leads me to decide that I know in my heart of hearts, you don't need me anymore."

"We can't thank you enough," Daisy told her. "You gave us much-needed clarity."

"I agree. Thank you, Dr. Specter," Nick added.

Leaning in the doorway, Dr. Specter said, "Make sure to send me pics of your wedding. Good luck."

* * *

Shopping for their newly purchased home outside Philadelphia was a thrill for Daisy. Nick enjoyed seeing her happy, so he put on a happy face and went along. Outside the furniture store, the late-afternoon summer sun seared its way into everything. Daisy consulted her shopping list. Her red curls were in a knot on top of her head. The light blue sundress exposed strong, shapely shoulders that were quickly turning a bright red. She folded the paper and stuck it back in her bag. "Well NT, it looks like we're done shopping."

He smiled at his childhood nickname—short for Nicholas Tucker—she occasionally used. Work colleagues and friends always called him Nick. "Thank God. It's hot as hell and I can't look at another piece of furniture." Nick pushed the trunk closed over a new area rug.

"Neither can I. We've spent enough of our budget for the month."

"And then some."

She ignored his comment. "Time to get home for drinks on the patio."

"Works for me!"

In a few minutes, they turned into their driveway and admired their new home, a four-bedroom fieldstone tucked into a cul-de-sac located thirty minutes outside Philadelphia. It sat on a half-acre and was within walking distance to restaurants, shops, and Mike's Farmers' Market—Daisy's favorite.

Daisy admired their house from the car. "I just love this house. It's perfect, isn't it?"

He turned to her. "Yes, it is. And you know what will make it even *more* perfect?"

Daisy shrugged. "Um, new paint? Plants out front?"

He gave her a sly smile. "When we have, like *four* kids running all over. Think how fun it will be making them!"

"I agree with the *making* part. How about we get married first, enjoy life for a year or so, and *then* think about babies?"

They stepped from the car and headed to the back where one end of a rug peeked out from the trunk.

"I think this will look great in the front hall, don't you?" She lifted one end from the trunk.

"Whatever you say, dear!" Nick learned long ago that once Daisy made up her mind, there was little chance of anything—or anyone—changing it.

* * *

On the flagstone patio, Nick and Daisy sipped vodka and club sodas. Only a quarter of the sun was visible above the orange-streaked horizon. Crickets played their happy songs and fireflies dotted the dusk with their love lights. They discussed final wedding plans when Annie, Daisy's mother, called.

"Hi Mama, how are you?" Daisy smiled into the phone. Whenever they spoke, the conversation was lengthy. And since their wedding was less than two weeks away, Nick knew this conversation was most likely going to center around last-minute details. *Time for another drink*, he thought and rose.

Daisy pointed to her empty glass and blew a kiss to Nick. He took it and headed back inside to pour fresh drinks. *I'll check email again while I can*, he thought, pouring vodka. Since he started his tenure with Mayor Basile, his inbox was constantly full. People usually wanted a response in a timely manner. He worked hard to adhere to his promise of responding within a few days unless it was something urgent. Twenty minutes later, he returned to the patio and handed Daisy her drink.

"Thanks." Her subdued tone cut a sharp contrast to the contented evening.

"How's your mom?" He sat down behind her on the lounge chair. She leaned back and rested her head against his chest. She sighed heavily and looked up into the summer sky. "She's okay. But she really misses Dad. Badly. So do I."

He rubbed her arms and kissed her head. "Oh, me too. He was the best. I'm so glad I knew him for so long."

"I wish so much he was here to walk me down the aisle," she said, her voice breaking. "I just can't wrap my head around the fact that he was here just a little bit ago and now he's gone." She wiped tears away. "It's so hard for me to understand how we can sit here under this beautiful sky, enjoying drinks and I hurt so much." Stars dotted the inky sky. "NT, do you think Dad is one of those stars above, twinkling down on us?"

He wrapped his arms around her warm body and held her tightly. He wished he could absorb her sadness. "I sure do, Daiz."

Three months earlier, Jackson Taylor was ripped from his family's life. Daisy experienced a breathtaking mix of emotions when she thought about how much she and her father adored each other. She never knew she could miss someone so much. He taught her the importance of clear communication among family and to *listen* to people, not just hear them. He was tough with her when she pushed, especially nights when she rolled home at four in the morning while still in high school.

After his passing, Daisy did not sleep or eat. She worried constantly about her mother who was alone in

Daisy's hometown of Cab Station, Virginia. Luckily, it did not take much coaxing on Daisy and Nick's part to convince Annie to move to Philadelphia.

"What am I going to do every day?" Annie had asked at the concept. "I can't very well pester you two."

Daisy took it upon herself to scour the local schools' websites and found a perfect job for her mother. "Mom, you need to apply for this teacher's aide job at Mulberry Elementary. It's only three days a week and since you're a former teacher, this suits you perfectly!"

"I insist that I am no more than a fifteen-minute drive to your house," Annie told them when she agreed to move.

Daisy agreed heartily, and now Annie called home a two-bedroom town house in a small suburb twenty minutes from her daughter and future son-in-law.

* * *

Daisy took the train into the city every day for work. Not one to waste time in traffic, she was grateful she could walk to one of the local train lines that ran in and out of the city. She thrived in her job as a field reporter for a major news station in Philadelphia: Live5 News. Always willing to travel, she was sent to small towns as far as four hours from Philadelphia to cover all types of stories.

The train was full of its regular early-morning commuters. Daisy settled into her usual window seat and took the newspaper from her bag. Old school as it was, she loved the slippery feel of a newspaper in her hand. Halfway through the sports page, she heard "Into the Mystic" float up from her phone. She looked down and saw it was Rick Thorne, her producer.

"Hey Rick, what's up? Is everything okay?" She quickly scurried from the Quiet Car to avoid the disgusted scowls from fellow commuters.

Rick replied, "Yes. Change of plans. I know you were expecting to go to Atlantic City today, but that's changed."

"Oh no. I was looking forward to going, as you guys say, 'downnashore.'" She laughed. "Where am I going today?"

"Impressive Philly accent!" Rick exclaimed. "I'm sending you out to Shunk in Sullivan County. And this is your first solo assignment!"

"Solo? Cool!" She balled her free hand into a fist and punched the air. *Yes!* "Thanks Rick. I won't disappoint you." *Can't wait to tell Nick!*

"Daisy, you're more than ready to tackle a solo job. I have ultimate faith in you, and you should too. It's your time."

He's right. It is my time, she thought and replied, "Thanks Rick. You're right, I'll be fine. What's the story?"

He chuckled. "You'll like this. Apparently, the skeletal remains of a body have been found." He slurped whatever he was drinking.

Daisy's interest was piqued. "Really? Tell me more."

"Sullivan County, specifically Shunk, is not known for finding bodies. In fact, if it turns out to be a homicide, this will be big news because there has not been a homicide in over *twenty-five years*. Obviously, you will be reporting on the shocking discovery."

"Do you know any other details? And how far away from Philly?"

"Not really. Other than the remains were found in the woods." He slurped again. "It's about three hours from here. When you get here, you and the crew will head out."

"I'm ready! See you soon."

CHAPTER 6

Randy Wright, the cameraman, paced back and forth in front of the news van like a shooting target at a county fair. When Daisy arrived at the station, he waved so frantically at her that it reminded her of someone drowning.

"You're finally here! Everything's ready! We should go before traffic gets *bad*!" Panic dripped from the last word.

Daisy gave him a tight smile. *You're a colossal pain in the ass.* Luckily, her sunglasses hid her palatable annoyance. He was a top-rate cameraman, but as the new kid on the block, she was stuck with him. If he only would not chew his nails to bloody stumps, Daisy could tolerate him somewhat better. *Just block it out*, she thought and climbed into the van.

Daisy loaded the address for the destination into Waze as Leo Stratman, the driver and technician, pulled out. On her personal phone, Daisy called Nick to tell him she was not going to Atlantic City, but to Sullivan County instead. "I know. I really wanted to go there, but there's a better story I've been assigned. I'll call you later. Love you." She hung up.

"What'd that thing say?" Leo asked and gestured at the phone.

"We need to get off at exit 131, which is under a half mile away," she replied.

"For God's sakes Leo, get in the right lane!" barked Randy from the back.

Leo glared at Randy in the rearview mirror and slapped the turn signal hard.

Daisy directed them to the rural destination. Randy set up the camera while Daisy adjusted her earpiece and microphone. Other stations caught wind of the discovery and were setting up.

Daisy secured her earpiece and listened carefully to Wesley Hines, lead news anchor, introduce the story.

"We have received a report that the remains of a *body* have been found in Sullivan County. This is a *shocking* discovery for a county that has not seen anything of this nature in over *twenty-five years.* For more details, we turn to our field correspondent, Daisy Taylor."

"Thanks Wesley. We are standing on Ridgerock Road here in bucolic Sullivan County, just outside the town of Shunk." Daisy pointed behind her and continued, "You can see behind me yellow police tape draped on trees indicating where the remains of a body have been found. Earlier this morning, two people were out for a walk when their dog began to dig furiously in the ground. The woman and man were shocked to see what appeared to be part of a skeleton buried in a shallow grave. Sheriff Drew Roth of Sullivan County Police Department informed me it seems the cause of death was blunt force head trauma. Speculation is that this is a homicide. This discovery is shocking because Sullivan County has not seen a homicide in over twenty-five years. Everyone in this quaint community is shaken, and the sheriff's department is determined to figure out exactly what happened. I believe

Sheriff Roth is going to share an official statement soon. I will be sure to pass it on as soon as I am informed. Back to you, Wesley."

He nodded solemnly. "Thank you, Daisy. Such a sad story." He smiled and added, "On a happier note, I speak for everyone here at the station by wishing you and Nick a lifetime of joy and happiness as you approach your wedding day next Saturday."

* * *

After Daisy signed off, she approached two officers with the intention of questioning them further about the discovery. Thanks to her father who had been sheriff of Cab Station for many years, Daisy was keenly aware of what tactics to use and not use when questioning the police.

She shook her hair and put on her thousand-watt smile. "Hello Officers. I'm Daisy Taylor with Live5 News out of Philadelphia. Do you have some time to spare for questions?"

Neither officer responded. They were momentarily rooted to the ground, gawking at the statuesque, stunning redhead in front of them. Daisy cocked her head and laughed. "Are you guys okay?"

Finally, the female officer said, "Oh yes, forgive us. We're not used to TV reporters from the big city out here!" She extended a hand. "I'm Officer Amanda Gillespie, and this is Officer Mike Atkins."

"Nice to meet you. I know Sheriff Roth gave a brief statement regarding this morning's discovery. I was wondering if you had any more information about this. Of course, it would be off the record."

Officer Atkins spoke up. "Ma'am, your best bet is to chat with the man over there." He turned and pointed to a tall, thin man engaged in conversation with the sheriff. "He's Medical Examiner Lee Christenson. He'd be the one to help you out."

Daisy turned to where the officer pointed. "Thank you so much. I'm a rookie and need all the help I can get!"

* * *

Daisy ambled over. She could still hear her father's voice, gently scolding her as a child when she bounded into the middle of an adult conversation.

"Daisy! You need to exercise some patience. Please do not interrupt your mother and me when we're talking." She would pay money—all she had—to hear his voice again.

Ahead of her, the sheriff placed his hat on his head and the two men shook hands. "See ya around, Drew," Daisy heard the ME say to Sheriff Roth. *Time to strike*, she thought and approached.

"Hello sir," she said. "I'm Daisy Taylor from Live5 News in Philadelphia. I'm sure you're very busy, but I was wondering if you had a few minutes to spare?"

He turned his strong chin to the side and met her gaze with wary dark brown eyes. "Philly, huh? Or should I say Killadephia? Heard the murder rate is pretty high there. True?" His response caught her off guard.

Heat pulsated in her cheeks. *So, this is how we're gonna play this, asshole?* she thought, and fired back, "I think *many* large cities are facing high murder rates. Guess you're lucky your town isn't a large, bustling metropolis, right?"

He nodded his head slowly and assessed Daisy. "Touché. What can I do for you?"

"Well sir . . ." she began.

"My name is Lee Christenson, ME. Pleased to meet you." He stuck out his hand. She shook it. He consulted his watch. "I have fifteen minutes, Ms. Taylor."

"I was hoping you could answer some questions about the discovery."

He sighed and glanced at his watch. "I can try."

"Great, thank you." She paused and jumped right in. "Do you have any leads on what exactly happened, or whose remains were found?" Daisy asked.

"Based on the small size of the skeleton, it appears to be that of a woman."

"Or a small man?" Daisy countered. *I love grilling people!*

"I suppose so. However, until we hear from my lab, we can't give a definitive answer."

"How long do you think the remains have been here?" she pushed.

"I'd estimate several weeks."

Daisy glanced around. "This is such a lovely area. It's shocking that a place this beautiful is the scene of a gruesome murder."

"Who said anything about a murder?" His dark eyes clouded over. "You know something I don't?" He bristled.

Daisy knew she hit a nerve. "Well, you don't know it *isn't* a murder, correct?"

"As I said before, until we complete all procedures, we are not making any assumptions or jumping to conclusions. Understand?" The conversation was over.

"Yes. Thank you for your time."

CHAPTER 7

As a student Rubi Lee detested homework, but she did it to shut up her teachers. Until one day in ninth-grade algebra when her teacher humiliated her for not understanding how to solve an intricate problem. The whole class laughed. Rubi Lee flipped off the teacher and never returned to algebra class.

But this new homework was different. Different because it *mattered*. Rubi Lee assigned herself an endless homework assignment: researching Daisy Taylor and her life after the horrific night in the garage. A rush of excitement tinged with nausea churned in her soul each time her fingers typed the name: *Daisy Kathryn Taylor*. Rubi Lee learned she moved to Philadelphia to be a reporter with Live5 News. A gush of triumphant glee flowed through her when she discovered her nemesis was three hours east. She downloaded the Live5 News app on her phone. "Nothing says fun like stalking my prey on a daily basis," she said and turned her attention to social media.

Facebook and Instagram were treasure troves of information too. Rubi Lee discovered much about Daisy's life. She learned that Daisy graduated from James Madison University in the top ten percent of her class, and recently finished journalism school in Washington, DC.

"She and the boyfriend live outside Philadelphia, how interesting." She continued to read on. Her mother, Annie Taylor, was a teacher's aide and lived nearby. "And she has three brothers? But Daddy died? Oh, poor baby. But that doesn't count." *She has everything I've never had*, she simmered.

Continuing her research, Rubi Lee googled Nicholas Tyson. *Yup, same guy. Dumb smile and unibrow*, she mused. "This jackass works on the mayor's staff in Philadelphia?" She laughed.

For the countless time, Rubi Lee stared at Daisy's Facebook page. The beautiful, smiling redhead—Nick's arms around protectively her—stared back. An enormous three-diamond ring glimmered from her left hand.

"Bitch. You don't deserve to be happy after you ruined *my* life!" Rubi Lee yelled, looking at their beaming faces. "You destroyed my and Zeke's chance of ever being happy!" She stood and paced the floor, eyes not leaving the computer. "We *never* had a family like you do. People like you think they're above everyone else!" She whirled around and slapped the table the computer sat on. Leaning within inches of the screen, she hissed, "That'll end soon enough!"

A link on Daisy's Facebook page led to a newspaper article and picture announcing her and Nick's engagement. The look of pure bliss on their faces made Rubi Lee felt as if ants marched over her skin. She clicked on it and printed it out. At the kitchen table she chain-smoked while she read it over and over. Black hatred simmered. Her plan grew like a tumor; its poisonous tentacles slithered their way into her brain. Daisy and Nick were going to be married in St. Matthew's church in Daisy's hometown of Cab Station, Virginia soon.

"Looks like I'm going on a road trip!" Rubi Lee took one last drag and ground the cigarette out on Daisy's face.

Inside a small duffel bag, she tossed items she would need. From the closet, she pulled something she would never buy—a pink dress with white flowers—but was wholly appropriate for an early autumn wedding. Bag packed, Rubi Lee sat on the bed and plotted her route to Cab Station. She was interrupted by a buzz on her phone. She ignored it. Her phone vibrated again. Rubi Lee stared at it. She read the notification out loud, "The skeletal remains of a body were found in the woods about two miles from Muncy Creek." *Damnit!*

* * *

Rubi Lee pulled into the gravel parking lot of St. Matthew's church. The crunching of the tiny pebbles under the tires reminded her of chicken bones she twisted and hacked up when she worked in the poultry-processing factory. The crunch made her blood run cold. Those heinous memories were forever etched in her mind. *Stop thinking of that. It's over*, she thought, brushing back her short, newly dyed blond hair with a headband. In the rear view mirror, she evaluated her heavily made-up face. "Good enough for now."

She approached the front door of the red sandstone church. Her gaze ran up the towering spire that soared above ornate stained-glass windows. The majestic beauty of St. Matthew's church made her breath catch in her chest.

Never having been inside a church, her hand trembled on the handle of the massive door. Rubi Lee pulled twice and once inside, she stood in awe at what met her eyes. The high vaulted ceiling was supported with crisscrossed, elaborately carved mahogany beams. The dark wood of each pew shone as if just polished. Stained-glass windows lined the white walls. For a moment Rubi Lee was bowled over by the startling beauty of St. Matthew's; she also felt ill at ease standing in such a grand, hallowed space.

"May I help you, young lady?" The voice startled her.

She spun around and saw a tall, slender man. His black pants and black shirt were sharply pressed. The white clerical collar peeked from his shirt. Thick gray hair was neatly combed to one side. A warm smile full of shiny teeth spread across his wizened face. He introduced himself as Reverend Roderick Brindley.

"Oh, um, hello." Rubi Lee kept her voice calm. "I ah, I wanted to see the church. It's really pretty." She was surprised by the flash of sincerity in her words.

"I know, the first time I entered, I was taken in by its grand beauty," he agreed. "Are you a new parishioner?"

Yeah, that'll be the day, she mused before answering. "No. I'm here for the wedding of Daisy Taylor. A little early," she chuckled. "But I wanted to know where I was going. Always a planner!"

"Ah, Daisy Taylor's wedding. This Saturday at four o'clock. The whole town is brimming with excitement for its golden girl! She and her lovely family have been very active members of this church for years." He stopped abruptly. He cleared his throat and continued, "Unfortunately her father passed away recently and is buried in our cemetery. What an outstanding man. He and his wife Annie helped to establish our Sunday School and youth programs. Finer people you will never meet."

She nodded politely. *STOP with your gross gushing over Daisy and her stupid family!*

"Are you a friend of Daisy's?"

"Ah, yes. We met in DC and became very close. I'm so happy for her and excited for the ceremony."

"I promise it will be beautiful and memorable."

"Yes, it will." Rubi Lee gave the obligatory smile.

"I'm sorry, but I have church duties to attend. My wife, Jenny, is waiting for me in the office. She keeps our books, you know. Anyway, enjoy your day. I'll see you Saturday."

Rubi Lee walked back to the vestibule by the doors. She saw a small, tucked-away staircase on the left. Tight, angled steps spiraled into darkness above. *Why not*, she thought and began the climb. At the top step, she panted heavily. *Man, I need to cut back on the smoking.*

Tentatively, she walked through a small arched doorway and stopped abruptly. *Holy crap, churches have balconies?* She stared at three stacked tiers of long pews running horizontally. Inching closer, she saw the balcony looked squarely down at the altar. *I know exactly where I'll be sitting on Saturday. This will be perfect*, she thought and gazed down at the sprawling church.

CHAPTER 8

"When is Win getting here?" Daisy called to Nick from their bedroom where she was packing.

"He said around ten," Nick responded, walking into the room.

She looked at the clock on the bedside table. "Good, that's only a few minutes. Mom and I'll wait for him. Then we can caravan down. Are you all packed?"

"Pretty much. Win said he'd grab my suit on the way in. And since he's my best man, who was I to say no?" He laughed.

"I can't wait to see him and Jaida. I feel so lucky the bureau gave them time off to be part of our big day."

He walked over to her and put his arms around her. "Me too. The four of us went through hell that night last winter; it's great they can be in our wedding." He rubbed his hands up and down her back. "We have a few minutes before he gets here . . ." He winked at her.

"As tempting as a quickie sounds I need to keep packing." Daisy squeezed him. She walked to the closet and assessed what to bring.

"Is Jaida meeting us down there?" He flopped down on the bed.

"Yes. She's flying in from Germany tonight. We're going to meet at the hotel tomorrow for lunch."

"Germany?"

"Yup. She's going to text me when she's in. She also—"
Daisy was interrupted by a knock and a familiar voice.

"Knock, knock, lovebirds! Guess who?" Winston Wang
leaned against the door frame. "I hope you're packed
because we have some serious partying to do!" He beamed
at his friends. Win's lively brown eyes sparkled beneath his
horn-rimmed glasses. The light blue shirt sat fittingly on
his wiry frame. It was tucked into gray flat-front pants.
Running shoes completed the ensemble.

"Win!" Daisy ran over and threw her arms around him.
Nick joined in.

"So great to see you guys! You both look awesome!"
Win stood back and soaked up his friends. "Check this out!
I've been practicing my moves!" He pulled out his phone
and the voices of a popular 1970s group singing their hit
song about young men filled the air. Winston marched to
the beat in a circle, arms flung in the air, and performed for
his friends.

Nick and Daisy turned to each other. She mouthed,
"OMG!" She did not bother holding back laughter. Nick
soon had tears running down his face.

"What?" Win asked, panting after his routine.

"I wish I had videoed that!" Nick replied.

He held up his hands. "I know, I know. You're *blown
away* by my moves!"

"For sure!" Nick laughed. "*That* aside . . ." He circled his
pointer finger at Win. "We're excited and honored you're
going to be part of our celebration. It means the world to
us." Nick squeezed his friend's shoulder.

During his freshman year of college Winston helped

Nick navigate college and fraternity life. Even though he was a few years older, the two stayed in touch throughout Nick's college career. They shared a house together in Washington, DC, where Nick, by mistake, learned his long-time friend was an undercover agent for the US Customs Agency. After almost losing his life three times in six months, Winston opted for a less dangerous occupation: Evidence Technician for the FBI in New York City. "It's a whole lot safer than being in the field!" he told Nick.

* * *

St. Matthew's church glowed from within. For most of the morning before the wedding, Reverend Brindley and Jenny vacuumed, dusted all pews, filled the crystal vases, and polished the silver cross on the altar until they saw their reflections.

Clear sunlight poked through the high clouds. A slight breeze swirled outside the church. Family and friends filled the pews, chatting and laughing animatedly. Vibrant fuchsia roses, creamy white gardenias, and lush periwinkle hydrangea burst out of their crystal vases. At the altar, Nick stood tall and handsome in his seersucker suit. The ten-person bridal party filed in; Winston and Jaida brought up the rear. Nerves threatened to kickstart heart palpitations for Nick while he waited for his Daisy. He tried to level his breathing by loudly exhaling.

"It's okay, man." Winston patted him on the back to keep him calm. Nick nodded and glanced at lovely Jaida.

"Be cool!" she whispered.

The first note of Daisy's entrance rose from the organ.

In the arched doorway she stood, glowing like an angel, her three brothers flanking her. Nick's breath caught in his throat. He flicked his eyes to the ceiling. *Thank you God for this beautiful woman.* His smile stretched to the point where his face ached. She stepped up on the altar and took his hands.

"Oh Daisy, I always knew you were beautiful, but you are the most gorgeous woman I've ever seen," Nick whispered. "I love you."

She blinked away tears. "I love you so much."

A few minutes later, Reverend Brindley beamed like a proud father as he concluded, "By the powers vested in me, I now pronounce you husband and wife. Nicholas, you may kiss the bride."

Cheers and applause erupted from the pews and echoed throughout the church.

He continued, "Ladies and gentlemen, I now present Mr. and Mrs. Nicholas Tyson!"

From the balcony, Rubi Lee ground her teeth. Perspiration trickled down her back. Struggling to paste a joyful expression across her face, she clutched her bag close. The weight of her knife calmed her. *I gotta try to get close to them somehow.* She knew she could not exit the balcony early. *Maybe they'll—*

A heavily made-up woman broke Rubi Lee's thoughts. "Isn't she simply stunning?"

Rubi Lee lied, "Oh yes, *so* stunning." Her mouth felt thick with those words. When the congregation began clapping, she forced herself to join in. *Just do it. You don't want to raise suspicion*, she told herself. She glanced around; disgust and contempt boiled deep in her soul. *God, look at all these effin' people who think that bitch is so awesome. If they knew the truth that she killed my brother, they'd hate her too.*

She narrowed her dark eyes at Daisy and Nick who relished in the applause and whistles. The glowing couple glided down the aisle to the door, followed by the bridal party. *You just wait.*

One of the rectors swung open the door and Daisy and Nick floated out into bright sunshine as man and wife. Nick stopped and kissed her again, foreheads touched, eyes locked on one another.

"Hold it!" Karen the photographer called out. *Clickclickclickclick!* The automatic shutter fired away, capturing the tender moment. "Perfect!"

The guests filtered from the church, chattering about the lovely ceremony and the grand reception at Cascades Golf Club. Mixed in was Rubi Lee. *Jesus, I think I'm gonna barf,* she thought as she watched Karen fawn over the newlyweds. Rubi Lee heard Karen order Nick and Daisy to the side of the church for more pictures.

"I'll be right there—need to change my lens!" Karen called.

Rubi Lee watched the photographer jog to her car for her lens. *Perfect.* Clutching the knife to the point of pain, Rubi Lee watched the newlyweds saunter around the corner. Keeping them in the crosshairs, she weaved through the jubilant crowd. Her hammering heart matched her quick steps. Goosebumps of excitement pricked her skin. *Hurry up!*

"Well, *hello*! Lovely to see you again!" a man's voice— British accent—came from her left.

Startled, Rubi Lee whipped around to see the genial Reverend Brindley, smiling broadly, standing in a small doorway.

Oh no! Damnit! She swallowed hard. "Oh. Hi. Yeah, nice to see you too." From the corner of her eye, she saw Karen striding across the lawn with her camera. *Shit! Too late.*

"Did you enjoy the ceremony? You must be so happy for your dear friend!"

"Of course I did! And yes, *so* happy for her!"

He clasped his hands to his chest. "As am I. Divine couple, those two."

Rubi Lee struggled to keep the frustration out of her voice. "They are."

"Will we see you at the reception?"

"Oh yes. I was, um, just heading to my car."

"Grand! See you there!" He turned and walked to where Daisy and Nick stood.

Rubi Lee simmered in a cauldron of frustration and rage. She pivoted and walked back in the direction of the parking lot. A new plan crawled through the darkness in her head.

I am going to make your life miserable. I will ruin everything and everyone you love, Rubi Lee promised. She turned away from the happiness outside the church parking lot. She could not bear that environment any longer. *If I couldn't get you here, I'll find another way to hurt you*, she decided. Down the stone path to the graveyard she walked.

* * *

The Cascades Golf Club ballroom brimmed with the vivacious energy of guests ready to cut loose. Twenty-five tables of eight were set with crystal glasses, shiny silverware, and gifts Daisy and Nick selected for their guests. In the center of each table sat a glass bowl in the likeness of a golf ball full of the same hydrangea. People crowded the four bars, but Ira, Daisy's former bartender colleague from the Black LaSalle in DC, was in total command. His team of bartenders was on top of the crowd. Drinks flowed and people were happy.

Karen and the wedding planner, Chantal, announced that the wedding party was going to be photographed on the eighteenth green.

"To the green we go!" Karen demanded.

No one listened.

She put two fingers in her mouth and whistled loudly. "The sooner we get this done, the sooner we can continue to party!"

Moans came from the groomsmen and bridesmaids.

"Oh hush. Take drinks with you!" Yvan, Chantal's assistance, admonished.

Karen, Yvan, and Chantal ushered the rambunctious bridal party outside to the emerald lushness of the eighteenth green.

After the group pictures were over, Nick and Daisy stayed at the edge of the green. He asked Karen to snap a few pictures there. He explained it was a special spot for them.

"I better take off my shoes. I don't want to puncture the green!" Daisy laughed.

"Do you remember this spot?" Nick asked. "That summer we were fourteen? When we learned who killed my great uncle?"

"I'll never forget it. Dad was right here"—she pointed with her toe—"when he arrested Mayor Hall." She cast her eyes down. "I wish he were here." A tear slowly slid down her cheek.

"Daisy, he *is* here, and he always will be," Nick said, patting her heart. They turned toward the setting sun over the eighteenth fairway. "This is almost as beautiful as you." He kissed her, grabbed her hand, and led her up the steps. "Time to party, Mrs. Tyson!"

Hours of dancing and eating continued as the wedding party and guests enjoyed themselves deep into the night. By midnight, the party began to wind down.

"I think it's time for us to go," Nick whispered in Daisy's ear with a smile.

Daisy turned and kissed him deeply. "Oh, it's *definitely* time for us to go."

Nick took her hand and whirled her around the dance floor to the band's last song. After the final note, Nick took the microphone and thanked everyone for their support and love. "We will see you all at brunch tomorrow."

They wandered to the front door of the club to get into the limo, but there was no car.

A low blast of what Daisy thought was a foghorn made her jump. From the corner of the driveway rumbled the stunning 1937 black LaSalle with Nick's grandfather and owner of the car, William Tyson at the wheel. Streamers adorned the narrow windshield. Balloons bobbed from the doorhandles.

"BB!" called Nick. "You're going to chauffeur us to the hotel?"

"Of course! What better a way for you two to start your life together than a ride in the old boy? I had him detailed just for you two!"

Family and friends ambled outside to wish the newlyweds goodbye. Nick helped Daisy into the rumble seat then jumped in. They both gave a wave before BB hit the gas. The crowd cheered when the LaSalle rolled down the driveway into the dark night. Daisy nestled her head on Nick's shoulder, and he wrapped his arm around her.

"Don't forget we're going to the cemetery in the morning before brunch," she murmured.

"I would never forget. We'll visit Hoot before we say hi to your dad."

"Perfect," Daisy whispered as she closed her eyes and dozed off. Nick looked down at her and smiled. He kissed her forehead.

"You have a real sleeping beauty there," BB said, looking in the rearview mirror.

"That she is, BB. It's been an exhausting, emotional, but joyous day for all of us."

CHAPTER 9

Thin fingers of sun snuck between the blinds and stretched across bare Nick's chest. He opened his eyes and gazed over at Daisy. She was on her side, back to him, sound asleep. He hated to wake her.

He scooched over and whispered in her ear, "Morning, Mrs. Tyson." He nuzzled her hair and ran a hand down her hip.

"Mmm, I love the sound of that." She smiled. She kept her eyes closed and murmured how much she loved him.

"I love you too, my sleeping beauty. And I hate to interrupt your sleep, but we need to be at brunch in two hours; plus, we have to visit your dad and Hoot first."

Daisy sighed and rolled over. "I guess we don't have time for a repeat performance of last night?" She slid over to lie on top of Nick.

He stroked her back and kissed her deeply. "You're killin' me," he laughed.

"You're right. We can take care of business later." She rolled off him and headed into the bathroom.

They showered quickly and dressed for the day. After a quick cup of coffee, the newlyweds strolled hand-in-hand out of the hotel into the sun-soaked morning.

Headstones of all shapes and sizes dotted the main lawn of St. Matthew's church. Daisy tiptoed over the lawn, careful to avoid stepping on plots. "NT, Mom said Hoot is buried near the large oak tree to the left of the front door."

Nick turned toward the church. "I remember. It's over there." He pointed at a mature oak tree. "I see a headstone with flowers."

Up against a gray marble headstone rested a bunch of white roses. Daisy looked down and read aloud, "Percy Robert Alexander. Oh, how we miss you Hoot."

Nick put his arm around his wife. "Hey Hoot, Daisy and I got married yesterday. I wish you were here to be a part of it, but I know you were looking down on us. Thank you for everything." He bent down and placed his hands on the gravestone. Daisy joined him.

"Same goes for me. Somehow, I think you knew we would end up together. Thank you Hoot. We love you." Silence surrounded them. Memories of childhood summer days with Hoot filled their hearts.

After a solemn minute, Daisy took Nick's hand and said it was time to visit her father. They walked over the bumpy ground through the tranquil cemetery to where her father lay. From behind, they approached the white granite headstone. Its newness reflected the warm sunlight. Daisy's heart leapt from her chest; her eyes filled with tears. Nick heard a small whimper escape.

"It's all right," Nick said.

"I need a minute." Daisy inhaled, wiped her eyes, and shook her head.

"You okay?"

She nodded, took his hand, and walked to the front of her father's headstone.

They stopped dead in their tracks. Daisy screamed.

Thick red letters defiled her father's headstone: *BITCH*. Red paint streaked from the letters onto the green grass.

The ground rushed up to meet Daisy. She fell to her knees. "Oh my God!" She frantically tried to scrub the paint from the coarse granite. "Nick, what's going on? Why would someone *do* this?" Her sobs broke the serenity of the bright morning. She did not feel the warm blood trickle from her raw fingertips.

Nick stood speechless and stared at the defaced headstone.

"Dad, I'm sorry someone did this. I'm sorry!" She wailed.

Her frenzied attempt at cleaning the headstone made Nick ill. He reached down and pulled her up to her feet. Daisy resisted and tried to yank away from him. Blood from her hands sullied her dress in mean, jagged streaks.

"Daisy! Daisy! Stop it!" He grabbed her shoulders. She stopped struggling and regarded him. "I'm as horrified as you are! We need to tell Reverend Brindley."

Deep down she knew he was right. She collapsed into his arms and sobbed.

From across the cemetery, they heard Reverend Brindley's polished voice. He trotted over, vestments flapping against his thin legs. "Good morning Mr. and Mrs. Tyson! Oh, what a magnificent ring that has! Lovely to see you after . . ." His cheery face flipped to one of fearful concern. "Dear God, what has happened? Why do you have blood on your dress?"

Daisy pointed to her father's headstone.

He gasped and gazed at Daisy and Nick. "Oh, dear God, no. This can't be!" He scurried over to the headstone to inspect the damage. "Oh no. Oh Daisy, I don't know what to say. I am so sorry."

"Why would someone *do* this? My dad doesn't deserve this!" Daisy cried. "Please Reverend, can you help get this cleaned off?"

He bustled over to Daisy and hugged her. "Oh yes, dear Daisy. I know someone who is an absolute wizard. She'll have it cleaned in no time."

"But we need to find out who did this. I think we should call the police," Nick demanded.

"But of course. Any person who would willingly deface a gravestone deserves a special place in Hell," Reverend Brindley replied.

Nausea turned Nick's stomach. He turned and wrapped his arms around Daisy. "Daiz, we'll find out who did this. I promise." He looked over her head at Reverend Brindley, who nodded. "As much as we don't feel like it, we need to calm down and get to brunch. It is still our wedding weekend, and people are waiting for us."

Daisy sighed, "I know. The thought of food is nauseating, but we don't want to worry anyone by not showing up—especially Mom." Fresh tears filled her green eyes. "Oh my God, she's going to die when she sees this." She turned away from the two men. "Give me a few minutes." Daisy walked to a bench and sat.

Nick turned to the reverend. "Reverend, we have to report this. Not only is it vandalism; it's also trespassing."

"Yes, it is. My hallowed ground—my *church*—and the

Taylor family's sacred tombstone have been violated under my watch."

Nick felt sorry for the older man. "Reverend, this is not your fault. How could you know this would happen?"

Reverend Brindley did not take his eyes from the ground. "Logically you are correct. Emotionally, however, is a different story." From behind, he heard Daisy approach and turned. "I know you're not okay, so I will refrain from asking."

"Thanks, Reverend. You're a smart guy." She held up the bottom of her blood-spotted dress. "I need to change before we go to brunch."

"Yes, you do." He looked at his watch. "Then we need to get a move on."

Reverend Brindley promised he would call with any news at all, even when they were in Hilton Head for their honeymoon.

"For now, I think we need to keep this to ourselves. Brunch is not the place to tell anyone about this," Daisy said on the walk back to the hotel.

Nick pulled her in and kissed her head. "I thought the same thing. It's been such a joyous weekend. Nothing good can come of ruining it for people, especially our parents."

* * *

On the way to pick up Annie Taylor, Daisy's mother, Nick gripped the side door handle until his hand ached. He turned and glowered at his wife. Dark sunglasses blocked out much of her face. Her diamond rings sparkled in the sun on hands that choked the life out of the steering wheel.

He asked, "Are you getting ready to try out for this year's Indy 500? Slow down, Daiz!"

She tilted her head down and stole a quick glance at the speedometer of her Jeep. "Oops. I had no idea I was pushing ninety. I'm so caught up thinking about Dad's headstone." The jolting vision of the snow-white headstone defiled by the blood-red scrawl of *BITCH* penetrated her mind.

"I'm a tornado of emotion and it's driving me crazy! We had the best wedding in the world, and bam! Some horrible person destroyed Dad's headstone. Who in the hell would do that and why?"

To Nick's relief, she eased up on the gas. He rubbed her forearm she rested on the console. "I can't take away how you feel. I wish I could. I don't have an answer either."

"The only comfort is that Reverend Brindley called the police. There has to be a way to trace the paint, right?"

"In today's age of technology, I would bet our life savings on it."

Sighing, Daisy replied, "I sure hope so." She turned into her aunt's circular driveway. Annie and her sister Liza were waiting in the driveway of Liza's home. Daisy and Nick honked and waved. "Put on a happy face. We can't let Mom suspect anything."

"Morning, everyone!" Daisy called. Pleasantries were exchanged. "Ready Mom?" Daisy asked as Nick took Annie's suitcase.

"Yes I am." Annie bent down and hugged her sister. "Thank you for everything. I love you dearly," she told Liza.

"Love you more!" She gripped her only sibling tightly. "Be safe. Text me when you're home."

"I will."

From her wheelchair, Liza waved and watched the car disappear.

Rain began to fall when they were outside of Baltimore. Daisy consulted her phone and saw they were driving into more rain. "Shoot, it's going to be pouring all through here, but clear by the time we get home."

"Hopefully the weather will cooperate when you two drive back down to Hilton Head," Annie said.

"Same here, but we're breaking up the trip," Nick said.

"Good for you." Annie closed her eyes and laid her head back. "It's a shame you had to delay for a week, though."

"It's fine. I want everything wrapped up at work before we leave," Daisy said. Nick agreed.

"What are your plans while we're gone?" Nick asked.

Annie opened her eyes and smiled brightly. "I am going on a community outreach trip with my church!" Giddiness hopped out of her words.

"Really? Good for you! Details please," Daisy said.

"Well, St. Stephen's established a program in which we ask corporations to donate school supplies for underprivileged children. Joyce Plimpton, a favorite colleague, told me about it. I told her to sign me up. She's done this trip for a few years and loves it."

"You work well together. She's really nice and I'm sure the students love her," Daisy said.

"Oh, they do. Joyce's last name, Plimpton, can be a mouthful for some of our little ones, so they affectionately call her 'Missus P'! She's one of the hardest working volunteers in our school."

"Where are you guys going for the trip?" Nick asked.

"A town called Shunk in Sullivan County, about three hours from home."

Daisy snapped to attention. "Shunk? I was there for a story a couple weeks before our wedding."

"The one about the remains of a body being found, correct?" Annie asked.

"Yes."

"Any more information?" Nick asked.

"Not that I know of, but I'll circle back eventually."

CHAPTER 10

A yellow school bus stood at attention outside St. Stephen's Church, ready for its volunteers to board. Two of those church members and close colleagues, Annie Taylor and Joyce Plimpton, boarded.

"Annie, this is perfect for us!" Joyce exclaimed, zipping up a purple backpack.

The two women became fast friends over their mutual love for educating young children, playing Words with Friends, and hiking. A last, and sad, element linked them: widowhood. "I have to tell you. Daisy and Nick's wedding was *so* beautiful," Joyce said as she settled into her seat. "Simply gorgeous."

"Oh, thank you. I can't believe it's over!" Annie said. "Jackson would have loved it."

"Yes, he would have." Joyce continued, hands clasped together, "The orchids accenting the dinner plates, the lovely gifts for the guests. I could go on and on. I'm sad I never had the chance to plan a wedding for anyone. But I'll be forever grateful for you and Daisy asking me to help with her flowers."

"Well Joyce, if anyone knows flowers, it's you! After all, you *did* own one of the most successful and popular flower shops before you became a volunteer librarian."

"You're right. That seems like a lifetime ago." Joyce

sipped her water. "Speaking of lifetimes, is the happy couple enjoying a romantic honeymoon in some exotic location?"

"They are, but nothing too exotic. They're in Hilton Head for ten days."

"I love Hilton Head! George and I went there many times. I just love Harbour Town."

"It's a very nice place. I talked to Daisy the other day, and they're having a wonderful time."

"I'm glad. On another note, I hope we get to meet some of the children we're helping."

"So do I. I know these families will appreciate our work," Annie assured Joyce.

"I've never been to Sullivan County. I've heard that the foliage is spectacular this time of year."

Pastor Carroll stood in the front of the bus for an announcement. "Okay everyone, please listen up." She went through the list of families who would be receiving the supplies. Along with each family name she gave the ages of the children who would benefit. She continued, "Some families can't get to the community center at this time, so I'm asking some of you to take the donations to their house."

Joyce and Annie's names were on that list. "Apparently, it is a small community, so if you don't mind a short walk?" Pastor Carroll raised her eyebrows in hopeful anticipation.

"Of course! Anything to help!" Joyce chirped.

"Thank you and bless you. We'll check into our hotel first then head out to our assigned homes. I look forward to a successful and blessed several days working with all of you." Pastor Carroll sat back down.

After the accommodations were sorted, the volunteers prepared to flood the community of Shunk with goodwill. After a brief introduction by the local community leader, the group received their assignments.

"We'll meet back here later this afternoon. Good luck and God bless!" Pastor Carroll sang out.

"Ready?" Joyce asked Annie.

"Yup. Looks like we're headed to 1169 Pinetree Way. According to Google Maps, it's only about a half mile south."

"The weather could not be better," Joyce remarked and tilted her round face skyward. "The warmth of the sun is lovely."

A black, metal mailbox sat atop a white wooden stake at the end of the driveway. In gold, *1169* was painted on the side. Annie consulted her list again to make sure it was the correct house.

"This is it," she told Joyce.

The worn-down driveway leading up to the small brick-and-siding ranch house was lined with miniature round bushes. As they walked past the blue sedan in the driveway, Annie glanced inside. She saw it was littered with empty soda bottles, chip bags, and other crap. *Not everyone is a neat freak like me*, she thought.

Up the three brick steps they climbed. Joyce looked for a doorbell and, not finding one, she rapped on the brown metal door.

The door squeaked open. The pale, skinny face of a young woman with dark, hooded joyless eyes peered from behind the door. Stringy blond hair was pulled back tightly from her angular face.

"Can I help you?" Rubi Lee's voice was gravelly. She coughed and set her gaze on the two women.

"My name is Annie Taylor, and this is Joyce Plimpton. We're from St. Stephen's Church outside Philadelphia. We are here as part of our community outreach program."

Rubi Lee's gaze bounced between the two women. She blinked in disbelief. *I can't believe this! Are you fucking kidding me? Here she is right in front of my face!* she thought, looking at Annie.

The lie came out like smooth silk. "Oh yeah, I heard about you. I'm Tanya."

"Nice to meet you Tanya," Annie replied.

"Hi there, Tanya. I'm Joyce Plimpton."

Adrenaline raced through Rubi Lee. Her armpits dampened as she fought to keep her hands in her pockets to avoid pulling out whatever eyelashes she had left—a habit left over from her broken childhood. Only a piece of gum would curtail her. *Crap! It's in the kitchen*, she remembered. *Keep the conversation going!*

"What, ah, what can I do for you?" Rubi Lee asked.

"May we come in? We have brought school supplies for your children," Annie asked.

"Yeah, come in." Rubi Lee stepped aside and held the door open.

* * *

Annie and Joyce stepped inside the front door, which opened at the base of navy-carpeted steps. Blond wooden floors shined brightly throughout the entire first floor. A beige three-seat sofa was pushed against a wall across from a small brick fireplace. An empty bookcase stood to its right. Two chairs of the same color were placed across from the couch. A rickety brown coffee table with Tanya's laptop open on it was placed front of the chairs. Rubi Lee panicked when she remembered the laptop was open. Information about Daisy covered the screen. *Oh shit! They can't see what's up on the screen!*

"Let me just send this email. Hang on a second." She went over to the laptop, pretended to send an email, and closed it. Annie and Joyce waited patiently by the steps and glanced around the tidy, nicely furnished house. A single lamp burned against the soft gray living room wall. An arched wall opened to a modest dining room which sat bare, aside from a small brass chandelier.

"Thanks for waiting. So you're here to deliver school supplies, right?" Rubi Lee asked.

"Yes, we are. In these backpacks"—Annie motioned to them—"are notebooks, pencils, paper. Everything for kids to achieve success. Speaking of children, where are yours? We'd love to show them what we brought."

Shit, kids! Think! Think! Think!

"Your kids?" Joyce asked again.

"Darn it. Y'all missed them. They're with their father. He took them fishing."

"Too bad for us. Do you mind if we sit and chat a bit? We walked here and I need a break," Joyce asked. "Perhaps you have some questions about our program?"

"Sure, make yourselves comfortable." Adrenaline still flying, Rubi Lee knew she needed to center herself. "Where are my manners! Can I get y'all something to drink?" She pasted on a faux smile.

"Water would be nice. We worked up a thirst by walking here," Joyce responded.

"I'll be right back." Rubi Lee went to the kitchen. As she filled the glasses, a feeling of euphoria swept through her skinny body. She tilted her head back and cast her eyes upward, a wide smile spreading across her face. *Thanks, Zeke, for putting her right in front of me. It all starts today. I won't let you down.* Her eyes fell on Timmy, her knife. She extended her hand and caressed the black handle. "Stay patient, my friend. You'll be needed soon enough." From a drawer, she took the tire iron and slid it up the sleeve of her sweatshirt. She placed the glasses of water onto a tray for better balance.

"Here you go." Rubi Lee offered them the tray.

Annie and Joyce took deep drinks and leaned back in the chairs.

"Thank you. I needed that," Joyce said.

"So, tell us more about your children," Annie said.

The statement hung in the air. Blindsided, Rubi Lee swallowed, her mind reeling. "I have two—a boy and girl—real close in age. I ah, am sharing custody with my ex."

"I see. That must be difficult," Annie replied.

Rubi Lee seized this sympathetic moment to her advantage. Pausing, she squeezed her eyes tightly and sniffled. "It's horrible, but I make do."

Joyce shifted uncomfortably and threw a worried glance at Annie. "Oh, poor girl. We're so sorry."

"It's okay. Me and their dad split a while back."

Joyce steered the conversation back to the kids. "What're their names?" she asked.

Names! Think! "Tammy is my girl and Hank is my boy,"

Rubi Lee lied, using her own parents' names.

"Lovely names. How old are they?" Joyce continued

"Eight and ten."

"Fun ages. What do they like to do?" Annie asked.

Shut up! Stop asking me! But Rubi Lee played along. She thought back to her own childhood with Zeke and the things they loved to do: play hide and seek in their trailer park, dip hot dogs in ketchup, catch lightning bugs, and dream of a better life. Rubi Lee answered them with this condensed version of her childhood—minus the better life part. "But they do love those damn games on their phones!"

Annie and Joyce laughed in agreement.

"I'm sorry we didn't get to meet them. They sound wonderful. You should be proud," Annie said.

Rubi Lee felt her adrenaline overtaking any patience. *Part one of my plan has to happen now*, she thought. "Thanks, I try." She stood, indicating it was time to go. Annie and Joyce took the cue.

"We've taken up enough of your time. Thank you for the water and conversation," Joyce said.

"May I use your bathroom before we walk back?" Annie asked.

"Of course." Rubi Lee turned and pointed down the hallway. "Second door on the right."

"Thanks. I'll be right back."

Annie wandered down the hall. At the click of the door handle, Rubi Lee slid the tire iron from her sleeve into her palm. Grip firm, she turned to Joyce who had no time to react. Rubi Lee swung and hit Joyce on the right side of her head. A grotesque *crack* filled the living room. Joyce dropped like Michael Moorer after a George Foreman one-punch. Blood oozed from Joyce's head like yolk. Rubi Lee stood over her; a triumphant smile danced across her face.

Annie searched for any kind of hand towel, as the towel rack was bare. *Hm, I don't see any and I don't want to root through her drawers. Oh well*, she thought and wiped her hands on her pants. She opened the door to the hallway. In her pocket, she felt her phone vibrate. Head down, she read aloud as she walked down the hall, "Joyce, Pastor Carroll said we should be back by four." Looking up, she saw Rubi Lee standing over a still Joyce.

Annie dropped her phone and rushed to her friend. "Oh my God! Joyce! Are you okay?" She fell to her knees by Joyce's head. Placing two fingers against Joyce's warm neck, Annie prayed for a pulse—nothing. Something warm seeped through her jeans. Looking down, she was kneeling in a pool of Joyce's blood.

The room suddenly became vacant of any air. Joyce's dead eyes stared at the ceiling.

Glued to the floor, Annie looked up at a smiling Rubi Lee. She screamed, "What *happened?*"

Rubi Lee slowly lifted her arm. In her hand was the bloody tire iron. She took a step toward Annie. "You're next!"

Annie shot from the room like a rabbit. She ran screaming to the front door. "Help! Someone help!"

"Not so fast!" Rubi Lee shrieked. She jumped on Annie's back and choked her with a double-armed, powerful hold. The two spun around like a top with Annie scratching and pulling at Rubi Lee's arms.

"Let me go!"

Rubi Lee squeezed hard. It became difficult to breathe. The four walls started to close in. Annie backpedaled and slammed into a wall with all 145 pounds of her. A sharp *oomph* pushed out of Rubi Lee's chest at the impact.

Annie pulled hard and pried one of Rubi Lee's spidery arms from her throat. She turned out of the headlock and ran to the front door. Safety and freedom were only ten feet away.

"Oh God! Someone help me!" But the walls absorbed her panicked scream. She grabbed at the doorknob. But Rubi Lee was too quick.

Intense pain filled Annie's head. Sudden blackness was all she knew.

* * *

Annie's eyes fluttered slightly. Fists of pain pounded her head. Clouds danced in her peripheral vision. Gently she sat up. Eyes at half mast, she scrutinized her surroundings and realized she was lying on a bed.

Joyce! Where's Joyce? she thought—then the grotesque image of her friend flooded back. *Oh my God! No! Joyce is dead!* Terror swept over her at the thought of that crazy woman bursting through the door at any minute. But the door stayed closed.

I have to get out of here! My phone! Where's my phone? She patted her pockets; it was gone. *Oh my God!* She shakily rose to her feet and made for the door. It was locked. She tried to raise one of the windows, but it would not budge. The other window did not yield either.

"Damnit!" She pounded on the glass, hoping to break the

panes. Nothing. She whirled around; her eyes fell on the chair. *That! I can throw it through the windows!* She yanked at it. Pain tore through her shoulder and traveled down her arm.

"Oh my God. *It's bolted to the floor!*" Annie made a second attempt to break the window with her hands, but the wind kicked up. She jumped at the menacing slam of the shutters. The brilliant sunshine vanished.

She screamed and pounded on the door. "Let me out of here! I'll do anything you want!" The talons of claustrophobia scratched at her soul. "Please! Let me out!" She battered until her hands ached. Annie felt swallowed up by the silent house. Drained and terrified, she slid to the floor in the darkened tomb.

* * *

The turning of the doorknob awakened her. Her blood ran cold at the eerie screech of the hinges. A sliver of light appeared from behind the cracked door.

"Hellooo Annie. Wakey, wakey!" Rubi Lee sang. She stood in the doorway, holding a knife.

Annie's eyes widened. "Please don't hurt me!"

"That's not up to me. If you misbehave, I'll be *forced* to hurt you. Or shall I say, my friend Timmy will." She waved the knife.

Annie was not sure she heard correctly. She could not help herself. "Timmy?"

"Yes, Timmy. Loyal, shiny, sharp Timmy. Timmy is always by my side, right Timmy?"

Annie did not know what to think. A gut check told her

that this young, waifish woman was extremely dangerous. "What . . . what . . . do . . . do you want from me?"

"Get up, turn around, and put your hands behind your back."

Annie obeyed. The handcuffs Rubi Lee slapped on her wrists sent cold tendrils of fear down her back. "Now, follow me."

Rubi Lee led her to the other bedroom. It was dark except for three candles on a dresser whose flickers sent an orange glow up the wall.

"Sit." Rubi Lee pointed to a chair directly across from the dresser.

Annie sat. "What do you want? I don't know you!"

Rubi Lee ignored her. "See all that?" She pointed at the dresser.

Annie squinted in the dark. The candles were surrounded by pictures, but she could not see of whom. Newspaper clippings hung loosely from the wall. She strained to see, but nothing was clear.

Annie's stomach churned. "Kind of. They ah, they look like, um, like pictures . . . and clippings from a newspaper? I'm sorry. I can't see very clearly. It's dark."

Rubi Lee snickered. "Maybe this will help." She flicked on a switch and the room came alive with blinding light.

Annie blinked at the assault of sudden brightness. The relentless pounding in her head subsided when she recognized what was in front of her. A small gasp escaped.

Pictures—lots of them—of a young man sat on top of the dresser near the candles. Other pictures of people she knew covered the walls. Annie gaped at them and became light-headed. Nausea sloshed in her stomach.

An engagement picture of Daisy and Nick was pinned to the wall; Daisy's face was covered with an X and a slash mark ran across Nick's. Annie raised her eyes and saw the entire wall was covered with pictures of her daughter and Nick. Every single one of them was slashed. "Oh my God. You're *her*." Tears slid down her face.

Rubi Lee grabbed Annie by the hair and pulled her close to the dresser. "Yup, your worst nightmare. In reality, you and *your family's* worst nightmare!"

"What do you want?"

"Revenge!" Rubi Lee spat. She grabbed a picture from the dresser and shoved it in Annie's face. "See this? You know who this is?"

Thick fingers of fear squeezed Annie's chest. Struggling to breathe, she was too terrified to do anything but close her eyes and shake her head.

Rubi Lee screamed, "LOOK at him! This is, *was*, my little brother!"

Annie cast her eyes to the handsome face of Zeke Dixon and stammered, "I'm sorry!"

"Do you want to know who is responsible for his murder?"

Murder? Why is she asking me this? I can't think straight! "I have no—"

"Your fuckin' bitch daughter!" she yelled. She shoved Annie to the floor and stepped on her chest.

"Please! Please! I beg you, don't kill me!"

"Kill you? Nah, I'm not gonna kill you—yet. I need you alive for a while—like weeks. But I *promise* I will destroy you, and your family, just like I destroyed your dead husband's headstone."

Annie's mind raced. Horror engulfed her. "What're you talking about? Why?"

"Oh, you didn't know? I left a little message on it for your daughter. And as to why? Because I could. And I want others to feel *my* pain." Rubi Lee tilted the tip of her knife over the candle flame until it blazed with heat. She knelt next to Annie, who tried to squirm away.

"No! No please!" The heat from the knife penetrated her skin. Annie wailed.

"I won't yet." Rubi Lee stood up and removed a picture from the wall. It was of Daisy. Crouching down, Rubi Lee stabbed the photo over Daisy's left eye. The heat burned a hole in the picture.

"You see, she destroyed my life when she killed my brother. And now it's *my* turn to destroy everything and everyone she knows and loves."

CHAPTER 11

"Hilton Head, here we come!" Nick exclaimed. Under a canopy of fluffy clouds, he pulled out of their driveway and within twenty minutes, they merged onto Interstate 95 headed south. He asked Daisy how the weather looked.

She consulted the weather on her phone. "Looks like clear skies for the next couple of hours."

"Good. In DC too?"

"Yep. I texted Ira and Henderson that we'd meet for lunch between twelve thirty and one."

"It'll be good to see those guys," Nick replied. "I know they were at our wedding, but we didn't really have a chance to talk."

"I know. We can be their captive audience."

"How long—" Nick was interrupted by "Beyond The Sea," Daisy's recently changed ringtone, their wedding song.

"It's Reverend Brindley." She said, "Hi, Reverend. Let me put you on speakerphone."

"How are the newlyweds?" he chimed.

"We're great. We're on our way to DC to meet friends for lunch. And from there, we'll drive down to Hilton Head."

"Sounds lovely. Anyway, I am calling with an update about your father's headstone. Thank the good Lord Jenny and I were able to scrub that horrid red paint from it."

Daisy sighed deeply. "Oh Reverend, that's great news. Do you have any idea when it was sprayed on?"

"I am not certain. However, I wanted to make sure that your father and Hoot's gravestones were clean, so Jenny and I circulated through that area on Friday morning to ensure that everything was in pristine condition. Which leads me to believe it happened Friday night, or—oh dear—on Saturday."

Daisy's mouth went dry. The reverend's statement hung like a dark, thick cloud.

"You're saying someone may have done that on our *wedding* day?" Nick asked.

"It's not entirely out of the realm of possibilities. Obviously I don't know for certain, and I am so very sorry. I did inform the authorities and they agree it was vandalism, desecration of a grave, and possible trespassing."

Daisy gave Nick the thumbs up.

"Good. Are they going to test the paint to determine the type and where it was bought?" Nick asked.

"Yes. And Daisy, I saved a few small scrapings for you. I know how much you enjoy a juicy investigation." The reverend chuckled.

"That's good news. Thanks so much. We're so appreciative," Daisy said.

"You're most welcome. Prayers that the police find the person responsible for this most reprehensible act."

"Amen to that," Daisy said.

"Jenny or I will be in touch. Enjoy your most deserved honeymoon!"

"Thank you!" they chimed in together and hung up.

"I love him. He's one of the most genuine, salt-of-the-earth men," Daisy said.

Soon, a comfortable silence filled the car. Nick glanced at Daisy. Her brow was furrowed, and she was twisting a tendril of red hair. "What's going on in that head?"

"Why would someone target Dad's headstone? Do you think it's someone from the past? Someone he arrested or locked up? But why write *BITCH* on it?"

"I don't know. Maybe it was directed at your mom? As you know, he ran into the bottom-feeders of society. It wouldn't surprise me if it was someone he arrested or put in prison."

Daisy pondered this. "I can't think of anyone else. This is scary, Nick. Something about the timing and our wedding. Someone tried to ruin our weekend."

"Yeah, the timing *is* coincidental. I wish we knew when this sicko specifically did it. If I had to guess, it was at night since the paint was dry, but I'm no expert."

"At least we know the cops have been told. We can touch base with the Brindleys when we get home. I'm glad it was cleaned off. I'm sick about it."

Nick removed his hand from the steering wheel and laid it on Daisy's thigh. "Tell ya what, let's try to focus on us, Hilton Head, and our honeymoon, okay?"

She took his hand and pressed it to her lips. "I will try. I can't promise however, that I won't think of it while we're gone."

"I know. But like we said, we've done everything we can to take care of it."

"You're right."

* * *

Henderson entered the Black LaSalle where Daisy used to tend bar. It soon became *the spot* after word spread that the former red-headed bartender survived a shootout with diamond smugglers and undercover agents, not to mention a United States Senator.

Ira glanced up from polishing glasses. "Henderson! It's great to see you man! You haven't been in for a while!"

"You as well!" Henderson replied. "I've been real busy, especially with physical therapy. Look, I can raise my arm all the way!" He proudly showed off the full range of motion in the arm and shoulder that took a bullet last December.

"Looks like all that PT was worth it! And you look like you took off some pounds." Ira appraised him over his glasses.

Henderson nodded and patted his shrunken midsection. "Damn straight!"

"Light beer then?"

"Sure." Henderson held up his wrist. "It's almost twelve thirty. Daisy and Nick will be here soon."

Inside the Black LaSalle, most tables were full. Ira saw Daisy and Nick walk in. He jogged around from the side of the bar, arms open wide. "There's my favorite bride! How are the newlyweds?"

"No complaints—other than we're thirsty!" Nick replied, embracing Ira.

"What're you drinking?" Ira asked.

"I'll have the IPA please," Nick replied.

"Light draft beer for me please," Daisy said.

"You got it!" Ira turned to Jimmy, his colleague. "Jim! One IPA and one light draft!"

Ira, Henderson, Nick, and Daisy shared laughter and conversation over a sumptuous lunch of sandwiches, wings, and pizza.

"I'm sure you're *real* glad you're in politics right now, huh Nick?" Henderson teased.

"Luckily, it's not the big leagues. Being on staff for the mayor is much calmer than being on the staff of a state senator."

"No shit. Truth be told, I'm surprised you continued in that field. Kinda thought you may have been too disgusted with that whole world," Henderson said.

"After that night in the garage, I was this close"—he held his thumb and forefinger about a tenth of an inch apart—"to quitting."

"What made you stay in it?" Ira asked. "You almost died that night, man."

Nick took a swig of water. "I thrive on the opportunity to better the place we live in. Philadelphia is a fantastic city with so much to offer. In the mayor's office, we have our hands full with a broken school system, crime, and other issues. However, the city's demographics have changed dramatically. Mid-lifers are moving into the city, out of suburbia."

"You like being back in your hometown, don't you?" Ira asked.

"Oh, you know it. And what makes it better is that Daiz works in the top station in the city. It was meant to be."

Henderson turned to Daisy. "I'm so proud of you for

stickin' to your guns and getting a reporter's job. You dug deep girl and did it." Henderson raised his glass. "Cheers!"

A loud *clink* made other patrons turn to see the commotion.

"You must love it," Henderson continued.

Daisy swallowed and patted her mouth. "I do. After the incident in December, I thought I would have to put everything on hold to heal my body and mind. But when Dr. Powell gave me the all-clear to finish school, I blew through the rest of my classes." She hesitated. "And we had to get out of DC." She nodded at Nick.

"What's it like working as a reporter? Do you stay local or travel?" Ira asked.

"I can't love it enough. It's a ball-buster job, but I love it. Every day is different because of myriad stories that need to be covered. As far as whether I'm local or I travel, it's both. For example, I've been to the Philadelphia Zoo to cover stories as well as down to Atlantic City. The farthest away I've been in my short tenure is three hours west to cover a special interest story."

"Oh yeah, that was to Shunk. You *have* to tell them about that," Nick put in.

"*Shunk*? What a name for a town!" Ira laughed.

"I know. Makes me think of a skunk. Kidding aside, it's a very beautiful place. Lots of woods, trees, rivers—total outdoorsy person's dream. Anyway, I was sent there to cover a story about the remains of a body found in some of the woods. Apparently, it was the first of its kind in over twenty-five years."

"Right up your alley. Was it a murder?" Henderson said.

"The authorities did not say much about it. It's a tightly knit community from what I gathered. The sheriff was helpful, but I sensed he was not comfortable talking about the discovery."

"As a former cop, I understand that. No one likes that kind of thing. But it happens," Henderson commented.

Soon, Daisy announced it was time to go. "I hate to break up the party, but we need to get going. We loved coming back here. Ira, I still miss working with you, but I don't miss some of the crazies who came in!"

"I know. I miss working with you too. We went through some unbelievable stuff together," Ira answered and stood to clear the plates.

"Great," Nick said and took Daisy's hand. "Well guys, we need to hit the road. We'll text you before we leave so we can meet up."

"We love you guys. Stay safe!" Daisy said as she and Nick hugged their friends and walked out of the Black LaSalle.

CHAPTER 12

"Time to get to work." Rubi Lee unlocked the handcuffs and told Annie to stand.

Annie froze. "What, what do you mean, get to work?"

Rubi Lee grabbed Annie's arm and steered her into the hallway. She jutted her pointy chin at the other bedroom. "Time to bury her."

Wide-eyed, Annie howled, "Oh God no! No!" She backed away into a wall.

"Just shut up." Rubi Lee shoved her toward Joyce. "Lift her up from under her arms. I'll get her feet."

"Oh God no!" Annie retched. "I . . . I . . . can't."

"Lift her up from the arms. Or else you'll join her." Light bounced from the knife in her hand.

Acid churned in Annie's empty stomach. She tried to avert her eyes from her dead friend. Tears splashed onto the dirty rug as she hesitantly bent down. "Oh Lord, please no!" Joyce's body still felt warm. Hot vomit bubbled up in Annie's throat. She turned her head and spit up on the rug. She collapsed into a sobbing ball.

"For fuck's sake! Now I have to clean up your puke!" Rubi Lee screamed. She stormed into the kitchen for bleach and a sponge.

Throwing the supplies on the floor, she ordered Annie to clean it up. "And then help me get rid of this body."

They wrapped the body in a tarp and moved it to the backyard. "Tomorrow we'll get rid of her," Rubi Lee said and lit a cigarette.

Annie was speechless. "Why did you kill her? You can't leave her out here!"

"I can do whatever I want. And why do you think I killed her?" A blue stream of smoke streamed from her mouth.

"I don't know!"

"You're not very bright, are you? She's a *witness!* Now shut up and get inside."

* * *

All night long, Annie's head spun. *Please God, let me pass out and wake up from this nightmare!* Sleep was out of the question.

Is this really happening? I've been kidnapped by this deranged woman when just yesterday, Joyce and I were handing out supplies! Finally, it dawned in Annie's terrified, rattled brain that Daisy, Nick, and Pastor Carroll knew she was on a community service trip.

Oh thank God! They'll notice I haven't called or texted . . . Annie lay in the dark and continued to pray. Just as her eyes grew heavy, the door banged open.

"Wake up. Time to get rid of her," Rubi Lee ordered.

Annie stirred slightly and struggled to sit up. "What do you mean?"

"Your friend. She needs to go."

Nonchalance oozed from Rubi Lee and turned Annie's empty stomach.

"Please no."

"Too bad. You don't have a choice." Rubi Lee strode to the bed and pulled Annie from it and dragged her outside.

* * *

An annoying, thick mist met Annie and Rubi Lee outside. Earlier in the morning, Rubi Lee parked the car out back, near Joyce's body.

Trunk open, Rubi Lee ordered Annie. "Help me shove her in the trunk!"

"No! Please don't make me do this. She's my friend!"

"*I don't care.* Get her feet!" Rubi Lee wielded Timmy. "Or Timmy will hurt you."

Timmy? She actually named her knife, Annie thought as her terror mounted. The mist grew into hard, cold drops. Annie turned away from Joyce and sent up a silent prayer.

"I said, get her feet!" Rubi Lee yelled.

The dark terror was tinged with shock. Annie bent down and cried, "Oh Joyce, God, forgive me!" Her back screamed as she lifted Joyce's feet. Strands of hair stuck to her damp cheek as she hoisted the body.

"Shut up! No one's here to help you!"

Joyce thudded into the trunk. Rubi Lee slammed the lid and ordered Annie to get in. The engine coughed and sputtered. Rubi Lee threw it in reverse then jerked it into drive. The wheels spun in a muddy puddle as they headed down Pinetree Way.

At a red light Rubi Lee turned to Annie who stared ahead, unblinking. "In the future when I ask you to do something, I think you should do it. Understand?" she ordered as she poked Annie with the knife.

Annie did not respond. Her mind raced like a rabbit at the events of the last day. *How did this happen? I was just on a bus with Joyce and now she's dead and I'm next. Please God, help me. I don't understand what is going on.*

The car bumped off the main road onto a dirt access road. Eventually, it led to Muncy's Creek and thick woods. Rubi Lee stopped on the side. From her pocket, she pulled Annie's phone and waved it in front of Annie's face.

"Who knows you're out here?"

Annie stammered and tried to focus. "Ah, my . . . children. And, um my pastor. Why?"

Rubi Lee sighed exasperatedly. She glanced around at the trees. "Send them both a message that you'll be staying longer up here. Make up some bullshit about hiking and looking at the leaves."

Annie fumbled with her phone, fingers shaking. She typed and showed Rubi Lee.

Rubi Lee read it. "Perfect. Send it and get out of the car."

Annie obliged. Her mind raced. *I know I'm going to die out here. My poor children!*

"Help me carry her into the woods," Rubi Lee barked.

Annie breathed deeply and walked to the back of the car where Rubi Lee stood. She recoiled at the smell and when she saw Joyce's pale foot slide from the tarp. "Oh my God!"

"Shut up. Just pick her up."

With quivering hands, Annie reached into the trunk and hoisted out her dead friend. Her lower back seized up and pain shot down her leg. She ground her teeth and blocked out the agony.

Rubi Lee hoisted the shovel from the trunk and indicated a path into the thick woods. "That way. Now."

After what seemed like a lifetime of trudging uphill through dense, beautiful woods, Rubi Lee stopped. Sweat and mist made Annie's shirt stick to her. Dizziness and nausea swirled like angry storm clouds inside her. "Please, no more. I can't go any farther."

Rubi Lee scanned the area. "This will do. Put her down."

Annie obeyed and then collapsed. Leaves and dirt tangled in her hair. She forced herself to focus on the birdsongs that danced through the trees. The fleeting reverie was shattered when she watched Rubi Lee kick Joyce down the hill. Annie folded into herself like a snail.

"Get up. We're not done."

Annie did not have the capacity to move or speak.

"I said *get up!*" Rubi Lee kicked Annie's foot.

This woman does not have a soul, she thought before rising. Stunned by what she just witnessed, Annie unfolded herself and quietly followed Rubi Lee down the hill. She ordered Annie to gather sticks and leaves to cover the body.

"We'll take turns digging a grave. Plus, I figure the animals will take care of this in no time."

Horror splayed across Annie's face. "*What? No!* You're psychotic! You can't leave her here! What about her family? Are you heartless?" The words poured out like a river.

"I don't give a *shit* about her family." Rubi Lee handed

Annie the shovel. "Get busy."

Annie's muscles ached after shoveling. Panting, she halted and looked at Rubi Lee. "You're not going to get away with this," she murmured.

"Wanna bet? No one knows *exactly* where you are, and no one will be able to trace me." She laughed and started to walk back to the car.

Annie stared at Rubi Lee's retreating back; adrenaline pulsated in her veins. Fight or flight instincts took over. *It's now or never*, Annie thought and made a fateful decision: She pivoted and ran. Blindly, she ran for all she was worth.

I have to find a road! I have to find help! She tried to dodge the roots that stuck up from the ground like small landmines. Annie ran around the occasional rock jutting from the earth. Rays of sun pushed through the leafy gaps in the lush green canopy of trees above and dappled the ground with shadows. She struggled to discern if what she saw up ahead of her were holes in the ground or shadows. *Please God! Don't let me twist an ankle!* Like a soldier trying to dodge enemy fire, Annie plunged deeper into the foreign woods. *I have to find a path or a road or something!*

Rubi Lee spun around to see Annie's dark head bobbing through the trees. "You're not gonna get away!" she bellowed. "Timmy and I are comin' after you!"

Annie glanced over her shoulder and saw Rubi Lee in hot pursuit. She forced her tired legs to keep going. *Oh my God! My chest is on fire!* Her back ached. *If I don't keep going, she'll get me!*

"Help! Help!" she screamed and plunged deeper into the foreign woods. Towering thick-trunked trees and bramble bushes obstructed her view of any type of path. Annie propelled herself forward, racing to get away. *I gotta find help! She killed Joyce! And now she wants to kill me!* Annie tore through the thick woods. *Screaming will get you nowhere. She'll hear you!*

"You're not gonna get away from me!" Rubi Lee yelled into the trees. "I can see you! You can't hide from me!"

Go! Go! Annie thought. *She's gaining on you! There has to be a path or a road somewhere!* A dead tree lay twenty yards ahead of her. *Oh no!* The dead tree crept closer and closer as Annie plunged forward. Vaulting the tree was out of the question, so she rolled over it but landed hard on her back. Layers of skin were scraped off her arm by the harsh bark. *Get up! Get up!*

Annie managed to stand. Before she had time to take a step, Rubi Lee leaped from the dead tree onto Annie's back.

"You're mine now, bitch!" Rubi Lee screamed.

The blow knocked the wind out of Annie. She gasped for air. Lying face down, she felt Rubi Lee's forearm pressing her face into the damp leaves and muddy forest floor. Annie was shocked at Rubi Lee's strength. Dirt and leaves filled her mouth. The musty flavor of earth made her gag.

"I should kill you right now, you fuckin' bitch!" Rubi Lee yelled in Annie's ear. "But I need you alive!" Rubi Lee straddled Annie and yanked her head up. Annie gasped and coughed.

"I'm sorry, I'm sorry!"

"If you ever, *ever* try something like this again, Timmy will cut your heart out while it's still beating and shove it in your mouth. Do you *understand*?" Rubi Lee yelled into Annie's ear.

Annie's face dropped back on to the fetid forest floor. Compliance had won. She whimpered, "I . . . I . . . understand. What do you want from me?"

Rubi Lee panted before answering. "Don't move." She pulled zip ties from her pocket. "I need you as bait to get *her*!" She twisted the ties around Annie's wrists and pulled her from the damp ground.

Annie's mind spun. *What is she talking about?* "Who? I don't know what you're talking about!"

Rubi Lee "Your spawn of Satan daughter, that's who."

Annie hesitated before answering. "Daisy? What did she do to you? She's never hurt anyone in her life!"

* * *

"Walk and keep your mouth shut."

Annie listened to Rubi Lee mumble nonsensically. She closed her eyes and tried to wrap her mind around where she was and what transpired in the last twelve hours.

This lunatic killed my friend! Come on Annie, think! You have to figure out how to keep yourself alive! God only knows how much time you have!

Back at the house, Rubi Lee cut the zip ties to cuff Annie back to the chair in the bedroom housing the shrine. She lit the candles on the dresser and tugged the shades down. She caressed the edge of a picture of Zeke.

"Oh, Zeke. You were so handsome. I'm gonna make this right." She picked up the picture and turned it to face Annie. "See her? She's the one who's gonna bring me the bitch who got you killed!" A hyena-like laugh filled the room.

"Please don't keep me in the dark," Annie begged.

Rubi Lee turned from the doorway and stared at Annie's filthy face, matted hair, and torn, bloody clothes.

"I guess I'll keep the door open," she sneered and walked out.

"Thank you."

Annie studied the pictures of Daisy, Nick, and Zeke that covered the walls. Annie counted eleven pictures of Zeke. She noticed that Rubi Lee had cut red hearts from construction paper to which she glued every picture of Zeke. *Hero worshipping*, Annie thought and shifted her eyes to the other wall.

Newspaper articles covered the other wall. Annie squinted at the bold-faced headlines: *New Hire at Live5 News Daisy Taylor*; *Nicholas Tyson newest member of Mayor Basile's Staff*; *Taylor–Tyson wedding at St. Matthew's.* Chills ran through her at the number of pictures and amount of research Rubi Lee conducted on her family. As a former teacher, she pulled from her vault of psychology training to assess her situation and her captor. Annie knew she was dealing with an intelligent, broken and dangerous woman who was hell-bent on revenge. People like her, Annie had learned, would stop at nothing to accomplish their twisted goals. Eyes closed, she prayed and pondered her situation. Suddenly, the voice of her late husband, Jackson, spoke to her. *"With every problematic situation there is always a solution."*

Tears formed in her green and a calmness washed over her. "Oh, my dear Jackson. I miss you so much." A kernel of hope and strength popped deep within her soul. Resolve and grit stirred her survival instincts. "Thank you, Jackson. I will survive this horrible ordeal."

"Who're you talking to?" Rubi Lee appeared in the doorway.

Annie sniffled. "No one."

She waggled Annie's phone in front of her. "Damn, your phone's blowing up. It must be nice to have people care about you."

Annie said nothing.

"I don't know what that's like. I used to, until Zeke was killed. By your daughter."

Annie grit her teeth. "My daughter *did not* kill your brother."

"Maybe not *directly*, but she's one hundred percent responsible. She—" Rubi Lee was interrupted by another text. She read aloud, "And I have not heard back from Joyce. Is she with you?" Rubi Lee clicked her tongue in mock compassion. "*So* sweet. Pastor Carroll is *so* concerned about poor Joyce." Pretending to be Annie, Rubi Lee replied to every text. "I told this pastor person that you and Joyce decided to stay up here for a while."

"No one is going to believe this, especially my family."

Rubi Lee rolled her eyes and chuckled. "Whatever. Anyway, I'm outta here for a few days. I'm going to lock you in this room. You can use the bathroom, but don't bother trying to run." She pointed to the floor at three paper bags. "Inside those is food and water. Nothing fancy, but you'll eat it."

"Where are you going?"

"None of your business. Don't try anything because I'll be watching." She turned on a small video camera atop the bookcase across the room. "Be a good girl." Rubi Lee patted Annie on the head and left.

CHAPTER 13

Inside the mostly full Black LaSalle bar, diners discussed politics, business deals, grandchildren, the weather. Ira Petrov, head bartender and partial owner, was training Jimmy, a new employee on the recently installed POS system.

"So, I just hit 'enter order' after I take the order, right?" Jimmy asked.

"Yup. Nothing more, nothing less."

"Sounds good to me. Next person who comes in, I'll do it."

"Great. While you're here, please check the two light beer draft kegs. I think we're running out."

"Yes boss!"

* * *

Because she and Zeke had been to the Black LaSalle several times, Rubi Lee knew it was a very popular lunch spot. *Perfect*, she thought. *Those assholes in there won't live to see dinner!* She turned right and glided the car into a spot two blocks away from the Black LaSalle. She lugged a backpack from the back seat and looped its straps over her bony shoulders. Yanking a hat on tightly, she marched to the front door and peered through the large windows of one of the most popular watering holes in Washington, DC. Bar seats sat open, so she wasted no time entering. Eyes darting left and right, she headed for one of the empty seats. No one noticed her, ever. *What else is new?* Gently, she placed the heavy backpack on the floor and nudged it up against the bar with her booted foot.

Jimmy saw her and shuffled to her. "Hello. Can I get you a drink?"

Rubi Lee did not make eye contact. "Yukon. And make it double."

"Be right back."

"Thanks."

He placed it down. Sipping her drink, Rubi Lee gazed around the Black LaSalle. *This dump hasn't really changed. Doesn't matter though, it isn't gonna be here long.* The door behind the bar swung open and Ira popped out. She immediately recognized the head bartender.

"I was about to offer you a drink, but it looks like Jimmy got ya," Ira said to Rubi Lee.

"Oh yeah, I'm fine." She pulled out her phone and scrolled. She could feel his eyes on her. *Please go away, asshole!*

"I don't mean to be pushy, but do I know you from somewhere?"

Eyes still glued to her phone, she replied, "I don't think so."

"Are you—"

"Ira! Gimme a hand with these kegs," yelled Jimmy, who served Rubi Lee.

Oh shit, I think he recognizes me, Rubi Lee thought. She hid her face in her phone. *But in ten minutes, that won't matter.* She glanced down at the backpack.

"Excuse me, can I get you anything to eat?" It was Ira. He cocked his head, eyes on her face. "Do I—"

"I could use a grilled cheese sandwich," she interrupted him, and picked up her phone.

"One grilled cheese coming up," he replied and headed toward the kitchen.

Rubi Lee knew it was time. She set the timer on her phone for ten minutes, threw back the last of her drink and scuttled out.

* * *

The blistering, orange fireball exploded from under the bar. Scorching flames tore through the front of the Black LaSalle. Glasses, plates, and silverware crashed to the floor. Windows shattered and rained shards onto the sidewalk, slicing unsuspecting passersby.

Ira was in the kitchen when the explosion happened. He and several cooks were thrown to the floor or against the walls. Pots and pans shot from their shelves and clattered to the floor.

Ira managed to get to his feet. Blood trickled from a gash on his head. He took no notice. "What the *hell*?" On wobbly legs, he hobbled to the front of his beloved restaurant. He was met with a sickening, bloody scene. Bodies of patrons and servers were strewn on the ground. People screamed in pain. Others lay burnt and lifeless. Trays that were once loaded with sandwiches, salads, and drinks lay strewn on the stone floor. Flames ate through the twenty-plus tables in the main seating area. The leather booths and tables were ablaze. Thick smoke filled the room and the fire alarm howled.

"Get out, get out!" He screamed into the kitchen. He pulled out his phone and called 911.

"There's been a ... fire ... or um ... explosion at the Black LaSalle! Help! Please send help!" He rattled off the address and ran to help any survivors.

Agonized screams and moans rose from the floor. Ira jumped into action and tried to drag any survivors through the backdoor to safety. The dead lay strewn on the floor. Even though he felt as like his skin was melting, Ira plunged headfirst into the thick smoke, hoping to save people. He did not see the body lying in his path. He tripped and when he looked down, a young, burnt face stared back—Jimmy, the young bartender he was training.

"NO! Jimmy!" Ira shook Jimmy's lifeless body. Smoke filled Ira's gasping lungs. He began to cough violently. *I gotta get out!* He knew he had to save himself before he succumbed to smoke inhalation. He stumbled out of the burning building, coughing violently. Gasping for breath, he fell into the arms of an EMT.

"Are you all right? Sir, are you all right?" the paramedic called to Ira. "Here, breathe!" She slapped an oxygen mask over his face. Ira sucked in several deep breaths.

Sirens wailed in the distance. Numerous fire companies raced to battle the blaze. Water shot from the hoses aimed at the building. Several firemen attempted to enter the building, but the intense heat turned them away.

"My friend and others are in there!" Ira screamed.

"Sir, we can't go in until we get the all-clear from the fire marshal! Given the intensity of the fire, I'm shocked you survived. I'm not sure how you did. You're a lucky man."

"I don't know about that," Ira murmured. He could barely raise his head to look at the fireman. Like an old, battered man, he shuffled across the street and fell to the curb. He did not notice the gash on his hand or the stench of smoke in his nostrils. He sat draped in a blanket, and tearfully watched the orange flames greedily eat up the wooden door at the front entrance. A gaping square hole took the place of the window above the brass handle to the two-story building. Its shards lay scattered on the ground. The massive window to the left, hand painted with THE BLACK LASALLE—was non-existent. Ugly jagged pieces of glass stuck from the frame like broken fingers.

Firefighters struggled to contain the flames which sprinted up the front of the stone building to the second floor. Two storage closets and two apartments were soon engulfed in the hateful flames. Smoke poured from the windows as the flames feasted on whatever was in their path. Wisps of burnt napkins, paperwork and receipts floated on air thick with the pungent aromas of melted plastic and smoke.

Through the cavernous hole in front, Ira spied flames dancing on the mahogany bar, inching closer to the inspiration for the name of the bar.

Oh Lord, please don't let the painting be destroyed. Ira thought of the enormous, breathtaking oil painting of a stunning 1937 black LaSalle proudly displayed behind his bar. Glass shelves on both sides held bottles which gave the impression they were sentinels guarding this treasured piece. Each week, he dusted the twenty-by-thirty-inch frame housing the most popular talking point of the bar. *Please God, spare the LaSalle!* he prayed as he helplessly watched his beloved bar and livelihood burn.

* * *

"Excuse me sir, I'm Officer Bart Sugarman. I know you've been through something traumatic, and I am sorry. May I ask you a few questions?"

Ira wiped his face. "Do I have a choice?"

The officer handed him a bottle of water. "Can you tell me what you saw inside? Do you have any idea what caused the blast? Were all of the inspections up to date?" He hurled questions at Ira, who patiently answered each one.

"You've been very helpful. Do you need assistance getting home?"

"No, I take the bus," Ira replied.

"Sir, I think you should go the hospital to get checked out."

"I'm okay. I need to go home and process this. My whole life is gone."

* * *

The following day, the fire marshal and his team sorted through the rubble of what was once the Black LaSalle. Across the street, a small group of curious onlookers and neighbors watched the action.

Tucked like a turtle into her hoodie, Rubi Lee smiled to herself when she heard murmurs that several people were killed in the blast. In her mind ran a one-sided conversation with Daisy. *Guess what, bitch? I destroyed your old bar, a place you loved! You deserved it! And as an added bonus, I killed some of your friends. I'm glad to know you'll feel what I feel. Too bad, so sad. Time to destroy Margaux Ford Park where my brother and uncle were killed.* She silently congratulated herself and turned to leave. She spied Ira out of the corner of her eye and abruptly turned in the other direction.

Ira stood in front of the charred skeletal frame of the Black LaSalle. Smoke lingered in the air. Puddles of beer trickled from shattered bottles. The acrid smell of burnt leather stung his nasal passages.

"Sorry sir, this is a fire and police scene. You can't be this close to the area," the fire marshal said to him.

Ira sighed deeply. "I understand. I just can't believe this happened. I've worked here for years. And now it's gone and so are innocent people."

"We will do everything we can to find out exactly how this happened."

"I hope so."

"Marshal! Got something over here!" an officer called.

The marshal patted Ira on the shoulder and hustled over. Ira tried to see and hear what was being said. To his left, he heard voices on a police radio emanating from a squad car. He inched closer to the fire marshal and the officer.

"We found what seems to be remnants of a pipe bomb. We need to follow protocol," the officer said to the fire marshal. He instructed a fireman to follow protocol, which meant calling the FBI and ATF.

A pipe bomb? Who would bomb the Black LaSalle? Ira wondered. From the left, several SUVs skidded to a shrill halt announcing their occupants' importance. Ira watched several suited women and men disembark. One of them marched toward Ira.

"Where's the marshal?" an agent asked Ira.

"There." He pointed.

"Thanks. Are you with the fire department?"

"No. I work, well, *used* to work here. And I'm part owner. Oh my God." Ira rubbed his head. "I can't believe what I'm seeing."

She softened her tone. "Were you here at the time of the explosion?"

"Yes, ma'am. I was working a double."

"Stick around. We'd like to talk to you. Please wait here."

The agents marched over and consulted with the marshal. In his hand was something not visible to Ira. One of the agents pulled on gloves, crouched down, and picked up some pieces of rubble.

"Bag this and close the area. Nobody within a hundred yards," the female agent said over her shoulder as she approached Ira. She extended her hand to him. "I'm Agent Cheryl Willoughby from the ATF. You are?"

"Ira Petrov."

"Can you please walk me through the events of yesterday?"

Ira recalled what he remembered. He fought through the queasiness churning in his stomach.

Agent Willoughby asked if anyone stood out at the bar that day.

"There was one woman who looked familiar, but I couldn't place her."

"What did she look like? Do you remember if she had a bag or anything like that?"

"I didn't see her come in, so I don't know if she had a bag." Ira thought, and continued, "Small frame and wore a dark hoodie. Oh, and I saw brownish hair sticking out."

"Did she eat or drink?"

"Yeah, both. Whiskey, then a grilled cheese sandwich. But when I looked through the kitchen door, she was gone. Then the whole place blew up."

"I see." She thanked him and gave him her card. "Please call me if you remember more about this woman." She turned to go.

"Wait. Can you tell me *anything* about what happened? Please?"

She sighed. "Mr. Petrov, what we *do* know is that it was a crude but deadly homemade pipe bomb. We found shreds of what appears to be a backpack or duffel bag stuck to some of the wires. But until our forensic team combs through all of this"—she spread out her arms—"we can't determine exactly what type of explosives were used."

Days dragged by for Ira. Every day he made the twenty-minute ride to the roped off, boarded up Black LaSalle, and every day he prayed for answers. He tried to remember any customer who may have had a grudge against the staff or owner. His thoughts repeatedly returned to the woman. Her angular, wan face hung in the recesses of his memory. *I know I know her. Think, Ira*, he thought, sitting in his living room, drinking a beer and staring at a wall.

Oh shit! He fell back into the couch. *Daisy! She doesn't know what happened. I don't want to ruin her honeymoon. I'll tell her later,* he decided.

* * *

Back at the station, Daisy struggled to acclimate from honeymoon mindset to work mindset. She busied herself reading stories and catching up on emails. Hilton Head seemed as if it was years ago. She heard her phone singing somewhere on her desk. Caller ID said it was Ira.

"Ira! How are you?"

"Hey Daisy, I'm okay." Melancholy was thick in his response.

"Ira, you sound weird. Are you okay?"

He sighed. "Not really. I have some bad news, Daiz."

"Hang on." Daisy turned down the music playing from her laptop. "What's up?"

Ira took a deep breath. "Um, there was an explosion. At the Black LaSalle. It was destroyed."

"*What?* No! Oh my God! What? Is everyone okay?"

Ira exhaled, "No. Jimmy and Debbie were killed along with seven patrons."

She had a hard time believing what he said. "Oh Ira!"

"The place is pretty destroyed. The upstairs apartment you lived in for a while is gone."

"Do you know what happened?"

"The FBI and ATF are investigating. I haven't heard anything definitive yet, but I did overhear they think it was a bomb."

"*A bomb!* Who would bomb the Black LaSalle? And *why?*"

"Exactly my thoughts. I have no idea. But Jeffrey, the owner, left me a message yesterday saying he was going to rebuild as soon as the investigation is done."

"Do they have any idea? Or do you? Did anyone come in who looked out of place or anything?" Daisy asked.

"There was a woman who came in and got a drink. Something about her made me look twice. I've tried to place her, but I can't. Then again, DC is a transplant city, so maybe I just thought I'd seen her before."

"I'm shocked." Daisy's voice lowered to a whisper. "I'm afraid to ask if the painting made it."

Ira was silent. "Well, about a quarter of it fell victim to smoke and fire. I had the firemen take it out and give it to me. I have it in storage and am going to call a restorer and see what she can do."

"Oh Ira, I'm so sorry. At least the whole thing wasn't destroyed. I know you feel like that painting is part of your family."

"Yes I do." Ira cleared his throat. "I have to go. I'll call soon. Best to Nick."

"Even though it will be rebuilt, it'll never be the same. Thanks Ira, miss you." Daisy hung up. Echoes of laughter, banter with her colleagues, stories of drunks, and her days of living above the bar ran through her mind like an old movie. *How could my bar be gone?*

CHAPTER 14

The night sky popped with dazzling stars. The moon shone brightly, slicing a fingernail sliver of a path down the road, beckoning anyone to follow. Rubi Lee's breathing quickened and matched her pounding heart. *Last time I was here . . . Get your shit together. You have a job to do!* She admonished herself. Months had passed since she witnessed her brother and uncle shot and killed inside the garage behind the park's office.

The Freedom Statues towered silently and cast eerie shadows onto the moonlit path. It was déjà vu for her as the events of the horrible night came back. *Stop! Focus on what you need to do!* Rubi Lee set the stopwatch on her phone and ran up the hill to the office. Once there, she saw it took close to a minute.

From her bag, she pulled her knife and jimmied the lock of the office door. Once inside, she figured out which desk was Henderson's. *Good, I have enough left*, she thought. Shaking the red can of spray paint, she left a message for him on the wall. Satisfied, she turned around to complete her mission.

The door to the garage loomed ahead. *Just go!* Breathing deeply, she pushed herself across to the door. Once inside the cavernous garage full of rakes, shovels, and other tools, the mental wrestling match commenced once again. She squeezed her eyes shut against it.

Inside the bag, she set the timer for five minutes and placed it in the middle of the floor. "This is for you, Zeke and Uncle Vic!" She sprinted from the garage through the office. Chest burning, she stopped and peeked from behind the statues. In the darkness, time dragged until the eruption of the magnificent fireball. Flames sliced the night as they tore through the garage and office. Pleasure flowed through her veins as she reveled in the fiery destruction.

Fulfilled, she disappeared into the night.

* * *

Several puffy clouds floated in the azure morning sky. Henderson buttoned his khaki park-issued shirt, slung his drawstring bag over his shoulders, and fired up his 1965 Harley-Davidson FLH Electra Glide Panhead Motorcycle. His afternoon shift as part-time security guard started at one o'clock, but he left earlier to stretch out his ride.

"Thank you, Lord, for this magnificent sunny day and for my job at the park," he said aloud on his ride. Eventually, he pulled up and saw there were plenty of would-be park goers ready for a lovely day. But their access was denied.

Yellow crime scene tape twirled in the soft breeze. Perplexed, he dismounted and trundled over to the officer posted at the gate. He showed his badge to the officers guarding the entrance and asked why no one was allowed in the park.

"We got a call last night about a fire in the garage," the officer replied.

"What do you mean?" He scowled at the officer.

"Apparently a fire ripped through the office and garage."

"The building past the statues? Up that hill?" He pointed.

"Yes sir."

"Oh, dear Lord. That's *my* building!" Henderson's heart pounded like a drum. "Please allow me access." It was more of a command than a request. Especially when he flashed the ID identifying him as a retired cop.

The young officer bumbled, "Oh, ah, yes sir, go ahead. The fire department is on site."

Unease stirred in his soul as he approached the charred building. Smoke hung on the breeze and stung his dark eyes. Henderson felt like a wrecking ball knocked him over when he saw where his once-homey office was located. Several firemen doused any smoking embers still aglow.

"Chief, what *in the hell* happened?" Henderson asked Fire Chief and good friend, Andre Clark.

The tall, usually gregarious man sighed. "Hello Henderson," he said, his tone as heavy as the lingering smoke. "We aren't sure at this point . . . we're investigating. This is *bad*, man. I'm sorry, so sorry. Isn't this your office space?"

"Yes, it was."

"Your stuff is ruined. So is the garage."

"God almighty, I can't believe what I'm seeing."

"I know." He patted Henderson's shoulder.

"Can I walk into my office?"

"Yes. Use caution though." He nudged the edge of Henderson's incinerated desk chair.

Henderson stepped into his small office. He inhaled sharply at the sight. The small two-seater sofa was black and soggy. Fire had melted his computer and file cabinet. The singed rug lay in a sad circle under the desk. Family pictures were flakes of ash.

Tears pooled in his eyes. *I've never felt so damn violated in my whole life. Not even as the only Black cop back in the day.*

"Get it over with," he mumbled as he turned to the garage door. The sight was gruesome. Thousands of dollars of equipment—rakes, mowers, tractors, shovels—all demolished. Next to a charred tractor sat Syd, his trusty golf cart, now a skeletal twisted frame. *I can't look at this any longer.*

He shuffled from the garage into the singed office. He turned to his left and opened the closet door. Surprisingly, his winter coat hung, unharmed. *Thank God for that*, he thought and shut the door. Streaks of something red jumped out from the wall. In red paint on the wall adjacent the closet read the words: *She's next.*

Henderson approached it and studied the words. "*She's next.* What does this mean?" Small drips dribbled from the two words, reminding Henderson of blood. He snapped a picture of it on his phone.

"Find anything, Henderson?" Chief Clark asked him when he rejoined his friend.

"Not in terms of what started this fire. But did you see the graffiti?"

"Graffiti?"

Henderson pointed at the red letters. Chief Clark closely scrutinized the message, his bulbous nose practically touching the wall. From his pocket, he took a glove and touched the paint. "Somehow this is unharmed by the fire. Which tells me this fire was possibly set on purpose—maybe a spot fire. Or the perp came back later and added this." He glanced at Henderson. "Do you think the message was meant for you?"

Henderson shrugged. "I don't know. But it was written on the wall in *my* office. I'm trying to think who the 'she' in question is."

A call came from the garage. "Hey Chief! We need you in here!"

Both the chief and Henderson hustled into the garage to see one of the firemen holding a blackened piece of pipe, roughly eight inches in length. "This looks like it could have been the cause. It's a crudely made pipe bomb," she told them.

"Good work. Bag it. This confirms my suspicion—this *was* done on purpose," Chief Clark declared. "Everyone clear the area! We need to seal off the building now!"

FBI and ATF agents arrived and searched through the debris. After consulting with Chief Clark, they inspected the area where the pipe was found. They picked several items out of the rubble and put them in evidence bags.

"Chief Clark, we gathered evidence that appears to be almost identical to another explosion last week—at the Black LaSalle in the city. After the lab analyzes this," she said, lifting the bag, "we will be in touch."

"Should we call this an accident? The media are lining up like hungry wolves," Chief Clark noted, frowning at the gaggle of news vans parked by the entrance.

"Right now, call it an accident. We will let you know how we are going to proceed."

"This isn't an *accident.* Whoever did this, did it on purpose," Henderson exclaimed loudly enough to catch the agent's attention.

"Why do you say that?" Her words were sharp.

Henderson held up his phone with the picture of the wall. "This is a message. I don't know what it means. As a former cop, I'm sure as hell gonna try to find out."

"Henderson, don't do anything irrational. Let the FBI and ATF handle it." Chief Clark placed his hand on his friend's shoulder.

"He's right. Let us do our job," the agent echoed.

"We'll see." Henderson walked away, the rolodex of friends and names spinning in his mind. *Who was this directed toward?*

CHAPTER 15

During Rubi Lee's absence, Annie ate all the food left for her, but hunger pangs gnawed inside. On the dresser sat a cup. *At least I can fool my stomach into thinking I'm full if I drink a lot of water,* Annie thought. But the first time she turned on the faucet in the bathroom, brownish tap water streamed out. She soon learned to let it run before putting the cup underneath.

On the third day of being locked up, Annie fought the dark despair slowly leaching into her soul. She felt it was perverse to hope for Rubi Lee to return, but she was trapped. Rubi Lee was her key to survival. Each day she lay on the bed and lost herself in sleep. She welcomed dreams of Daisy and Nick's wedding. Of dreams about her three sons and their children. Of dreams about her beloved Jackson, whose sudden death threatened to drown her in a quagmire of pain.

Sweat drenched the coarse blanket upon which Annie lay. Each twist and turn felt like she was stretched across sandpaper. She prayed for sleep, but her mind raced with the overwhelming understanding that her life was in jeopardy. Lying on her back, staring at the popcorn ceiling, Annie inhaled deeply and wrapped her head around the unthinkable thought she could no longer ignore: *This woman may kill me.* She squeezed her eyes against the idea. Tears rolled from her think cheeks onto the flat, yellowed pillow.

I may never see my children or grandchildren again. I may never see Daisy and Nick's children, if they have them. Please God! No! This can't happen. Daisy won't let it. I know they'll figure out something is wrong.

The clomping of footsteps in the hallway jolted her. The lock rattled and the door swung open. Rubi Lee walked in with a brown bag and set it down on the dresser.

"Good afternoon. I see you didn't die on me," Rubi Lee said.

Annie slowly sat up. She squinted at Rubi Lee. *What's different about her?* she wondered. *Her hair is different*, Annie realized. It was shorter and dyed light brown. Rubi Lee admired her reflection. She noticed Annie staring.

"Got my hair done. Do you like it?"

Annie knew she had to play the game. "Yes, I do. It's very flattering."

Rubi Lee turned back to the mirror. She cocked her head and studied her reflection. "You know, I think you're right. I don't want people to think I'm cold-hearted. Especially Bump. He seems to really like me."

This was the first time Annie heard Rubi Lee mention that name. "Who's Bump?"

"Someone I've been seeing. You'll meet him eventually."

Annie jumped on the opportunity to talk to Rubi Lee about a boyfriend. "That's an interesting name for someone."

"I know. His real name is Chuck, but people have always called him Bump."

"Why?"

"'Cause, as he said, he was dropped on his head as a baby and as he said, always bumps into stuff."

What an awful name to give a child, Annie thought. "I see. I'm glad you found someone who cares about you."

"I guess he does. He thinks I'm beautiful and as long as he's gettin' what he wants, I'll keep him around." The tone was as cold as a sharp icicle.

Oh no, she's going to destroy someone else too, Annie thought. She jumped on the chance to compliment Rubi Lee. *Play her game.* "You are a very pretty girl," she said.

Rubi Lee turned and ogled Annie as if she had four eyes. "Really?"

"Yes." Annie gazed squarely at her. "You have high cheekbones, and intense eyes. And your porcelain skin is lovely."

Rubi Lee turned back to the mirror. A slight smile turned up the corners of her mouth. In the mirror, she lasered Annie with a stare. "Nice try. *Me* attractive? Nobody except dumb Bump has ever said that to me."

"Oh, that can't be true. I'm sure someone other than your friend Bump finds you beautiful. Someone such as your parents?"

"Parents?" Rubi Lee spat and shook her head. "Tammy and Hank Dixon, parents? Sure, if you can call a chronic pill popper mom and a worthless piece of shit drunk dad, then so be it. My only family were my brother and uncle—but they're dead. Thanks to *her*." Rubi Lee pointed at a picture of Daisy.

If I try to defend Daisy, she's liable to become even more unhinged and kill me. "I'm so sorry about them."

Rubi Lee whipped around and faced her. "Just shut up! What the hell do you know about *being sorry*?"

"Nothing, I'm sure, since your life is perfect. Well, it was until you knocked on my front door. What were the odds of that?" Rubi Lee cackled. "You made my job easier. You came to me instead of the other way around. But I would have found you anyway."

A cold feeling roiled through Annie. *She's been planning this for months*, she realized. *I must redirect her thoughts away from killing me.* Annie took a stab at a topic. "Since you like to get your hair done, do you like to wear makeup?" In the mirror she could see an almost imperceptible glow suddenly blossom in Rubi Lee's face.

"When I was little, I was a ballerina for three years until we had no money. Dad drank it away. When we put on recitals in the cafeteria at school, our teachers used to put makeup on us and I loved it, especially lipstick." From the dresser, Rubi Lee plucked a tube of lipstick. She twisted it and said to Annie, "Kind of like this." Like a child with a crayon, Rubi Lee manically colored her mouth with the garish, dark red stick of color until she resembled a relative of The Joker. "There, that's better." She puckered her lips and blew herself a kiss. "I guess you're right. I do look *kind of* pretty. The bartender at that shithole bar where your daughter worked thought I was hot."

Annie forced herself to look at the ghastly face. Bringing her eyes to Rubi Lee's, she asked, "You went to the Black LaSalle? Why?"

"Why? To destroy things and people your daughter held dear to her heart. My first stop was that bar where I saw some of her former colleagues." In the mirror, Rubi Lee played with her hair. "Oh, and did I mention there was a *terrible* fire there and people were *killed*? Such a shame."

I am with the devil! This woman is evil in the flesh! Goosebumps popped on Annie's arms.

"That park where she murdered my brother? Seems the garage and office were destroyed by fire too. Hmm, such an unfortunate coincidence. Don't cha think?" Rubi Lee continued to admire herself.

"How could you do that to innocent people? They did *nothing* to you! Including my daughter!" Annie yelled. "You'll *never* get to her. She is a strong woman, and you will ultimately fail!"

Rubi Lee lunged at Annie and grabbed her by the neck. "How dare you tell me what I will and won't do?" She tightened her grip. Annie struggled to breathe. "I know she lives and works in Philadelphia. I know she got married recently because *I was there*. You have no idea how long Timmy and I have waited to get our hands on her. She destroyed my life, and I will destroy all of yours!"

Inside her chest, Annie's heart throbbed against her ribcage. She tried to inhale. In a forced soft voice, Annie said, "Please let go. You're hurting me." Arrows of fear struck Annie's heart. "Please, I can help you," she whispered as she held Rubi Lee's hateful glare.

Rubi Lee released her grip and stood up. "Help with what? Tracking down your spawn? No need. I know where she is . . . and guess where I'm going next?"

* * *

Rubi Lee threw her overnight bag into the back seat of her car. On her phone, she hit the video camera icon. Annie sat in the chair, like a child in time-out. *Good, the camera is working perfectly.* "Go ahead and cry like a baby!" She said to the phone and started the car.

The interstate rolled on. Eventually, Rubi Lee's thoughts turned to Bump. *He's the perfect in for me at the cop's station. I need all the information I can get, but it's gonna cost me. I need to convince him that I like him, and he can trust me. There's only one way I know how to do that. Sex works every time. I can deal, as gross as it will be. Time to get that ball rolling.* She scrolled through her contacts and sent him a text.

* * *

Bump was in the middle of washing his 1992 Chevy Blazer and did not hear his phone ping. *Man, I wish I had one of them huge Ford pickups. I'd get big monster truck tires and go four-wheeling all the time. I wonder if Tanya likes four-wheeling?* He hosed off the rusting blue vehicle. *I'll ask her*, he thought as visions of him and Rubi Lee racing over rough, woodsy terrain in a red pickup filled his mind. It was rare that a day went by in which half of Bump's thoughts included her. "She's the best!" He turned off the water and checked his phone.

"Speak of the pretty little devil!" He read her text: *Call me when u can.* His heart swelled at the row of hearts she sent after the message.

He still felt nervous around women because of the incident. For years, Bump tried to rid his mind of the incident; he could not. When he was fifteen, he was head over heels in love with Stacy Bennett. Tall, blonde, and rich, Stacy commanded the hallways of their small high school. Wrapped in tiny miniskirts, plunging necklines, and heels, she left boys drooling and girls wanting to be her. One day in the crowded hallway, someone tripped him, and he fell into her as she was applying lip gloss.

The stick of gooey gloss flew from her hand and smeared her white top, right over her right breast. "You *idiot*! Look what you did!" She shrieked at him and pointed at her shirt.

"Oh Stacy! I'm so sorry! I didn't mean to! I promise!" Panic raced through him. He did not know what to do. Kids stopped, pointed at her and laughed.

"Get away from me!" She shrieked as he approached her to clean it off. "Now I have to go through the rest of the day with everyone staring at my chest!"

Before Bump knew it, Stacy's hulking boyfriend slammed him up against the locker. "What the fuck are you doing, you pervert?" Spit flew into Bump's terrified face.

"I'm s...s...sorry! It was an accident!" Bump felt a dampness in his pants. Face on fire, he looked down. A yellow puddle formed at his feet. Laughter rang up and down the hallway.

"Oh my God! You pissed your pants!" Stacy laughed and pointed.

"You're fucking *gross*!" the boyfriend yelled.

The hallway suddenly caved in around Bump. Sneering, laughing faces and pointing fingers suffocated him. He ran through the snickering crowd and out the doors.

Suddenly his feet and pants were soaked. "Oh shit!" He snapped out of the nightmarish flashback from high school. Looking down, he felt relief. *It's okay, Bump. It's only the hose and you have a girl who likes you. But she can never know about the incident. Never.* "I can't lose Tanya. I need her and she needs me," he reasoned as he replaced the hose and called her back.

"Hi Bump. We should meet for a drink. I feel like I haven't seen you in a long time," Rubi Lee purred when he called her.

"Okay Tanya, where and when?"

They decided on a spot, one on the outskirts of town.

"I'll see you in an hour. Don't be late," Rubi Lee said and hung up.

"I gotta get ready for her!" Bump said, walking into his first-level brick apartment. He stripped off the wet clothes and quickly rinsed off. From the bathroom cabinet, he took a can of AXE, sprayed a huge cloud, and waltzed through it. After a long day working outside, he did not want to smell like a bag of wet onions.

He pulled up outside the bar twenty minutes early. The two beers he tossed back helped settle his nerves.

"Hello Bump!" She sat down beside him and pointed at his bottle. "See you got a head start?"

"Oh, yeah. I was thirsty and, ah . . . a little nervous." He tried to laugh.

Please, she thought and tried not to roll her eyes. "Oh, how sweet. You have *no* reason to be nervous." She reached over and ran her hand down his thick thigh. "I'm not gonna hurt ya!"

"Good. I didn't think so!" He took a swig of beer and told Rubi Lee how pretty she looked.

"Aw, that's sweet. Thanks Bump." Rubi Lee assessed him and heaped on false praise. "You look nice too. Cool cargo shorts."

His face lit up like the sun. "Thanks! Picked them out myself at Target. I can't really afford anything else. Wish I could though."

After several beers and shots of Yukon, Bump, feeling emboldened, turned to her and asked, "Where do we go from here?" His smile exposed the gap in his child-like teeth.

Here we go. She threw back her double shot of Yukon. "My granny is in town, so your place sounds good." She ran a finger down his cheek, over his lips.

Bump dug in his pocket and tossed a few crumpled bills on the bar. He leaped from the barstool and practically ran for the door.

Perfect, I'll have him right where I want him. Rubi Lee continued with her plan.

"Damn. My phone is out of juice. I need to text Granny that I'm going to be out late. Can I borrow yours?"

Bump eagerly handed over his phone to her.

"What's your password? I won't tell."

"2867. Guess what that stands for?" He giggled.

"Hm, let me guess," she flirted. "Bump?"

"Yep!"

Of course that would be his password. He is stupider than I thought. She pretended to send Granny a message. Rather, she sent one to her old phone—just in case.

* * *

She stepped inside his tiny, cluttered kitchen. Harsh yellow light shone down on the cracked brown linoleum floor. An old white refrigerator hummed in the corner next to a sink choked with dirty dishes. The sour stench of leftover food and dirty laundry assaulted her. A flash of déjà vu was palatable. *God, that smell. It's like our trailer growing up. Go with it. You have a mission.* She stepped into the living room. A faux leather three-seater couch sagged against an ecru wall. A rickety black table upon which lay empty beer bottles, Bump's laptop, and comic books sat in front. Rubi Lee picked one up and flipped through it.

"Comic book fan, huh?"

"Yup. I love the pictures and the words are easy to read. Reading was never my thing."

She nodded. "I'm sure comic books were probably more interesting than whatever you were working on." She gestured toward the laptop.

"Oh yeah. I'll close that. Not a time for work!"

"No it isn't." She sauntered over to him and lifted her hand to his cheek. "How about you go get us a few drinks and we can get, ah, more comfortable?" Her eyes lingered on his.

"Ah yeah! Right away! Don't go anywhere!" Bump hurried into the kitchen and reappeared with two beers. He gestured toward the soiled sofa. Hours went by as Bump spilled out his life and how he wished he was rich.

"I'd buy the biggest house ever and the hugest truck!"

Rubi Lee's mind was turning and plotting. She knew she had him in the palm of her hand and she could get him to do anything. As the night wore on, Bump yawned continuously, a signal to Rubi Lee that they should move to the bedroom.

"I don't know about you, but I think it's bedtime," he slurred.

"I was wondering when you were going to say that." *Do it now.* She inhaled, held her breath and leaned over to Bump. She kissed him hard on his thin lips. He responded by jamming his tongue into her mouth. Rubi Lee fought the Yukon threatening to expunge itself from her stomach. Slowly, she pulled away and whispered, "Time for bed."

Bump led the way and put his beer on the dresser and moved to the bathroom. From her bag, she took out two pills.

Plink plink. She dropped the pills into his beer and watched the fizz. Wearing only boxers, Bump reappeared and motioned toward the bed.

"You can't waste good beer!" She handed him the bottle, which he greedily slugged.

Minutes later Bump was passed out on the bed.

That was easy. Now where is his work laptop? On the kitchen counter, Bump's state issued laptop sat open. Rubi Lee pulled up a chair. *Wonder what his password would be? Of course. Bump.*

She typed in the password and bam, she was in. After scouring through arrest warrants, traffic violations, names of the deceased, and other things she deemed impertinent, she found what she wanted and took a picture: missing persons' names for the past ten years, recent reports of bodies being found ... *This is going to make my life easier now. I can get into the system and keep track of all police action and movement.*

She slowly crept back to Bump's bed and lay down. She watched his chest rise and fall. Little gurgles escaped his slightly parted lips. Rubi Lee gazed longer at Bump. *What am I gonna do with you when this is over? I'll figure something out.* She sighed, pulled up the sheet, and slept.

The next morning, Bump rolled over and saw Rubi Lee sleeping on her side. He couldn't remember anything but smiled because she was there.

* * *

After bidding Bump goodbye, Rubi Lee followed the directions from the GPS to the hotel. She chose one a half block from the news station where Daisy worked. She put out her cigarette on the ground before checking in. She remembered to pick up the butt—she did not need to leave any DNA anywhere.

"Good late morning! Checking in today?" asked the freshly shaven, baby-faced man at the reception desk.

In a thick, sugary Alabama accent, she replied, "Yes I am. It's been a long drive."

"And what's the name the reservation is under?"

"Tanya Holston."

Manicured nails tapped adroitly. "Ah yes, here it is. You are staying two nights, correct?"

"If that's what the reservation says, then yes sir."

"Where did you arrive from?"

"Oh, Alabama. To see my sick momma. I grew up there."

"That explains your enchanting accent. And I'm sorry about your mother." He looked sadly at Rubi Lee and continued, "How would you like to pay for your stay?"

"I'd like to pay with cash."

"Of course. May I see some ID?"

Rubi Lee produced a driver's license and handed it to the clerk. He looked at the license, peered at Rubi Lee, then back at the license.

"I've cut and colored my hair," Rubi Lee laughed. "I needed a change."

The clerk nodded and agreed with her. "These pictures are always the worst, aren't they?"

He handed over the key. "Turn left at the end of the hallway. Your room is down on your right."

Rubi Lee lay down on the bed and closed her eyes. She dozed off for a few hours and dreamt of confronting Daisy at the news station. Setting a trap and using Annie for bait was the only way she was going to get Daisy. In the darkness of the hotel room, she spent most of the night finalizing how she would send her a message.

* * *

Before leaving the hotel lot, Rubi Lee pulled on a black long-haired wig and square sunglasses. A white physician's coat completed the outfit. She drove to Children's Hospital of Philadelphia where she learned, the previous night, about a maintenance workers' strike. Because this hospital was one of the nation's best, she knew all the local stations would be covering the strike.

From across the street, Rubi Lee spotted the Live5 News van pull up in front of the station. Heart in her throat, she watched the side door slide open. Sun bounced off the red curly hair of her quarry. Daisy stepped from the van, laughing with the cameraman.

There you are, you bitch. Rubi Lee's heart fluttered. Sticky sweat dampened her palms as she gripped the steering wheel. For a split second, she fantasized about punching the gas and plowing into the van, à la Brady Hartsfield in Stephen King's *Mr. Mercedes.* She watched Daisy point to a group of protestors as she spoke on her phone. After hanging up, she dashed back into the van.

Rubi Lee looked at her phone; it was a little after five. Less than an hour before the six o'clock news. Less than an hour before Daisy would receive her message.

She took inventory of the protestors. A young girl and her mother stood nearby. The girl turned her pretty face upward and said something that made her mother laugh. *I don't remember my mother ever hugging me, just yelling at me . . . all the time.* The mother handed the young girl some money, and the girl crossed the street to a local deli.

"Perfect," Rubi Lee murmured as she exited the car and waited outside the deli. When the girl exited, Rubi Lee was standing at the door.

"Excuse me, I know you don't know me and I'm not some weirdo. But I need a favor. It's worth a hundred bucks."

A wary scowl and a step backward. Her dark eyes took in Rubi Lee. "What do you mean?"

"I have this sign." Rubi Lee held up a piece of

cardboard. "And I need someone to carry it in the protest line. Can you do that for me?" She flashed a fresh one-hundred-dollar bill.

The girl's eyes bulged. "Wow, that's a lot of money."

"It's all yours if you want to help me." Rubi Lee waved it around.

The girl narrowed her eyes and stepped back. "Um, this sounds weird."

"I'm sorry. I should have told you. It's a joke. It's for a bachelorette party and if I were seen holding the sign it would ruin the surprise."

The girl relented a bit. "A *hundred bucks* to hold a sign? What does it say?"

Rubi Lee showed her the poster.

The girl read the four words aloud: "I have your mother." She frowned at Rubi Lee. "This seems like a really weird joke."

"I know. Believe me, it wasn't my idea. But it's a code as part of the bachelorette scavenger hunt." Rubi Lee lied as easily as butter melted on hot toast.

"Whatever. I'll do it."

"You need to carry it when the newscasters are reporting live—especially the red-headed reporter from Live5 News. She's a friend of the bride."

The girl shrugged, pocketed the money, and carried the sign across the street.

Rubi Lee hustled down a side alley. From behind a vile dumpster, she observed the girl show her mother. The girl pointed in Rubi Lee's direction but saw no one.

Finally, Daisy reemerged from the news van and

began her broadcast. *Showtime!* Rubi Lee smiled.

"Okay, three, two, one, you're live!" the cameraman called to Daisy who stood in front of the protestors.

Now! Go! Rubi Lee willed from the alley. A sinister smile crossed her pallid face when the young girl stepped into the picket line, sign in hand.

CHAPTER 16

Wesley Hines, the lead anchor of Live5 News, began the six o'clock broadcast with the story about the protest at Children's Hospital. "Let's go live to our reporter at the scene, Daisy Taylor." He smiled. "Oh, I'm sorry, it's Daisy *Tyson*. Congratulations on your recent marriage and welcome back."

Daisy looked in the camera, green eyes bright and alert. Her genial smile was warm and welcoming.

"Thanks Wesley. I'm here at Children's Hospital of Philadelphia where the maintenance workers have gone on strike. According to the union spokesperson the workers have not gotten a raise in five years. I inquired about the timing of the strike, as a flu epidemic was sweeping through the city. She replied that the timing was perfect because the workers were needed, and their strike would garner the attention of hospital administration. Currently, there is no timetable for a meeting between the union and the administration. Unfortunately, Wesley, it appears the strike will last awhile."

"I see a significant number of protestors on site. Daisy, can you talk to some of them?" Wesley asked.

"Sure, let me move across the street. As you can see, many are carrying signs advertising their grievances." Daisy approached a middle-aged man and asked, "Excuse me sir, can you tell us exactly what you are protesting?" Daisy aimed her microphone his way.

"Damn straight! No raise in five years, no overtime pay! And there ain't enough people to work! We gotta get what's due us! It ain't fair to those kids in there!" He gestured toward the hospital.

Daisy heard Wesley say through her earpiece, "Daisy, seems you have a young enthusiastic protestor behind you!"

"Thank you, sir." Daisy turned to see a girl jumping up and down behind the man being interviewed. In her hand, she held a sign written in red letters. The girl with the sign smiled and waved at Daisy.

"Hello, I see you are part of the protestors," Daisy said.

A shy smile crept over the girl's face. She blinked several times before answering. "Yeah, I'm helping my mom."

"I'm sure she's proud of you." Daisy pointed at the sign. "What does your sign say?"

The girl read out loud, "I have your mother."

Daisy frowned, unsure of what to say. She cleared her throat and quickly replied, "Well, that certainly *is* an interesting sign. Where did you get it?"

"Some lady gave it to me. She said to make sure the red-headed reporter sees it."

Confused, Daisy continued smoothly. "I see. Well, I guess that's me!" She laughed. "I think it's time to turn things back to you, Wesley!" Daisy removed her earpiece.

The girl continued, "The lady said it was a joke for a bachelorette party?"

"A bachelorette party? Can I see it please?" Daisy read

it to herself: *I HAVE YOUR MOTHER.* The red letters leaped out against the white background.

Daisy turned to the girl and asked her what the woman looked like who gave her the sign.

"Um, she was short. I think she had dark hair and a white doctor's coat."

"A white coat? Like a jacket?"

"No, like doctors wear."

"I see. Did she pay you?"

She whispered, "A *hundred* dollars!"

"That's a lot of money. Did she say anything else?"

"No." She fidgeted with her hands. "Can I go now?"

"Yes. Thank you." She watched the girl skip over to the sea of protestors. "Something is weird here. We need to go," she said to Randy.

"What in the hell did that sign mean?" Randy asked as they climbed into the van.

"I don't know, aside from what the girl told me."

"What did she say?" Leo asked.

"Apparently it was for a bachelorette party. But it's a little unnerving, especially since she said it was for the redhead."

"Yeah, but you're married. What's the deal with the bachelorette party?" Randy pointed out. "And the redhead thing *is* odd."

Daisy shook her head. "I don't know. But the girl specifically said that the person who gave her the sign said, 'the red-headed reporter.' I want to watch the tape again. Maybe we'll see who gave it to her." Her phone buzzed against her thigh.

"Hey Wesley, what's up?" Daisy frowned as she

listened to Wesley. "That weird sign? We don't know, but we're going to watch it again. Let me check the tape and get back to you."

"Rewind and then play it in slow motion," Daisy ordered. They watched it until the girl appeared in the frame. "Stop! Over my right shoulder! Zoom in!"

They leaned closer and studied the small screen. "There she is. I didn't see anyone give it to her, did you?" Randy asked.

"Unfortunately not."

Leo scratched his sweaty head. "I guess you're right. And like you said, the kid mentioned your hair color— and your mother."

"You're right," Daisy replied. "But my mother? Why? I'm not sure about this. Maybe I should call my mom." She dialed.

"Hi, this is Annie, I can't come to the phone right now, please leave a message. Have a great day."

Daisy was not surprised. Oftentimes, her mother turned off the ringer. "Mom! It's me. Give me a call when you get this." Daisy sighed and twirled a tendril. "This is really strange, guys."

Leo clumsily patted her shoulder. "I'm sure she will call you back soon." He started the engine and they drove through the city back to the station.

Daisy slid heavily into her office chair and spun around to face the sprawling, bustling city below. "Dark hair, doctor's coat . . ." Daisy chewed on these words over and over. She tried her mother again. Voicemail. *The worst thing you can do is panic, so don't*, Daisy told herself.

* * *

Nick's personal phone buzzed. Only a handful of people knew that number. Which meant that whoever was calling had damn good reason.

"Excuse me," he said to the two staff members in his office. "Hi Daiz. I'm in a meeting. What's up?"

Daisy relayed the story of the girl and the sign.

"What? What are you talking about?" Nick politely gestured to the two staff members to leave.

A torrent of words tumbled from Daisy. "I called Mom and left a message. I have no idea who that girl was. But she told me some dark-haired woman paid her to hold the sign."

Nick exhaled loudly. "Daiz, you know better than anyone how many weirdos are running around. It's possible it was a mistake."

Daisy tried to control the anger starting to simmer. "Then tell me *why* the girl said the woman told her to make sure the *red-headed reporter* saw it. How can you be so dismissive?"

Nick knew that tone. *Tread lightly.* "I'm sorry. I wasn't thinking."

"I didn't mean to get nasty." She sighed, "I'm going to call Pastor Carroll. Maybe she's heard from Mom."

"Good idea. It's okay, Daiz, we'll get to the bottom of this."

Daisy sighed. "I sure as hell hope so. You know Mom, she doesn't operate this way."

"No, she doesn't. Let me know what you learn."

* * *

"Hello. This is Pastor Carroll from St. Christopher's church," she sang.

"Hello Pastor. This is Daisy Taylor Tyson—Annie Taylor's daughter."

"Daisy! How can I help you, dear?"

"I can't get ahold of my mom, and I know she went on the community trip with you. I'm a little concerned."

"Is she not answering her phone?"

"No, but that's not completely unheard of. Mom often turns off her ringer."

"Oh, that is a little strange she hasn't contacted you. Maybe she forgot to call," she offered. "One second! I just remembered I have some unread texts sitting in my phone. One could be from her? Hold on." While on speakerphone, the pastor scrolled through her phone searching for the text.

"Daisy? Your mother texted me about staying longer to enjoy the beautiful scenery in Sullivan County. Apparently, there is a train ride one can take to see the gorgeous fall foliage. Plus, there are lots of hiking trails. Joyce Plimpton is staying there too."

Daisy knew her mother was a nature lover; something felt off, though. "I got one from her too, a few days ago. It's just odd she hasn't called or texted again."

"Daisy, at the risk of upsetting you, perhaps she needs some serenity and time to process your father's passing."

Daisy sat and said nothing; she could not speak. Powerful waves of guilt took her breath away. Tears stung her eyes. *Oh no. That never dawned on me. I was so caught up in wedding planning and my own grief. I didn't talk to Mom enough about Dad's passing.*

"Oh Pastor Carroll, I was so caught up in my own world of wedding planning, work, and who knows what else. How could I be so insensitive? I'm sorry, Pastor." Daisy choked up. Her voice broke. "And now I can't get ahold of her."

Pastor Carroll's softened her tone. "Daisy, you are not insensitive! You and your mother are so close and when a family—especially one as close as yours—experiences a death, it does turn one's world upside down."

Daisy could not disagree. "We talked about Dad and still do, but it doesn't feel like it was enough. Mom needs me, especially now! I think I may go crazy if I can't get ahold of her!"

"All of us grieve differently. What is important is that you recognize your own grief and how to work through it. Your mother will need you, but for now, she may have needed a change of scenery, to go somewhere new. Sometimes a different, unfamiliar environment helps us to see things more clearly."

I guess so, Daisy thought. *But I still feel awful.* "Thanks, Pastor. Mom probably is trying to figure out where to go from here." Daisy realized that the wedding was all-consuming and her mother may not have allowed herself to grieve properly.

Pastor Carroll agreed. "Give her time."

A thought suddenly struck Daisy. "Can you please give me the number of the community center? Maybe I could get someone from there to help me?"

"Sure. I'll text it to you. Don't worry, I'm sure she's fine."

"I sure hope so. Thanks, Pastor."

Daisy called, left a message, then called her mother again with no luck. *I hope Pastor is right,* she thought. "Something does not feel right." She turned in her office chair and gazed out the window.

"What do you mean?" Randy the cameraman stepped into Daisy's office.

Spinning around in her chair, Daisy shared with Randy her concerns about her mother.

"Maybe the pastor is right? She may need time." Randy chewed a nail and spat it out.

Daisy glared at him. "Randy, that's gross," She shook her head. "Considering we've never been through a family death, I don't know what to expect. But I feel certain she would have called me."

"Where is she anyway?"

"She texted me and told me she was staying to enjoy the fall foliage where she and her friend did community service. And Pastor Carroll said there's some train people can ride that goes through the woods for people to see the changing leaves up close."

"Where? A train ride through the foliage? Sounds absolutely wonderful."

"Sullivan County, the place we went to cover a story on a body being found, first one in over twenty-five years."

"I remember. I'm sure she's fine."

"I hope so. But I'm going to call the sheriff. Something is not sitting well."

* * *

"Hello Sheriff Roth. This is Daisy Tyson. I'm one of the reporters who covered a story in your county regarding the discovery of a body. It was about two months ago. Anyway, I'm hoping you can help me locate my mother. Here's my number. Please call me back as soon as you can. Thanks." *I have to get out of this office*, she thought.

The unusually warm fall day was a surprise for Daisy. She fumbled in her bag for a hair tie and piled her curls in a topknot. Two blocks down from her office was a playground adjacent to an elementary school. She plopped down onto a swing and swayed slowly back and forth. *I loved the swings as a kid, especially trying to flip over the top.*

Thinking about being a child again triggered the memory of the young girl holding that sign. *"I HAVE YOUR MOTHER." What the hell is going on? It can't be coincidental that I haven't heard from Mom and then suddenly, I see a sign that was directed to me? No way.*

Her thoughts were disrupted by her phone ringing. *Please be Mom.* It wasn't.

"Hello, this is Daisy Tyson."

"Hello Mrs. Tyson. Sheriff Drew Roth here."

She stopped swinging. "Thanks for returning my call sheriff. And please, call me Daisy."

"You're welcome, Daisy. What can I help you with? You sounded worried." His warm voice was soothing.

Daisy explained how her mother and friend volunteered for the community outreach program in his county. She also told him about her phone call to Pastor Carroll.

"I would be glad to help you out but I'm out of town."

Daisy's heart sank. "Oh, I see." She inhaled deeply. "I'm really worried."

"Daisy, wait. I will call my Deputy Chuck Willis and have him go to the community center for you. The head of the center may be able to help, but I can't say for certain."

Daisy perked up and thanked him for helping her out. She sat for a while longer until the sides of the made-for-kids swing started to pinch her hips. In the heat of the early evening, Daisy walked back to pack up and head home. *Thank God it's Friday*, she thought and headed to the train station.

* * *

Drew Roth was a man of his word. Immediately after hanging up with Daisy, he called his deputy.

"Sheriff's Department, how can I help you?" Bump answered. "Hey Sheriff . . . Yes I see. I'll be glad to run over to the community center for you. What is the woman's name?"

"Thank you, Bump. Her name is Annie Taylor."

"Glad I can help you out. I'll call you back later, sir."

"You don't need to call me, but Mrs. Tyson needs to call her daughter. Thank you for your assistance, Bump. Have a good weekend."

Bump grinned when he hung up. Glancing around the empty station, he opened a desk drawer. He ran his hand to the back of the drawer and pulled out the burner phone Rubi Lee gave him. *Tanya'll think this is cool!*

* * *

Even though Nick grilled Daisy her favorite dinner, filet, she only picked at her plate. He knew her mind was on her mother and the strange events of the day. She explained what Pastor Carroll said about the grieving process and how everyone goes about it differently.

"It's late. I'll clean up. You get ready for bed." Nick kissed her and took their plates.

"You're the best." She yawned and took her phone with her. Normally she put it on silent mode, but not now.

She slept hard for two hours until her phone dinged. Daisy's heart pounded as she snatched her phone from the bedside table.

Nick groaned and rolled over. "What does it say?"

"It's from Mom. She says she is fine and is sorry for not contacting me and she'll call soon."

"Well, that's good news. You can call her in the morning. We need some sleep."

She ignored him. "Nick, something isn't right. I can feel it. It's almost one in the morning; why is she texting this late?"

Nick sat up in bed and turned on his bedside lamp. "Maybe she can't sleep?"

"Maybe, but she *never* stays up this late. I'm going to call her." She put it on speakerphone so Nick could listen.

The phone rang and rang until the same greeting floated from the phone.

"She *just* texted me. How can she *not* answer her phone?"

Nick sighed and flopped back down on his pillow. He

slung his arm across her thighs. "I don't know, Daiz. It's possible she put it on silent. You did say she turns off the ringer. And after what Pastor Carroll told you, it's possible she wanted *and needed* some solitude and felt like since she texted you, that was enough."

Daisy lay back down. "I guess you might be right. She needs some time. But I'm calling her first thing in the morning."

"Great, now let's get some rest," Nick said, rubbing her arm.

CHAPTER 17

In the morning, Nick awoke to the enticing, bold aroma of fresh coffee. He threw on his robe and wandered out to the kitchen. Daisy sat at the counter, both hands hugging her coffee mug. A steaming cup waited for him.

"Good morning." Nick gave her hug from behind and kissed her neck.

"Morning. Hope *you* got some sleep. I've been up for hours because I'm worried about Mom."

"I'm sorry, and I am too." He sat down and took her hands.

"I've called her three times so far and still have gotten the *same goddamn stupid message!*" she cried.

He squeezed her hands tightly. "Daiz, I'm sure she's okay. You called the sheriff who said he'd get the deputy to look for her. As far as we know, the deputy did." He took a swig of coffee. "I've been thinking about that sign too. We need to figure out where it originally came from."

Daisy stood, put her mug in the sink, and took a box of cereal from a cabinet. She poured some into a bowl and began to eat it.

Nick laughed. "*Dry* cereal?"

Daisy glanced down. "Oh boy. *That's* bad." From the fridge, she grabbed the milk and poured some into her bowl.

"I have a great idea."

"Yes?"

He put the newspaper down. "We're going to the area around the hospital to see what stores have video cameras. Maybe one of them caught something."

Daisy tilted back the bowl and slurped the milk. "Great idea." She paused. "Even though I got a text from her last night, something just doesn't feel right."

Nick agreed. "We should watch your video footage from the broadcast. Randy always shoots some video before you go live, right? He might have caught something too."

"I'll text him and ask him to look. I'm impressed with how you have this all figured out."

"While you were tossing and turning all night, I kept thinking about that girl holding that sign during your broadcast. It's very strange."

"Sorry if I kept you up." Daisy rubbed his cheek. "And yes, it's bizarre."

"You didn't keep me up. Anyway, I was thinking we need to head down to the area near Children's Hospital where you saw the girl with the sign. There's bound to be video of it somewhere since there are different businesses down there. Seems logical, right?" Nick suggested.

"Yes. We have the whole day."

* * *

They pulled up in front of Children's Hospital and scanned the area. It was a brilliant Saturday, and all the stores were open. Customers strolled in and out, coffee cups in hand, children or dogs in tow.

They scrutinized the block. "Lots businesses on both sides of the street. Fingers crossed they have video cameras," Nick commented and took Daisy's hand.

Across the street the protestors marched, signs in hand. Some of the picketers waved at Daisy. She flashed her smile and returned the wave.

"Fans?" he teased.

"I chatted with some of them yesterday—great people, I hope they settle soon."

Up and down the block they walked. The stores close by yielded nothing.

Nick kicked the curb. "Damnit. In today's world, how can you *not* have any surveillance cameras? I don't get it."

"Keep in mind. Some of these stores are old and so are the owners." She patted his back. "Come on, there are two more. I'm feeling lucky." She gave his hand a squeeze.

They hit paydirt at Stanley's Shoe Shop, a sliver of a store whose owner, according to the crooked sign in the window, specialized in resoling worn shoes and tooling leather goods. A buzzer bellowed when they pushed open the glass door and entered. Inside the store, belts, shoes, jackets and other goods sat on shelves or hung on hangers. Dust sat on everything. The distinct aged, smoky aroma of leather hung in the air. A television with an antenna was propped up on a shelf in the corner. The movie *Rocky* was playing.

"I feel like we stepped back in time," Daisy whispered to Nick.

"Yeah, kind of like Foley's hardware store," he replied.

"Remember how we used to ring every sample doorbell there?"

"And laugh at the toilets on display? I *loved* that store."

"Hello folks, can I help you?" A slight, older man with a cropped ring of white hair stepped from behind the drawn curtain near the counter. By his side was a white-muzzled black Labrador retriever who ambled over and leaned its well-fed body into Daisy's legs. Daisy rubbed the dog on its back.

"Oh Gracie, don't bother those nice people!"

"Not at all! I love dogs!" Daisy stroked the portly canine. "Are you the owner?"

"Yes, I am. Bill Stanley is my name, but you can call me Stanley." He cocked his head and looked at Daisy. He bobbed his finger at her. "And you are the pretty newscaster I see on television!" He smiled at her. "Oh, am I *allowed* to say things like that in this day and age?" He chuckled.

Daisy blushed and thanked him for the compliment. "Yes sir, I'm Daisy Tyson and this is Nick, my husband."

Stanley did a double-take, his green eyes lighting up. "And you're one of the higher-ups on the mayor's staff! I recognize you both! How did I get so lucky to have *two* celebrities in my humble store?"

"It's nice to meet you, sir. Thank you for your kind words. Daisy and I are wondering if we could look at your video from your camera that faces the street? We are interested in yesterday afternoon's footage."

He cocked a bushy eyebrow. "Sure. Are you investigating a story?" He shifted his gaze to Daisy.

"We're looking for a particular person who was seen on the street during my broadcast."

"I won't ask why 'cause it ain't my business." He turned and gestured to them. "Follow me." They went to a small back room that housed stacks of video equipment.

Nick whistled and then commented, "This is high tech stuff you have here."

Stanley showed them how to work the equipment. "I'll leave the two of you to it. Time for me to save some soles!" He chuckled as Gracie ambled out with him.

Daisy and Nick fast-forwarded the videotape to four o'clock yesterday afternoon. Their eyes were glued on every person who passed by Stanley's. Suddenly a dark-haired woman wearing a doctor's coat appeared walking from the left side of the screen. Under her arm was a sign. Nick stopped the video and moved it forward frame by frame. She walked quickly down the street which made it difficult to see her face, but some of the wording on the sign was visible. They tilted their heads to read the exposed letters: *VE, THER.*

"Damn, I can't see any more," Nick whispered.

"The *VE* is on top of *THER*," Daisy muttered, head tilted the right. "This has to be the same person. No one else carried a sign like that."

"I know. It's not a normal picketing sign like the other ones," he noted.

"'*I HAVE YOUR MOTHER.*'" I'll never forget. Here look." She scrolled through her phone.

"Here it is." She turned her phone to Nick.

"Zoom in on her," Daisy said.

They both looked intensely at the woman. The image was a bit fuzzy, but her forearm was exposed. "Zoom in on that."

Daisy pointed at the white, tattooed arm. Her stomach

clenched and her heart hammered. "Holy shit! Jesus Christ, that's Rubi Lee!" Daisy shouted.

"*Rubi Lee*? It can't be her!" Nick moved his head closer to the screen. "How do you know?"

"Because of *that*!" Daisy pointed at the tattoo of a snake curling up Rubi Lee's pale, skinny arm. "I'll *never* forget seeing that snake the night she tried to kill me!"

Nick glanced at his wife who was white as a sheet. "Are you okay? You look like you're about to puke."

"I think I might throw up! That psycho is *running free*! Oh my God!" Daisy's hand trembled as she brushed away her hair. "What're we going to do?"

Nick turned his eyes back to the frozen image. "That definitely looks like a snake. After that night, I assumed she was caught and locked up."

"I did too. But she's not. That's her." Daisy pointed again and paced.

Nick squinted. "Sure looks like her, hard to tell. It's grainy."

Daisy's face flamed, as did her anger. She whirled around to her husband. "Are you doubting me? Look, Nick! It's her! I know it! That snake tattoo is all I need to know."

"Fair enough. Let's see if we can borrow this video. How about you go and ask Stanley for it, and I'll call Winston."

"Fine. But you need to call the DC police too. They can check to see if there's any record of that psycho's arrest." Daisy took a deep breath. "But I know they don't. She's out there, Nick, whether you believe me or not." She turned and headed back to talk to Stanley.

* * *

Nick dialed Winston, who did not answer. As he left Winston a message, a dark thought ran through his mind: *If Rubi Lee is alive, then we are all in danger.* He called the DC police was put right through to Chief Rickards, someone he befriended from his days in the senator's office.

"Chief, I need you to pull all arrest records from December 27 until now. Please look for the name Rubi Lee Dixon among them."

"It's gonna wait, but I'll do it. I'm in the middle of something. I'll call you back later," Rickards replied.

"Thanks." Nick hit end call and gazed into space. He ran his hand over his face, his head spinning with thoughts of Rubi Lee out on the streets. *What if that was Rubi Lee on the tape? What if that psycho is running wild?* His thoughts retreated to the night in the garage where Daisy was almost killed by Rubi Lee. *If she's out there, we could have a big problem.*

Daisy returned with the video. "What did Win say?"

"I left him a message and I talked to Chief Rickards who is going to pull arrest records to see if Rubi Lee's name appears. Fingers crossed it does." *I wish I felt as confident as I sound,* he thought.

CHAPTER 18

Daisy pressed the speed dial number of her mother and held her breath. One ring, two rings, three rings.

"Damnit!" Daisy screamed at her phone. "Why did I even bother?"

She turned and buried her face in Nick's chest. He smoothed her hair and held her.

"I thought she was dead or arrested! How could Rubi Lee still be out there?"

He held her at arm's length. "I don't know. Maybe she hid or had someone help her escape?" he responded and noted a look of dread came across Daisy's face. "What?"

She began to pace in the small office. "Oh no. Oh dear God. Nick, she has Mom. I just know it!" Daisy yelled.

"Wait a minute. How do you know that?"

"In here Nick, here"—she tapped her stomach—"I *know* deep in my gut Rubi Lee's alive and has Mom." She collapsed into a wobbly chair by the door. "That sign *I HAVE YOUR MOTHER* tells me all I need to know. What're we going to do?" She dropped her head in her hand.

"I'm not saying you're wrong, but you have to admit, we have no proof. After we hear from the cops in DC and Winston, we'll know more. For now, we need to take this tape home."

"What is wrong with you? You saw that snake! I can't

believe you don't agree with me!" Daisy stomped past him toward the front of the store. Stanley was punching holes in a belt up front. Lowering her voice, she addressed the man. "Thank you, Stanley. We appreciate you letting us keep this tape." Daisy patted the old man on the arm.

"Hope you found what you were looking for."

"We did. Thanks."

On their way to the car, Nick's phone rang.

"Hey, Nick. I got word you were looking for me. What's up?"

"Win, hey man. Thanks for getting back so soon. Long story short is that Daisy's mother has gone missing. And we may have video proof of Rubi Lee being alive. Daisy is freaking out. She thinks Rubi Lee is the reason her mom is MIA. I called Chief Rickards in the DC office, but he hasn't gotten back yet. Please help us out."

"*What?* Of course! But *Rubi Lee?* What the hell . . . I thought . . . ?"

"It's too long a story to go into now, but see what you can dig up on her."

"Will do. Nick, give Daisy a hug and kiss for me and tell her I'll see what I can do. I'll call you back soon. Take care, brother."

"Thanks Win, I'll tell her."

Daisy glanced at him, hope in her eyes. "I don't think I can sit around here and wait for other people. We need to go find her." Daisy's stomach rumbled loudly enough for Nick to hear. "But I need to eat. My head is starting to throb."

They went to their favorite lunch spot, famous for its

authentic Philly cheesesteaks. After ordering the decadent, hot cheesy sandwiches, they sat at a scratched red plastic table to wait. Daisy fiddled with the salt and pepper shakers. Thoughts of Rubi Lee and her stomach-turning existence filled Daisy's head.

"Nick, that video tape is terrifying. She found us and she's out there." Daisy waved her arm toward the city. "And to think, she was right at the hospital when I reported the story about the strike."

"I know. I wish we could find the kid who had that sign." He stuffed the last of his cheesesteak into his mouth.

"That'll never happen. The point is she found us and now we need to find *her*."

Sandwiches finished, Daisy reached over and wiped melted provolone from Nick's chin. "It's a three-hour drive to Sullivan County. Time is not on our side. We need to get going *now*." Her green eyes bore into his. "No" was not even a remote option for an answer.

Nick began to reply when Daisy's phone dinged. He heard her inhale sharply.

"Look at this!" She handed him the phone.

He read aloud, "I'm staying up here for longer than I said a few days ago . . . the trails and waterfalls are gorgeous and I want to see them . . . The reception is horrible. I'll try to call . . . OXOX."

"OXOX? Mom would never, ever sign off that way. *Ever.*"

"You're right, she wouldn't. We need to get there."

* * *

The enormous cheesesteak and mind-numbing ride up the turnpike lulled Daisy to sleep for most of the ride. The stomp of the brakes startled her awake. "Where are we?"

"At the police station in Shunk."

"Oh, I must have dozed off." She yawned and stretched.

"Dozed off?" He chuckled. "You were out cold for the *whole* ride. A sleepless night will do that."

"I was tired-and stressed. Not to mention a five-pound cheesesteak sitting in my belly." She yawned and stretched her arms over her head. "Give me a minute before we go in the station." She retrieved a brush from her bag, ran it through her curls, and checked her reflection. She sensed Nick looking at her.

"*What?* I am a TV reporter, and I can't go in there looking like I just rolled out of bed."

Nick chuckled, shook his head, and got out of the car.

Inside the small police station, Deputy Chuck Willis was sitting at his desk when Nick and Daisy entered. He glanced up from the comic book and greeted them. "Hi there. I'm Chuck, but everyone calls me Bump. Can I help ya?"

Nick and Daisy introduced themselves and stated why they were there.

Mouth slightly opened, Chuck stared blankly for a beat at Nick and Daisy. Suddenly, a lightbulb went off. "Oh yeah! That lady who Sheriff told me about! Yeah, Sheriff asked me to go to the community center to ask about her!"

"Thank you for doing that. We're so worried," Daisy said. "What did they say?" Her heart pounded.

Bump stared up at them and scratched his large head. "Oh, I didn't go yet."

His nonchalant tone stoked a fire inside Nick and Daisy. They looked at each other before steamrolling the deputy with their glares. "What do you mean you haven't gone yet?" Nick asked.

"I was—" Chuck began.

Daisy interrupted him. "Before you even *think* of giving us some lame excuse, when did Sheriff Roth ask you to do this?"

"Hmm, let me see." Chuck mumbled and shuffle papers on his desk. "Oh, here it is." He held up a pink piece of paper. Squinting at the paper he continued, "This was written on Friday. So yeah, I guess yesterday."

"He asked you *yesterday* and it's now *late* Saturday afternoon. You still haven't gone?" Nick's voice rose.

"Um, I was . . . ah . . . fishing. But I was going to swing by tomorrow morning."

"*Fishing?*" Nick yelled. "Do you understand . . . ?"

Bump turned scarlet and fumbled over his own words. "I'm . . . I'm sorry. I didn't mean to make you all mad." He shrunk back into his seat.

"This woman, my wife . . ." Nick pointed at Daisy. "Her *mother* is *missing*! And you sit around here with your thumb up your ass?! You were given—"

Daisy grabbed Nick's arm before he really let loose and rained all over the deputy. She threw Bump an icy stare. "Calm down. He got the point," she whispered to Nick and led him to the door.

Bump tried to apologize again and said he would go to the center right then.

"Don't bother, *Bump*. We'll do it." Nick shot daggers at him and slammed the door.

Outside, Nick ranted, "Do you believe that guy? What an asshole! He has *no* interest in helping us contact your mom!"

As upsetting as the interaction with the deputy was, Daisy remained calm. "Nick, let's just find the community center."

"Definitely, but first I need to take care of that one." Nick nodded at the police station.

* * *

Inside the police station, Bump called Rubi Lee again and told her about his encounter. "Tanya, I'm sure you're gonna love this." Babbling like a little boy, he told her what happened.

He was met with her chastising him. "You don't have to call me every time someone walks in, okay? I'm busy."

Bump withered into himself, feeling as if she slapped him. *Maybe she's havin' a bad day. Yeah, that's what it is. I know some of her patients have been pretty tough.* He tried another tactic. "Well I just thought you'd like to know it was a news reporter and her husband lookin' for her momma."

Rubi Lee gasped. "Why didn't you say that in the first place? A reporter? Wow! Was she as pretty as me?" she teased.

"Oh Tanya, no one's as pretty as you. And she's too tall."

A euphoria swept through Rubi Lee. *Yes! She's here!*

Yes! "Bump, you're such a nice guy. I can't believe I'm such a lucky girl to have you as my boyfriend." Rubi Lee silently gagged on that last word, as if she just swallowed lumpy, rotten milk. She knew *boyfriend* would seal the deal.

Bump was speechless.

"That's the cool kind of stuff I want to hear. Good job, Bump! Makes my day go quicker."

Bump blushed. "Thanks Tanya. Maybe I'll see ya later?"

"Sure, I'll text you."

* * *

After several minutes of driving on a windy, bucolic road, the community center appeared out of the woods. The building was a log cabin and faced a calm, massive lake. Inside, the smell of a burning fire welcomed them. Not a soul was around.

"If there is a fire, someone must be here," Nick said.

"I agree," Daisy responded as she combed over the bulletin boards for any helpful information.

"Hello folks. Can I help you with anything?" An older man wearing overalls and a flannel shirt appeared from a side door.

Daisy told him about her mother's church outreach program, and that they were looking for her.

"Do you have any information, like names or addresses of the people who received the supplies?"

The old man shook his head. "Sorry ma'am, I'm just the custodian of the building. We get many groups rentin' the place out. Once they're gone, they're gone."

Daisy's face fell.

He quickly tried to cheer her up. "You could check with the deputy at the police station. He is responsible for booking the building."

Daisy stared at him in disbelief. "We were just there, and Chuck was no help. But thank you anyway."

Nick's phone buzzed. "Okay, great, thanks guys." He slid his phone into his pocket. "We have the sheriff's address." He shook the man's hand. "Thanks anyway."

CHAPTER 19

Woods Lane twisted through tall pines and paralleled a dazzling, lively river. Daisy and Nick admired the scenery and slowed down when they saw mailboxes appear.

"The address is 6105, right Daiz?"

"Yup. There it is." She pointed.

The dirt driveway stretched on and on. Finally, they saw a sprawling rancher at the end. Colorful plants lined a brick walkway to the red front door. A black pickup sat inside an open garage.

"Oh good, someone's home," Daisy said.

But there was no answer when they knocked.

"Damnit! We can't win!" Nick mumbled.

"Maybe someone is out back?" Daisy suggested.

From the back of the house, they saw a man standing waist deep in the river, a fly-fishing rod in his hand. Nick and Daisy hustled to the river's edge and called out to him. They waved their arms until he caught sight of them.

He pulled out an AirPod from his ear. A perplexed frown wrinkled his forehead. "Can I help you?" he asked, his tone abrupt.

"We hope. Hello, Sheriff Roth. I'm Nick Tyson and this is my wife . . ." Nick began.

Water snaked around Roth's sturdy long legs. He eyeballed Daisy and Nick until his eyes rested on her. A flash of recognition crossed over his square face. "I remember you. You're the TV reporter. We spoke a little bit ago. And we met several months back."

"Yes sir, I am. We're so sorry to interrupt your day, but we're praying you can help us, please." She struggled to keep her voice level. "Please." Daisy held his eyes.

He sighed and undid the waxworm at the end of his hook. "You win, fish. Here's a free lunch!" He tossed the worm into the water, stepped over the rocks, and waded out of the river. "Okay. Let's go to the back deck and talk."

Once seated on the three rockers, he asked, "What can I do for you folks?"

Daisy swallowed hard and took a deep breath. Nick took her hand and she filled Roth in with everything that transpired in the last day.

His gaze never left Daisy's face. "You believe your mother is in danger? You don't think her texts are legitimate?"

Nick and Daisy shook their heads.

The sheriff told her that he asked his deputy Chuck to investigate the matter and it might be best to go ask him.

Daisy told him they started with Chuck and about going to the community center. "Bump dropped the ball, sir."

Roth curled his lips inward. "Well, I'm sorry about that, folks. Bump isn't quite all there, if you know what I mean." He tapped his head. "Often it takes a kick in the pants from me to get him to do his work." He chuckled.

Anger simmered inside Daisy, who was far from amused by the laissez-faire attitude of Roth. She leaned forward in her chair; her gaze shot arrows into Roth's face.

"This is *my mother*, and we believe she is in great danger—in *your* county, specifically your town of Shunk. Pardon me if I fail to find the humor."

Roth heard her message loud and clear. He stood and said, "You're right. I apologize. I'll call now and get him to look through the community center records. Can I interest either of you in something to drink?"

Daisy glanced at Nick, who stared with hard hazel eyes at Roth. His right knee was bobbing rapidly, a sign of intense anger. She rested her hand on Nick's knee and responded, "No thank you. Would it be a better idea for you to go to the station and help Bump? Sounds as if he may need it."

"No. I need to be here for my wife—she's not well." He glanced away. "I'll call him and instruct him to look up the addresses of the people who received donations. And I promise you, I will go house to house if necessary to find your mother."

"Call him *now*, please. We have no time to waste, understand?" Nick's voice was barely audible. "The amount of time already lost is inexcusable."

Roth nodded and pulled out his phone. "Bump, please pull the records of residents who received donations from that outreach program from St. Christopher's church." He listened and continued, "Search from August on. I'm sending the two people from earlier today to the station to get them. Do it *right now*, please. They will be there shortly."

"Do we have your word that Bump will do it by the time we get there?" Nick asked.

"Yes sir, you do. If not, call me."

Daisy and Nick thanked Roth for his help. Time was of the essence since the dusk started to settle in. They needed as much light as possible.

"I swear to God I'm going to strangle that guy if he doesn't have the records ready," Nick stated through clenched teeth as he slid into their car

"Nick, I know he did. We can get your posse to help look too." Daisy rubbed his arm.

"Thank you for having the level head."

"It's a struggle, but I'm trying."

Bump was standing at his desk with a folder in his hand. "Howdy! I think you're looking for this. I printed each group's name and those from the community who got the stuff. I found an address list for the church group too!" A glowing smile filled his face. He handed the list over.

Daisy and Nick scrutinized the list; little did they know that one name—Tanya Holston—had been omitted.

* * *

The ride home was quiet. Nick stole a glance at Daisy, who was twirling a red ringlet around a slender finger. A small crease sat between her brows. He did not disturb her when she was deep in thought. Nick's phone buzzed and he answered it. All he said was, "Thanks, I'll tell her."

"Who was that?"

"My aide, Peter. They did some recon in town, and it seems everyone minds their own business. I'm sorry— nothing new to report."

Daisy sighed and scrolled through her phone. "Nick, what if Rubi Lee *has* done something awful to Mom? It's like no one gives a crap there's a crazy woman on the loose who kidnapped my mother!"

He knew better than to try to contradict her. "I know, but remember, I don't think anyone around here knows about it. And another point: We're not from here so I don't know how high a priority we actually are."

Daisy turned in her seat. "Nick, you're a *higher up in the mayor's office.* If *anyone* has weight, it's you!"

"Daisy, calm down, you're yelling. We'll get back up here and find her. I promise."

"I'm so damn frustrated! What else can I do?" She pounded her fist on her leg and leaned her forehead against the passenger window and watched the different colors speed past. "I know! I'm going to hang flyers if I don't hear from her by tomorrow!"

They turned into their driveway, happy to be home. Daisy typed in the code of their garage door when her phone rang. The number had a DC area code. "Hello?" She whispered to Nick, "It's Henderson. How are you doing, Henderson?"

"Hey Daisy! Things in DC are all right, but I have some news you probably want to know about."

Daisy flicked her eyes to Nick. "Go ahead, you're scaring me though."

"There was a fire in my park and the garage was completely destroyed."

"Oh Henderson! Are you all right? Wait! You mean Margaux Ford Park?" She put him on speakerphone.

"Yes." He was silent for a beat before he continued, "I'm fine but the garage is gone and so is a bunch of the equipment—including my beloved golf cart."

"Oh Henderson! I'm so sorry but thank goodness you're okay! Does the fire marshal know what happened?"

"I did overhear him saying it was possibly a pipe bomb."

"No way! A *pipe bomb*! What the hell?"

"I don't know, but there's more. There was a strange message left on the wall of my office. I'm not sure what it means."

"A message? What did it say?"

Henderson sighed, "*She's next.* I just sent you the picture."

The picture came through. As Daisy studied it, an epiphany exploded in her head. "Henderson, I'm so glad you called, but I have to go. I'll call you later."

Daisy continued to stare at the picture as the epiphany solidified. "Nick, two places—*two* which have been blown up. The Black LaSalle and now the park. It's Rubi Lee, I know it!"

"Why would she blow up two buildings?"

"Because she's after me and these are warnings. It's startlingly clear." Daisy paced around the room. "There's more. He sent this picture." She stopped, tossed him her phone. "It was sprayed on the wall in Henderson's office."

"You think the 'she' in the message is you?"

"Who *else* would it be? Yes, me!"

"And it looks similar to what was sprayed on your dad's headstone." Nick's face suddenly grew hot and red.

Daisy continued, "Rubi Lee tried to kill me the night in the garage at Margaux Ford and now that's destroyed. She knew I worked at the Black LaSalle and it's gone. And now Mom's missing! And I think she's been kidnapped by this psycho!"

Nick looked out into the dark night, his mind racing. "And if she's out for you, she is probably out for anyone connected to you."

Daisy stared out the living room window with him. "That's what I'm afraid of." She turned to Nick, who pulled her in close. "How could Rubi Lee have escaped from the garage that night? There were cops and the FBI *everywhere*, right?" she wondered aloud.

"Yes. Keep in mind though, they were in the middle of a shootout. I'm sure they looked for her, but she's sneaky. She may have been hiding, like me. Who knows where, but since there are no records of her arrest, she's out there."

Daisy sighed. "I *hate* feeling this helpless. I hate relying on other people to get information." At this, her phone buzzed. She broke from Nick's arms to find it. Looking around, Nick told her it was in the kitchen.

"Oh yeah. Be right back." She hustled into the kitchen.

A moment later, her plaintive wail echoed throughout the dark house. "Oh no! Please God, no!"

Terrified, Nick ran into the kitchen where Daisy sat, shaking. "What? What is it?"

"This." She choked on the word and handed him her phone. "It's from Wesley," she whispered.

Nick read aloud. "Daisy, sorry to change your location assignment. But another set of remains were found in Sullivan County. Since you've been there, you need to go tomorrow."

Nick looked into her green eyes and knew what she thinking. "Don't go there. We don't know whose remains they are. We need to stay positive."

Daisy sat in silence. Fear of the remains possibly being those of her mother was etched in her face. "I know, but I don't feel anywhere as positive as you do. Especially knowing that woman is out there."

CHAPTER 20

The police cruiser turned into 1169 Pinetree Way, and Sheriff Roth stepped out and strolled up the three front steps. He rapped loudly on the flimsy metal door. He saw a window curtain move to one side and a woman look out at him.

Rubi Lee's heart stopped in her chest. *Fuck! Cops!* Her mind raced. She had to get to Annie.

"Just a second!" Rubi Lee called calmly through the door. She raced to Annie's prison and flung open the door.

"What's going on?" Annie sat tied in the chair.

"None of your business." Rubi Lee reached into a bedside table drawer for the duct tape.

"No please! I won't make a sound! I promise!" Annie whimpered.

Rubi Lee took the roll of thick duct tape, tore off three strips, and slapped them over Annie's mouth. "I know you won't." After she double-checked the ties around Annie's wrists and ankles, Rubi Lee ran back to the front door.

"Sorry, had to change. Can I help you?" Rubi Lee asked timidly. *Stay cool!* Calmly, she brushed her hair out of her eyes and prayed her thudding heart was not visible through her flimsy shirt.

"Hello ma'am. I'm Sheriff Drew Roth. I didn't mean to startle you."

"No, not at all. Can I help you with something?"

In his beefy hand was a piece of paper. Before speaking, he ran his eyes over it. "I am calling on all the new residents of our county. I like to say hello and check on all our community members, especially the new ones. Think of me as a welcoming committee!"

Are you serious? A welcoming committee? Rubi Lee thought and played along as he continued.

"I wanted to personally welcome you to our quiet community and answer any questions you may have. According to this document, you are . . . ?" He ran his eyes over the list.

Rubi Lee was glad she spent time rehearsing introducing herself with a new name. Smooth as silk, she answered, "I'm Tanya, Tanya Holston."

Roth extended his hand. "Welcome to Shunk, in scenic Sullivan County, Miss Holston."

She gave his hand a brief shake. "Thank you." Rubi Lee managed a smile. "It's nice you're checking on the new residents." She nonchalantly tugged her shirtsleeves down to cover the inked snake—but not before Roth noticed it.

"Snake, huh?" He motioned at her arm.

"Um, yeah. Dumb teenage thing."

"I get it." He laughed. "Another reason why I stopped by was because I wanted to inform you that two disturbing events have recently occurred. Yours, and everyone else's safety, is our priority. We also want to request that our citizens keep an eye out for anything strange."

Rubi Lee's antenna went up. She shifted her weight. "What do you mean by strange?"

"Do you mind if I come in? Sitting is more comfortable at my age."

Stay cool, she thought. "Well, my house is a mess and—"

"I won't be long." He looked past her through the door.

"Sure, ignore any messes."

Roth nudged open the door and stepped in. He gazed around the living room, and nothing was out of order. The room was clean and tidy. "Mind if I sit?"

"No."

He lowered himself down on the two-seater couch. "What do you do for a living?"

"I'm in health care." *Don't say too much*, she told herself.

"Given what's going on in the world, I'm sure that keeps you busy."

"Yes, yes it does." She cleared her throat. Needing to change the conversation, she asked the sheriff how long he had been in law enforcement.

"Over twenty-five years." He smiled at her and said nothing else.

Rubi Lee nodded. Perspiration dampened her underarms. "Wow, long time." The ticking of the clock on the mantle echoed as the two sat in uncomfortable silence.

"Yes, it is." His dark questioning gaze did not falter. After a few seconds dragged by, he surprised her. "I don't suppose you've heard about the grisly discovery of skeletal remains?"

Rubi Lee swallowed. "No sir. I'm, ah sorry to hear that. My ah, cable isn't hooked up." *God, what if he knows something? Stay calm!*

"Well, it was a bit of surprise. But since you're new

here, you probably wouldn't have heard anyway."

"No, didn't hear anything."

He inched forward on the couch and leaned on his knees. "Where did you say you were from?"

"I didn't. I'm from Alabama." Rubi Lee tried to keep the impatience out of her voice.

"Never been there." He looked around the house. "Nice place. Mind if I walk around the back of the house? An old friend lived here years ago. We used to sit on a bench out back and talk. But he died."

Shit, Rubi Lee thought. *Don't be short. He's already nosy and if I say no, he'll stay longer.* She manipulated her face into a tight smile. "Not at all, help yourself."

"Thank you." He pushed himself up and headed for the door.

Rubi Lee walked behind him. "Nice to meet you, Sheriff. Thank you for coming out and I'll be sure to keep my eyes peeled. If you'll excuse me, I have some work I need to do."

"Likewise, and welcome to Sullivan County."

* * *

Rubi Lee narrowed her dark eyes at the sheriff's every move. Her stomach churned like an angry ocean as Roth wandered into the neglected backyard, stepping over clumps of tall grass, broken clay pots, and wayward branches. He glanced around and shook his head at the dead vegetable garden adjacent to the house. He ran his hand across the iron-backed bench he referred to earlier before walking toward the front of the house. She assumed he was returning to his car. Unexpectedly, he pivoted to the right and strode to the back of the house.

The cable box was mounted on the wall next to the shuddered bedroom window where Annie was imprisoned. A weathered black cord hung like a skinny snake over the same window. Rubi Lee watched the sheriff pull out his glasses, lean forward, and tilt his head up to where the cord dangled. To her horror, she saw him reach toward the shuddered window and tug on the cord. He cocked his head to one side and leaned closer to the window. Hot redness bloomed in Rubi Lee's face as she witnessed him run his hand over the shiny nails she used to keep the shudders closed.

Fuck! He heard her! Heart in her throat, Rubi Lee frantically searched for her bag where Timmy was hidden. Shaking the bag's contents over the floor, she seized the knife and held it close to her face. She whispered, "Timmy. There's a nosy cop here. He may need to meet you."

She slid Timmy into the back of her waistband and like a cat, slid noiselessly through the open screen door. Treading lightly, she approached the broad back of Sheriff Roth. He held the cord in his hand and was knocking on the shudder of Annie's prison.

Blood pounded in Rubi Lee's ears. *Go! Go!* Gaining on the sheriff, she reached around to the handle of the knife and slowly extracted it from her waistband. She overheard the sheriff mumbling something about windows and cable boxes. *I can't take any chances*, she thought. Edging closer, she gripped the knife. Several feet stood between her and his back. He scratched his head and she heard him say, "Maybe these windows were nailed shut before she moved in. But this cable shouldn't be dangling here." On his toes, he reached up and tugged the cable free from being stuck on the top of the shudder.

Go do it! Now! Rubi Lee closed in on the last few feet between her and Sheriff Roth. Gripping the knife gave her confidence. Adrenaline propelled her forward. Up went her arm, Timmy shining in the sun. Rubi Lee licked her lips in excited anticipation of what she was about to do.

Out of nowhere, Rubi Lee heard music. It was Roth's phone. *Fuck!* Paralyzed, she watched him pull out his phone.

"What's up Bump? I'm helping a resident with her cable."

Bump! The idiot had to call now of all times! You're one lucky son of a bitch. Glaring at the sheriff, she rapidly slid the knife back into her waistband.

Roth startled when he turned around to see Rubi Lee standing there. "Yes Bump. Tell him I'll email him the info when I get back. Thanks."

"Is there something wrong?" Rubi Lee asked innocently. The blade of her knife was cold against the base of her spine.

"This shutter is crooked, and I thought I heard a humming coming from the house. You know it's unhooked, right? Can't watch any good television without that!" He bent down and plugged the cable into the box for her. "Now you can watch whatever you like!"

"You're right. I've been so busy I forgot about that! Thanks for helping me."

He glanced once more at the windows. "As far as those?" He pointed. "You're missing some great sunshine! Open 'em up!"

"I will. Thanks again for coming over, Sheriff." Turning away, she signaled the conversation was over.

"You're welcome. I best be going. I'll see you around." He gazed at the house once more, tipped his hat, and walked back to the driveway.

* * *

Annie heard the entire exchange through the thin walls. *NO! NO! Oh God! Please help me! I'm in here! Please!* Her throat was raw from grunting. Her shoulders cried out in pain when she tried to slide the bolted chair closer to the voices. Hot sweat mixed with tears poured down her face. Over the duct tape they fell hard, especially when she heard the male voice begin to fade. Annie strained her ears but heard nothing.

NO! NO! Come back! Anger, fear, and frustration crashed over her in vicious waves. She panted heavily through her nose. Her heart rate shot up. Annie threw her head back and pushed the primal scream from her raw, inflamed throat.

* * *

Rubi Lee needed to get out of the house. After the unexpected visit, she had to clear her head. She hid her hair under a black baseball hat that matched her black shirt. She checked on Annie who sat like a wet lump in the chair. "Good girl. You followed directions. Maybe I'll get you a treat!" Rubi Lee taunted her.

A red warning light came on when she started up the

car. "Now what?" Ten miles left until the car ran out of gas.

At the local gas station, she rammed the hose in the tank and glanced around. The metal door to the garage service bay was open. She grabbed her bag from the car and wandered over.

Several cars sat ready for a mechanic to work their magic. One car caught her attention: an early 90s Pontiac Trans Am with a black phoenix painted on the orange hood. She and Zeke used to talk about the cars they would buy someday. He had his heart set on an original Ford Thunderbird that he wanted to restore. She, on the other hand, pined for the Trans Am.

She wandered over for a closer look but stopped abruptly. *Oh my God!* Parked next to the Trans Am was the car she stole in Washington, DC. "Shit! It's the car I took!"

Panic flamed inside. She looked at the stolen car. Besides some external wear, the car appeared to be in good condition. *Who found it and towed it here?* She wedged herself between broken cars and side-stepped to the back. She bent down to see a plate from Washington, DC hung like a loose tooth below the back fender. *I can't let that plate be traced*, she decided.

She glanced around the oily garage when her eyes lit on a pile of old license plates in the corner. Thanks to Zeke's lesson of removing and replacing plates, she quickly tore off the DC plate and replaced it. She stuffed the plate in her bag and skittered back to the car.

On the way home, she pondered her next move with Annie. It was time to lure Daisy into the trap. Lost in thought about Annie, she almost drove off the road when she saw a Live5 News van drive past her. *Wonder why they're here?* She pulled to the side and watched the news van stop on the side of the road, adjacent to the township building. Other news vans crowded the area. Keeping her eye on the Live5 van, she saw Daisy pop out. Rubi Lee's eyes widened. *I gotta get home!* Before she spun out, she opened the Live5 News app on her phone.

Back home, Rubi Lee stood in the doorway and gazed at the woman. Annie did not move an inch. "Wake up. I have something to show you."

Annie slowly turned her head. She tried to sink into the chair as Rubi Lee approached.

"What? You don't trust me?" Leaning down, she tore the duct tape from her face. Annie yelped. "I think you'll enjoy this." Rubi Lee held the phone out.

CHAPTER 21

After Daisy received the call that she was headed back to Shunk, she quickly printed out a stack of flyers with the latest picture of her mother. As the copier spit out flyer after flyer, she tried to stay calm and not speculate if the story she was soon to report would be about her mother.

"Daisy we are live in five." Wesley's voice shot through her earpiece as she paced near the news van. *Come on Nick, get here!*

The county coroner was on her way to announce the finding of another body in Sullivan County. Daisy prayed with all her might that it would not be that of her mother. She tried all night to push that image out of her head and woke up feeling sluggish and irritable. All the coffee she poured down her throat now sloshed around in her stomach and filled her bladder. She did not know if she had to vomit or pee or both.

The grim-faced coroner arrived and adjusted the microphone set up on the podium.

"Good morning. At nine o'clock this morning the partially decomposed body of a white female was found in a shallow grave several hundred feet above Doe Path in the woods two miles north of the interstate. As of now, the identity of this person is unknown. We cannot yet determine if this was an accident, suicide, or a homicide.

We will take the deceased to the morgue for an autopsy. My department is analyzing the clothes and the area surrounding where the deceased was found. As I get more information, I will pass it on through the sheriff. Thank you." The waifish woman walked from the podium into a room with several officers.

* * *

Rubi Lee hit the Live5 News app and turned the phone around. "Watch this."

Annie raised her eyes. When Daisy appeared, a breath so sharp caught in Annie's throat she thought she may faint. It dawned on Annie that she had not seen her daughter for almost a week. "Oh Daisy. I—"

"Shut up and listen!"

Annie sat agape as the cameras rolled. An ache so deep, so visceral throbbed in Annie's soul. For a split second, she feared she was having a heart attack. The ache to hold her beautiful daughter in her arms threatened to overtake her. *Stay strong, she needs you to stay strong*, Annie thought, watching as Daisy put on her television face and looked at the camera.

"Thanks Wesley. This is Daisy Tyson reporting live from Sullivan County. The coroner just gave us a briefing on the body that was found earlier this morning. She reported the body is that of a badly decomposed female. This is the *second* body to be found in six months. Police are asking for help from the public. If anyone saw or heard anything, please contact the authorities. They are working day and night for any leads in the deaths of two unidentified women—a first for this country community. The police hope to find answers soon. Back to you, Wesley."

Rubi Lee turned the phone away from Annie. "And to think, your precious daughter is not even ten minutes away from here!" She laughed. "And she has *no clue* you're here! This is great!"

* * *

When Daisy's live report was over, Nick complimented her, "Nice report."

She wrapped her arms tightly around him and asked, "Did you hear back from Winston or anything more about Mom?"

"Sorry, nothing about your mom. But yes, I did hear from Winston." He sighed. "And it's not good news."

She pulled away and looked up at him. Sadness emanated from her eyes. "Tell me."

"The FBI and ATF suspect the two DC fires were related because of the evidence—a crude pipe bomb—found at both sites. They're reviewing surveillance video and conducting interviews to see what they can uncover."

Daisy sighed and asked about the red paint. "Dare I ask if that paint matched the red paint on Dad's grave?"

"Win said that test was inconclusive because they lacked a sample from your dad's gravestone."

"I see." Daisy absentmindedly twirled a tendril of her hair.

"What are you thinking?"

"Do you think there are any paint particles left on the

gravestone or around it?"

"How did I know that was what you were thinking?" he replied. "It's possible, but keep in mind it's been a while since Reverend Brindley cleaned it off."

"I know, but it's worth a shot. Nick, I'm *desperate*. Still no word from Mom. I know she's here somewhere. I just feel it in my bones. And if that paint *is* a match, then at least we have something."

"I'll call Winston back." Nick kissed her on her head and walked off.

Randy, her cameraman, breathlessly loped over to her, camera bouncing on his thin shoulder. "Daisy, Daisy! Sheriff Roth is making a statement. We need to shoot some film. Move over to the podium!"

"I'd like to thank all of you who are here to support our effort in finding out what happened to the victim," Sheriff Roth began a moment later. "I just received more details about the most recent discovery." He put on his glasses and read. "It appears the deceased is a middle-aged woman wearing a blue dress. We also discovered a thin silver bracelet near the scene. We will put a picture of the bracelet on our webpage. If anyone can identify the bracelet, please call our office immediately. Currently we are canvasing the entire area in the woods and checking with our residents to see if anyone saw or heard anything. We will let you know if we have any more information in the coming days. Does anyone have a question?"

The cacophony of reporters vying for Roth's attention reminded Daisy of being at a football game. At five feet ten inches, Daisy stood out among others and got his attention.

"Sheriff Roth! Sheriff Roth! Daisy Tyson—Live5 News,

Philadelphia. Are you inclined to label this as a homicide?"

"At this stage we are not ruling anything out."

"Do you know *how* the woman died?"

"Again, too early for a definitive answer, but it looks like blunt force trauma to the head. The woman also suffered several broken bones."

"Sheriff Roth, this is the second discovery of a body in six months. Do you think you are looking for a serial killer?"

Roth stared at her. "We are in the nascent stages of the investigation. I cannot comment on that right now. Thank you all for coming." After answering several more questions, he tipped his hat and disappeared into the hallway behind the podium.

Nick listened to the sheriff and swelled with pride at Daisy's command of her emotions, considering the woman in question could be her mother.

"Great job, Daiz." He hugged her.

"I think I'm going to puke. Mom has a silver bracelet." She turned and ran to a bathroom.

CHAPTER 22

The black SUV sped from Washington, DC to Cab Station, Virginia. The driver turned left onto the church's driveway and meandered up the paved driveway that bisected part of the cemetery before lurching to a stop in front of St. Matthew's church.

Jenny Brindley was busy shearing the hedges and did not hear the vehicle. Suddenly, a hand was on her shoulder. She whirled around, electric shearer rotating, and nearly beheaded the owner of the hand. Loudly she shrieked, "Oh dear Lord! You nearly lost your head!" Jenny turned off the implement and caught her breath. She blinked and brushed her hair from her face. "Can I help you?" She stared at the suited-up man and woman.

"We hope so."

"Jenny! What on earth?" Reverend Brindley hustled from a side door at his wife's scream.

Turning to Reverend Brindley, Jaida said, "Good to see you again, Reverend."

"Yes. You both look vaguely familiar." He studied them.

"We were at the Taylor–Tyson wedding. I'm agent Jaida Campbell and this is Agent Winston Wang. We were maid of honor and best man."

"Oh yes, of course! What brings you here in such a grand fashion?" He gestured to the idling SUV.

"Is there somewhere we can talk?" Jaida asked. "Can you show us Daisy's father's gravestone?"

"Yes, of course. Follow me. I received your message, and I sincerely hope I can help you."

He led them through the pristine cemetery to the headstone of Jackson Taylor. Winston got down on his knees and ran his hand across the stone. He leaned in close and gave it a good look over.

"You did a nice job cleaning this." Winston looked up into the expectant face of the reverend.

"Oh no. Perhaps it was too good a job?"

"Maybe, yes." Winston rose from the ground and brushed off his pants.

Jaida inspected the back of the stone. "Win, check this out." She pointed at a small red dot stuck on the base.

Winston knelt close and pulled out a small X-ACTO knife. He scraped the red dot and placed the sample in the small plastic evidence bag Jaida held.

"Bingo!" he said, standing up.

"What did you find?" Reverend Brindley clasped his hands to his chest like a child.

"Reverend, we ask that you not tell anyone about this. Do I have your word?" Jaida leveled her dark blue eyes at the man.

"I will not say a word. I am a man of the cloth." He smiled.

"We can't thank you enough. We hope this will point to the perpetrator," Winston said, shaking the reverend's hand.

"I'll pray for you."

"Thank you for your time. Be well," Jaida said.

In the car Jaida called the Forensics Department in Washington, DC and asked where the closest field office was located. "This paint chip needs to be analyzed ASAP."

When she hung up, Winston said, "That was quick. What did they say?"

"We need to drop it off at the field office in Harrisburg. It'll be analyzed there, and they should be able to pinpoint the type and who makes it. Then they will cross reference all stores that sold it around the time of Daisy and Nick's wedding within a hundred-mile radius. If they get a hit, they will request surveillance tapes from the stores."

"You got a lot of info quickly!" Winston laughed.

She chuckled and grabbed his arm. "They know when I want something done, they better do it right away."

"That type of power must be awesome!"

"Oh, it's *intoxicating*." Jaida flashed a triumphant smile at her partner. "I'll call Nick. He wants to be kept in the loop."

"I think you should tell him to keep mum about our part in this, don't you?" Winston looked at her.

"For sure."

* * *

After they dropped off the paint sample, Win and Jaida followed Nick's suggestion and sped out to Sullivan County.

"I'll call the sheriff to tell him to expect us," Jaida said.

They nudged the SUV into a tight spot outside the police station. Inside, an assistant led them to Sheriff Roth's office.

"Sheriff, we are investigating the disappearance of a woman. She is the mother-in-law of Nicholas Tyson, a higher up in Philly local government." Winston saw the effect of his sentence when the sheriff's mouth fell open. "Here is a recent picture of the missing woman, Annie Taylor," Winston said, holding up a picture for Sheriff Roth.

"I know exactly who you are talking about, but I didn't know about her son-in-law. May I?" Sheriff Roth took a long look at the photo. He moved to his desk and opened the top drawer. He pulled out a battered file and leafed through the papers. Halfway through, he removed a photo of an unidentified person—one of the two murder victims—and compared it to the one Winston had.

"Thank the Lord," Roth said and showed the other picture to Winston and Jaida. "It's not a match. If it's any consolation, I know how distraught her daughter is about this. She and her husband paid me a visit. At home."

"Did they?" Jaida asked.

"Yes. I had just baited my line to reel in a fat trout when they interrupted me. Can't say I was happy about that."

Jaida and Winston were stunned into silence. Jaida flattened Roth with a glare that would have made boulders melt.

He cast his eyes to the floor like a scolded little boy. "But, but I'm here now to help!"

"I sure hope so. We need to find her. Where do we go from here?" Jaida asked.

"I asked my deputy, Bump, to look into this matter, but I think he's come up empty-handed. I expect him to come in the office today. He was away on vacation."

Winston and Jaida gawked at Roth. "Your deputy is supposedly working on this case and is on *vacation*? Are you serious?" Jaida barked.

Sheriff Roth cleared his throat before responding. "Ah, yes ma'am. I'll call him and tell him he needs to return."

"*Now,*" Winston said and pointed at the phone.

Roth left a message on Bump's phone. "How else can I help? People around here are getting a little nervous with these two bodies being found and someone who may have gone missing."

"*May?* Come on, Roth." Winston stepped closer to him. "I know you're aware of the severity of this matter, especially now since the FBI is involved. I would like you to keep our involvement to yourself. Agent Campbell and I are going into town to get a feel for things."

Jaida ordered Roth to call them the minute he heard back from Chuck. "Oh, and how well do you know the residents in the county?"

"I've been sheriff for twenty years and our population is very small—around a thousand permanent residents. I know almost all of them."

"Has anyone new come into town?" Jaida asked.

"I have a list of all county residents and we can certainly check. I'll call our local realtor too. She would have a record of real estate transactions. Depending on the month, we are a fishing destination, especially during trout season. We get a lot of day trippers coming here to hike our trails and see our streams too."

"We can rule out a stranger who is responsible for her disappearance," Winston commented.

Roth cocked a thick eyebrow. "And why's that?"

Winston explained about the threatening sign on the evening of Daisy's report from Children's Hospital of Philadelphia. "Plus, Daisy and Nick saw video of a woman whom they know tried to kill Daisy last winter."

This statement caught Roth short. "*Kill* her? What do you mean?"

Jaida explained the events of the night in the garage at Margaux Ford Park and that Rubi Lee Dixon was intelligent and dangerous. "From profiling I've done of other criminals, I can safely state that she blames Daisy for Zeke Dixon's death. Which means Rubi Lee will stop at nothing to exact revenge for the death of her brother."

Roth let out a tense breath. "Thank you for this information. We will do everything we can. Let me get you all that list of homeowners." Roth hustled out of the room.

Jaida looked at Winston and rolled her eyes. "Looks like I lit a fire under his ass, right?"

"You did. Furthermore, who the hell allows the deputy *who's in charge of a case* leave on vacation? Jesus!"

"This country bumpkin cared more about a fuckin' *fish* than a life!"

Roth returned with the list and promised he would let them know when he heard from Bump.

"Is there a place we could get something to eat?" Winston asked.

"Good Eatin' Diner. Great place. Take the main road and it's about two miles down on the right," Roth responded.

"Thanks. You're welcome to join us," Winston offered.

"Sure, I'll be along. Go ahead and order without me."

* * *

A handful of cars and pickup trucks were scattered in the lot. Good Eatin' Diner was a rectangular cement block outfitted to resemble an elongated train car. BeBop music pumped out of an old jukebox in the corner. Décor and posters reminiscent of the '50s gave the feel that time had stopped. Aromas of sizzling pancake batter, bacon, and coffee mingled together to permeate the air.

A waiter approached them with menus. "Sit anywhere you want. I'll be with you in a moment."

They sat in a booth with a roadside view.

"Did you ever think we'd face Rubi Lee again?" Jaida asked.

"Between you and me, I thought she'd be arrested that night. But she's a slippery snake and I'd say she's desperate."

"And we both know—all too well—how desperate people act." Jaida sighed and picked up the menu.

The waiter sauntered over and pulled a pen from behind his multi-pierced ear. "What can I get you two?"

"Do you have any specials?" Jaida inquired.

"Sure do, our trout BLT is the best around. Comes with fries, fruit, or slaw." He yawned.

"*Trout* BLT?" Jaida asked. "Hard pass. I'll have a burger, medium rare, fries and chocolate milkshake."

"Make that two, but I'll have slaw, not fries. Thanks."

Roth showed up a bit later and ordered coffee with an egg salad sandwich.

"Before we get to that, Jaida and I are a little perplexed about this Bump/Chuck name thing."

Roth laughed. He explained that they were one in the same person and how Chuck got the name Bump.

"Got it. We'll refer to him as Bump then."

"Do you have the list from the realtor?" Winston asked.

"Yes I do. Here are the new residents."

"What can you tell us about these people?" Winston asked.

Roth donned his glasses and scrutinized the list again. He exhaled, "Well the Goldbergs and the Hartzells are older couples. Dougherty, bless him, is wheelchair bound, and Dalton is a widow. Holston is a young woman from Louisiana. Met her the other day. Very nice. Works for the health care system."

"How about any of the other residents? Anyone holding a grudge or disgruntled about anything?"

"Not that I know of, but Rita over there would know. She has worked here for years and knows everybody." He pointed at a woman in the kitchen.

"Thanks Sheriff, you have been helpful. We'll consult with Rita," Winston said.

Jaida and Winston watched Rita, a stout ball of energy with a shock of platinum hair, cruise around the diner chatting with customers.

"We should wait a bit. The lunch crowd is pretty big right now," Jaida observed.

"True." Winston watched Rita. "More importantly, don't you think the sheriff would have investigated a missing person more thoroughly? Especially since two instances of human remains were found earlier?"

"Win, you've talked to Roth. Until we mentioned that night last December, I got the impression he'd like this investigation to slowly disappear. He seemed more interested in fishing and crap like that."

"Agreed. After we talk with Rita, we can do some follow up with the residents on the list."

The diner slowly emptied. Jaida saw that Rita was at the cash register. "Time to go. I got this." Jaida put cash on the table and approached the register.

"You're Rita, right?" Jaida and Nick introduced themselves.

"Yes. Can I help you folks?" Magenta lipstick was carefully painted over her thin, aged lips.

"We are working on a missing persons investigation and wondered if you could help us?" Winston asked.

"Missing person? How exciting! It must be someone important." She clasped her hands against her ample chest.

"Actually, she is," Jaida replied. She gave Rita a quick recap of Annie's disappearance.

"Oh dear Lord. Poor woman, not to mention her family," Rita responded.

"Are there any new faces around here you've noticed? Anyone strike you as a loner? Or a 'quiet' but friendly neighbor?"

Rita tilted her head to the left and gazed up to the ceiling. She pursed her magenta lips together. "Oh, like a Jeffrey Dahmer type?"

Hope glimmered for Jaida and Winston. They waited as she thought. Their hopes were dashed.

"No. Not that I've noticed. I'm so sorry, wish I could help more."

"Well, if you think of anyone or anything, please call us." Jaida handed her a card.

"I will." She turned and added, "Have you tried Vernon's Farmers Market just down the street? Lots of folks go there—great place. Mike, the owner, has a sharp eye and would know if any strangers or weirdos were around."

Jaida and Winston thanked her before driving to Vernon's.

* * *

Vernon's Farmers' Market was a bustling beehive. The building was an aged, cavernous garage. The front doors were rolled up to the top, giving the market an open, airy feeling. Vendors selling anything and everything haggled with customers. In their dark suits, Jaida and Winston stood out among the casually dressed people enjoying their shopping. They stood near the soft pretzel stand, inhaling the mouthwatering aroma of hot, buttered pretzels sprinkled with cinnamon.

"Can I help you? You look a little lost."

Jaida and Winston turned to see a bespectacled middle-aged man in a short sleeve shirt. His green eyes were patient, and a friendly smile played across his face.

"Oh hello. We're agents Campbell and Wang, from the FBI."

His eyes lit on the badges hanging from lanyards around their necks. "The FBI, huh? This is a first. I'm Mike and I run the show here."

"We're working on a missing persons case."

"I've seen the flyers, but that's it. People are more interested in the skeleton parts in the woods. Word travels faster than shit through a goose around here."

"We understand. Do you have any recollection of anyone coming in you don't recognize?" Jaida prodded.

Mike scratched his chin and shook his head. "We get lots of people in here during the three days we're open. But we're a small town. Sure, we get some characters in here, but no one has stood out. That's not to say a wanderer hasn't come in. I'll keep my eye out, though. Most of the shoppers are local. Do you have a description?"

"Caucasian female, early twenties, on the skinny side, tattoos?"

Mike scowled. "Possibly, but I can't say for sure."

"Okay. But if you can recall anything or anyone, please let us know," Jaida requested.

"Or if someone stands out for the wrong reason." Winston handed him a card as he thanked Mike.

Jaida and Winston walked through the market and stopped at a deli counter. "Can I interest you in a bag of cheese?" a vendor asked, holding up a plastic bag.

Jaida smiled, "I think we'll pass, thanks." They walked into the sunshine to the car.

Winston smacked the hood of the SUV. "Damn. We struck out big time. We need to circle back to Roth and tell him we learned nothing new here. And we should pay a visit *to these people* right now." He slapped the list of names Roth gave him.

CHAPTER 23

The unshaded lamp held a dull dusty bulb. Enough light emanated for Rubi Lee to see Annie lying listlessly on the bed. Over the ten-day period, Annie's skin turned sallow, and her clothes hung on her thinning frame. She could not run the risk of her prisoner dying from malnutrition; she needed Annie robust and healthy.

"Wake up!"

Annie did not move.

"I said *wake up!*" She shook Annie, who gradually opened her eyes. "Get up!"

"I'm trying," Annie rasped. Rubi Lee was taken aback at the purple bags under Annie's sunken blue eyes. Her cheekbones jutted out and her skin was ashen.

"Jesus, you look like shit."

"I feel like shit."

"What do you eat?"

Annie felt like she was in a scene from *The Twilight Zone*. "What?"

"Food! What food do you eat?"

Annie gawked. "Food? Since when do you care about what I eat? You've been feeding me that fast-food garbage, so of course I look and feel awful."

"You need to eat because I need you alive for now. I'm going to the store, so you better tell me what you want. I can't have you die from shitty food. And when I get back, we're going on a road trip."

Annie understood that if she wanted to see her daughter again, she had to play along with this woman. "Um, fruit, vegetables. Turkey slices and cheese."

* * *

With Annie next to her, Rubi Lee sped down the twisty roads through Sullivan County. Annie ate in silence. *Apples, turkey, and cheese never tasted this good*, she thought. Soon the road turned narrow and bumpy. Annie felt as if she was on a terrible carnival ride as the car bounced over rocks and plunged into potholes that dotted the road. She stopped in a heavily wooded area. Rubi Lee got out and came to the passenger's side and opened the door into the knee-high brush.

"Get out," she demanded.

Annie stepped out into the tall brush. The long grass tickled her bare legs. Curious dragonflies buzzed around the two women. Rubi Lee shoved her in the direction of a thin path that snaked through the ground cover. Annie followed as it wound through the woods. She stopped at the base of a towering, rocky bluff.

"Keep going. Follow the path."

"If you're going to kill me then do it now. You keep threatening, but there's no follow through," Annie panted. "I think you're afraid."

"Hardly. I have a plan. Start climbing!" Rubi Lee snarled. She tingled with pleasure as she watched Annie struggle to keep her footing on the rocky terrain. They reached a small plateau and Annie fell to her knees. Rubi Lee kicked her foot.

Up ahead and deep in the woods, automobile-size rocks jutted from the side of the bluff, creating deep, thin caves that penetrated ten feet into the heart of the mountain.

Rubi Lee pushed Annie into the cave. "Go in and sit down. You obviously are weak and can't handle a stupid hike."

Annie lowered herself to the cool, moist earth, grateful to be sitting. Closing her eyes, she inhaled deeply and conjured images of her family. The faces of her three sons and Daisy filled her mind and helped her process the situation. She raised her eyes to Rubi Lee. "You'll never get away with this. Never. A person as sick and evil as you gets caught." Annie narrowed her gaze at Rubi Lee. *"Every. Time."*

"Bullshit! Someone as smart as me doesn't get caught! I've already killed three people since I got my hands on you. And guess what? I'm still roamin' free, aren't I?"

Annie raised herself from her rocky seat and stared at her. Rubi Lee's eyes shimmered like black diamonds. Annie knew she was telling the truth.

Rubi Lee spit on the ground at Annie's feet. "And then it will be five after I kill you and your daughter."

Tunnel vision enclosed Annie. Eyes fixated on Rubi Lee, the rest of the cave fell away. *I will never allow that! You will never have the chance to murder another person! I will pound your head into the wall again and again for all the people you murdered!*

Hurtling toward Rubi Lee, Annie felt a primal scream start in her gut, burn its way through her stomach, and repel out her mouth. She lunged at Rubi Lee and slammed her hard against the wet wall. She clamped her hand over Rubi Lee's face and shoved her head against the uneven cave wall. "Never! You will never, *ever* get near my daughter!" she roared, her voice echoing in the damp chamber.

Half-blinded by Annie's fingers, Rubi Lee clawed at whatever she could. She found Annie's neck and raked her fingernails across it, drawing small lines of blood.

"You vile animal!" Annie screamed and squeezed Rubi Lee's face until her fingers ached.

Panic washed over Rubi Lee. Screaming, flailing, Rubi Lee lifted her foot and kicked Annie hard in the knee.

Annie screamed at the crack of her kneecap. She let go of Rubi Lee, who pounced on her.

"You bitch!" Rubi Lee screamed. She threw Annie to the ground and wrapped her hands around Annie's throat. Rubi Lee's eyes were wide with craven evil.

"Killing those people wasn't my fault! It's your daughter's! Me and my brother were doin' just great with our uncle! If Daisy didn't get involved, none of this would have happened! I blame her for *everything!*" Rubi Lee screamed at a gasping Annie.

Annie felt her windpipe being crushed like a matchstick. *Oh my God! The last thing I'm going to see of this world is this face of evil!* Annie gasped, trying to maintain consciousness, but Rubi Lee's grip was too tight.

"*No!* Wake up damnit!" Rubi Lee shook Annie's bony shoulders. Eventually, she coughed, and her eyelids fluttered.

Rubi Lee slumped against the wall, relieved. "It's time to go."

* * *

Nearing the house, Rubi Lee let out a stream of expletives when she caught sight of the uninvited black SUV sitting in the driveway. Stopping short, but within eyeshot, she slammed the gearshift into park. "Ah shit, that looks like a cop car! How'd they find me?"

Annie rubbed her bruised throat; she gasped at the sight of the vehicle. *Police! Thank God! They're here!* Like lightning and with no forethought, Annie reached for the door handle and pulled.

"Don't even think about it!" Quick as a snake, Rubi Lee pulled her knife from the driver's side door compartment. The five-inch blade nicked Annie's thigh when Rubi Lee plunged it into the seat. Blood trickled out. Annie cried out in pain and reached for her thigh.

Rubi Lee grabbed Annie's jaw. "Next time, it'll be your fuckin' throat." She released her and stared at the two people inside the vehicle. "We're outta here."

About two miles down the road, she pulled over. From the back seat, she retrieved a bandana and dangled it in front of Annie's face. Her breath was hot and frantic against her hand as she bound Annie's mouth.

"Come on." Rubi Lee popped open the trunk and shoved her in. "Keep quiet or you will never get out of this car."

To burn time, Rubi Lee scrolled through Annie's phone for several minutes. Countless texts from Daisy clogged it. "Looks like Daisy is worried about you. Too bad Mommy's in the trunk and I have her phone."

Twenty minutes later, Rubi Lee turned the car around

and headed home. Even though the driveway was empty, an unsettling feeling churned in her stomach.

On the front door was a note. Her heart pounded out of her chest as she read: *Miss Holston, sorry we missed you. We came by to ask you some questions. Please call when you get home so we can find time to meet. We left our cards are here too. Thank you.* Rubi Lee read the names on the business cards: Winston Wang and Jaida Campbell.

She almost tore the note and cards into pieces but stopped short. *If I tear these up, they'll know I was here*, she thought. She reread it hastily and realized they would be back. Always one to think on her feet, she hurried into her messy bedroom. Into a bag went clothes and other necessities. Hastily, she emptied the contents of the kitchen cabinets into several bags and seized four bottles of water from the refrigerator. She locked the front door and hurried to the car.

Clumsily, Rubi Lee wrenched Annie from the trunk and untied the bandana wrapped around Annie's face. As she started the engine, she issued a stern warning to Annie, "Don't say a word. I don't need to hear your whiny voice."

Annie obeyed.

"We're off to the big city of Philly!" Rubi Lee told Annie when she pulled out.

On the way, she purchased two burner phones with cash. By late afternoon, they pulled into the hotel. Rubi Lee exited the car but not before gagging and handcuffing Annie.

Time to use Bump, she thought, dialing him before checking in.

He picked up in one ring. "Hey Tanya. Wut's up?"

"Hi Bump. What're you doin'?'"

"Not much. Just finished work and am sittin' here watching TV. You wanna come over and hang out?"

"I can't right now. Remember when we talked about being rich? And you told me what your wishes were if you had money? What if I told you I could make your wish come true?"

Bump sat up at this question. "Yeah I do. What do ya mean? You kind of already did by being with me."

Gross, Rubi Lee thought. "What if I told you we can make that happen?"

"What do you mean? You hit Powerball and you're gonna share?" He laughed.

"You're kinda close. I just got a letter from some law firm telling me that I had an old rich aunt who died."

"Oh Tanya, I'm so sorry."

Rubi Lee tried not to laugh. *Good, he fell for it.* She continued, "And she left me *a lot* of money. Supposedly, I'm her only living relative. You know what that means, Bump?"

"That you're really rich now?"

Rubi Lee's chuckle sounded like a branch scraping against a wall. "Not at this exact moment in time, but soon I—or should I say, *we*—will be."

Did she just say we? Bump cleared his throat. "*We*, Tanya?"

For fuck's sake! Do I have to spell it all out? Patience did not come easily to Rubi Lee. She took a deep breath. *Just say it*, she thought and continued. "Yes. We. You and me could live together. And you don't have to work anymore."

Bump's thick eyebrows shot up. He tried to process

what she just offered. "Did . . . did you just say *live* together?"

"Yep. I don't mean like, *right now*, but eventually." Rubi Lee paused. "Why, do you *not* want to live with me?"

Bump was silent. Euphoria and desire coursed through his body. He leaped from the couch and danced around his cluttered living room.

"Are you there, Bump?"

"Yeah, yeah. I'm *always* here for you, Tanya. You know you're my girl."

"And just think, Bump! You can quit a job your grandparents made you take and spend your days hunting and fishing!"

"Really? I can quit?" Bump envisioned himself skulking in the woods, hunting rifle pressed into his shoulder, the early-morning mist damp on his face. Flashes of him fly-fishing with Tanya at his side made him smile. He shook his head at his good fortune. He glanced up. *Thank you, Dad, for Tanya.*

"Well, don't quit now, but in a month or so."

"Oh, okay. Tanya, this is great! We need to celebrate!"

"I know. But I'm going to be out of town for a few days—need to sign the papers to get my money. When I get back, we'll celebrate. And Bump, get ready. I mean a *big* celebration."

"You're making me feel like I need to take a cold shower!" He joked. "Call me when you're home. I'll miss ya, Tanya."

"Yeah, okay. See you soon."

* * *

The glass doors to the hotel slid apart. The overpowering aroma of manufactured floral air freshener made Rubi Lee's nose burn. Behind the white granite check-in desk was a middle-aged woman.

"Welcome! Checking in?" she asked.

What do you think? "Yes."

"May I have your name?"

"Dixon." She immediately realized her mistake. *You dumbass! Holston!*

"Hm, I don't see a Dixon. Did you make a reservation?" Her blue eyes scanned the computer screen.

"I'm so sorry. I meant to say Holston."

The receptionist cocked a painted eyebrow at Rubi Lee. "So, which is it, hun? Dixon or Holston?"

"Holston, Tanya Holston."

"May I see some ID? A driver's license will do."

Keeping her head down, Rubi Lee handed over her driver's license.

"Ah there we go. Holston."

"Sorry, still getting used to using the name of my ex. Dixon was my married name, but I'm not anymore."

"I get it," the woman said. "Men. Who needs 'em?" She returned Rubi Lee's ID.

"Amen to that."

"Okay hun, your room is on the first floor near the back exit." The woman instructed Rubi Lee how to get to her room.

Rubi Lee pulled the car around to the back and parked in front of the room. "Don't try anything." She uncuffed

Annie before they entered the room.

Rubbing her sore wrists, Annie breathed a sigh of relief and took in the generic hotel room: two single beds, a cramped bathroom, and a thick brown rug. Annie breathed a sigh of relief. *Thank you God, for getting me out of that house. Please give me strength*, Annie thought before she asked to take a shower.

Rubi Lee pondered the question. "Yes. Keep the door open, though, until you get out."

Annie acquiesced. The hot steam rose and entwined itself with the piney aroma of the green bar of soap. Annie stood and relished the hot cascade pouring over her tired body. She closed her eyes and fantasized about being home. Visions of tulips and daffodils showing off their brilliant colors temporarily erased her new reality. An image of Jackson laughing at one of her corny jokes danced through her mind. "Oh Jackson, my love. I ache for you." *I wish I could swirl away down the drain like the water and be with you . . .* Her warm trance was broken by Rubi Lee.

"Towel off and put on those clothes on the sink. Hurry up."

Annie dried off and dressed slowly to extend this freedom. She shuffled out of the bathroom where Rubi Lee paced, chomping on gum. In her hand was a small white plastic bag with red lettering on it.

"Sit down." She pointed to the bed and continued. "Because I'm not the totally horrible, twisted monster you think I am, I'm gonna let you see your criminal daughter today. Isn't that nice?" Dark, reptilian eyes bored into Annie.

Raising her head slowly, Annie stared back and asked,

"Why should I believe you?"

"Because I have a little present for her, one that I plan on giving her in person." Keeping her eyes locked on Annie's, she reached into the bag and withdrew one of the burner phones.

"I don't understand. Why are you giving her a phone?"

"To torture her. I can't wait to call her and hear her panic. Especially when I let her hear your old voice."

* * *

Rubi Lee weaved through the tight city streets toward Daisy's office. In the back seat, Annie sat in pained silence, hands cuffed behind her back. Outside, the world went about its normal business. Watching people hurry by, she begged, *Please, please turn and look in the car! Please see me and help me!* Her wish was not granted.

Rubi Lee turned into an empty church parking lot. Across the bustling street, the glass building that housed Live5 News and other businesses soared thirty stories into the crisp blue sky. They parked and waited.

Around noon Daisy appeared. "Look. There's your spawn of Satan." Rubi Lee pointed to the sky-high building. "She thinks she's such hot shit. If people knew she was a murderer and . . ." She continued to mumble nonsensically.

Annie craned forward in the seat as far as the seatbelt would stretch. Through the filth and dead bugs on the windshield, she stared at her only daughter.

Daisy got into her Jeep and pulled out. Rubi Lee soon pulled out of the lot and fell in line four cars behind Daisy.

Annie felt new worry lines carve their way into her

face. *How am I going to save my child from this monster? It's a mother's job to protect her children! I'm failing at the most basic job of a mother! I have to try to deter this monster from hurting my daughter!* Annie felt angry heat start at the base of her neck and creep its way to her face.

"What do you plan on doing, Rubi Lee?"

Rubi Lee cut her eyes to the rear view mirror.

"You'll see. For now, shut up, sit back, and enjoy the ride!" Eyes locked on the Jeep, she watched it merge onto a main artery and pick up speed. Rubi Lee followed suit. A thin-lipped smile spread across her face. *I'd love to just smash into her car. But you need to be patient, Rubi Lee. Your time to get even with her will come and—*

Her daydreaming stopped abruptly when a rusted white van cut in front of her, obscuring her view of the Jeep.

Slamming on the brakes, Rubi Lee laid on the horn. "Fuckin' asshole!" She punched the gas and the car lurched forward. Flipping the middle finger, she raced by the van. Rubi Lee yanked the car back into the right lane behind two cars crawling at a turtle's pace.

"Hurry the fuck up!" she screamed and watched Daisy's Jeep speed up. *Shit, I'm gonna lose her!* Slicing her eyes to the passenger's side mirror and seeing room on the right, she jerked the car onto the shoulder. White-knuckled, Rubi Lee raced down the cup-strewn, broken-glass-littered shoulder. Gravel and small pebbles kicked up and pinged off the car. She barely missed a discarded tire.

"You're gonna kill us!" Annie screamed as the guard rail came closer. All her muscles constricted. Eyes squeezed tightly, she braced herself for the impact.

198

"Shut up!" Rubi Lee wrenched the car back in the exit lane and blew through the yellow light at the bottom onto Independence Avenue. "I need to find her!" She popped up in her seat like a prairie dog, eyes searching for Daisy's Jeep. Twenty yards up, she spied it turning into a mall parking lot. "There she is."

Rubi Lee pulled into the enormous parking lot of the local mall. Donning a white baseball hat, she counted to five before she trailed Daisy.

Inside the mall, the aroma of greasy fast-food grills wafted up Rubi Lee's pointed nose. She watched Daisy meander around the shoppers. Jealousy simmered inside as she watched men and women do a double-take when the statuesque redhead—oblivious to the attention—walked by. *All the more reason to kill you, you bitch*, Rubi Lee thought, picking up her pace to make sure she crossed paths with her nemesis.

* * *

Daisy strode through the mall, her boot heels clicking on the shiny white marble floor, a bag from a major department store swinging at her side. *I need to get back by one thirty for a staff meeting*, she thought and consulted her phone. She had picked up a birthday present for her boss Wesley, and now she was headed toward the exit to the parking lot. Up ahead, a separation in the floor's tile formed a small crack. She did not see it.

An acute pain shot up the outside of her right leg. Her three-inch heel landed on the side of the crack. Daisy felt like one of those people on *Funniest Videos* as she struggled to keep her balance to no avail. Her ankle buckled under her and like a child learning how to ice skate, Daisy fell with slap a onto the cold floor.

"Ouch! Ow! Ow! OW! Damn that hurt!" She cried and clutched her ankle. Behind her, snickering and laughing echoed in the cavernous mall. A group of teenage boys pointed and laughed. *Little assholes*, she thought.

"Yo, stop it you imbeciles!" A tall, reed-thin boy with bad acne darted forward and helped her up. "Are you okay?" he asked, flipping aside a mop of blond hair.

"Yeah, I'm fine, aside from embarrassing myself." Daisy brushed herself off. "See what happens when you never look up?"

"Yea, my mom says the same thing," he replied and cut his eyes to his friends. "Sorry about my stupid friends laughing at you."

"Not your fault. Hopefully I'm not on TikTok by now!" she remarked. "Thanks for the help."

"All good. Make sure you look up though!" He turned back to his friends, and they ambled off.

Limping slightly, she approached an empty bench by the soaring, splashing fountain in the center of the mall. She took off her boot and rubbed her ankle. She did not think it was sprained. As a kid, she twisted her ankles numerous times; thankfully this did not feel like that.

After a few minutes of rest, Daisy dropped her phone back into her bag. Rising carefully from the bench, she glanced up and saw a woman roughly her mother's age strolling and laughing with a younger woman who was pushing a baby carriage. They ambled toward Daisy, arm in arm. Both were tall, shared the same heart-shaped faces and full smiles. Mother and daughter. Daisy froze. An arrow of pain shot through her soul, to the point she could not stand.

She fell back onto the bench. Tears sprang to her eyes. She could not tear her gaze away from the women. *That should be me and Mom! Please God let her be okay!*

Extracting her phone, Daisy dialed, then paused. *I know she won't answer*, Daisy thought and pressed call anyway. Straight to voice mail the call went. She quietly cried into the phone, "Please Mom! *Please* call me! I need to know you're okay. I'm so worried about you. I love you." Daisy hung up and sat watching shoppers bob in and out of the row of stores. Her mental capacity was shot; being back to work by one thirty wasn't on her mind anymore.

* * *

From the safety of one of those stores, Rubi Lee watched Daisy. She delighted in the way Daisy angrily threw her phone back in her purse and wiped her eyes; Rubi Lee figured she called her mother. *Good, she's upset. Serves that bitch right. I've never enjoyed a game so much in my life.*

When Daisy stood to leave, Rubi Lee palmed the burner phone in her sweatshirt pocket. She glanced around to see a pack of teenage girls fifteen feet away from her, sashaying without a care in the world. Snippets of teenage up-talking floated her way.

"Right? My mom thinks she's, like, *so* good at yoga."

"That new art teacher thinks they're really cool."

"We should Snap and send it to Hannah. She's fun to make jealous."

Pencil-thin legs clad in black tights carried equally thin bodies. Rubi Lee glanced down at her own skinny thighs. *Good thing I wore black pants too. Helps to blend in.* She detected a pungent aroma of orange, cinnamon, and flowers swirling around the girls like a cloud. Rubi Lee crinkled her nose and shook her head.

Sunglasses on, hood up and head down, she lagged a few feet behind the girls. Through their bobbing heads, she spied Daisy moving closer.

Even better, she's limping a little bit. Don't get ahead of yourself. Timing is everything. Licking her dry lips, Rubi Lee reveled in the warm gush of euphoria pounding through her body. *Show time!*

Clack, clack, clack. The sound of a pair of brown ankle boots on one of the girls grew louder as Rubi Lee hustled to catch up to the group. Instinctively, her right hand flew to her eye and she began to tug on her eyelashes. *Stop! Be cool! Don't draw attention to yourself!*

Heart pounding, she saw Daisy approaching her, a shopping bag slung over one of her forearms. *Perfect, right into a bag.* She turned on the phone and clutched it in her left hand. Sweat tickled her scalp.

Rubi Lee stepped to Daisy's left. Just as the group passed Daisy, Rubi Lee, pretending to scroll on her phone, stepped into Daisy's path and lowered her left shoulder.

The powerful jolt knocked Daisy off balance. Like a snake, Rubi Lee's hand silently darted into the bag and slid the phone inside.

"Whoa!" Daisy wobbled like a new colt finding its legs. Catching herself before she fell again, she tried to stammer an apology. "Are you okay? I'm sor—"

"Watch it!" Rubi Lee mumbled. Her cheeks glowed with her victorious smile. *Score! Done! Zeke, you'd be so proud.* Sauntering off with the pack off girls, the *squeak, squeak, squeak* of her sneakers was in perfect unison with her pounding heart.

* * *

Daisy turned and watched the figure dressed in a black sweatshirt and black jeans stride off and disappear into the mall. Cocking her head to one side, a crinkle formed between her eyebrows. *Woman or man? Or was that a kid?* She shrugged it off. *Someone's having a tough day*, she rationalized. Too exhausted to do any more shopping, Daisy returned to the parking lot.

* * *

Rubi Lee jogged across the parking lot and slid into the driver's seat. "Mission accomplished!" She announced gleefully. "You just wait for my second act."

"What did you do?" Annie asked.

At first, Rubi Lee ignored her. She drank from the can of soda, relishing in the scene from the mall. She belched and turned to Annie. "That bitch is so lucky I didn't bash her ugly head in. But there's plenty of time for that. I'm very patient."

"She has done *nothing* to you and you know it!" Annie raged.

Rubi Lee lifted the can and poured the rest of the soda down her throat. "Oh yeah? Maybe in your opinion." Rubi

Lee wiped her mouth with her sleeve. Glaring at Annie, she continued, "Ever hear of an eye for an eye?"

Gnashing her teeth made small quivers pass through Annie's cheeks. Her teeth ached. *Where is she going with this?* "Of course. It's part of Hammurabi's code."

"Whatever that is." Rolling her eyes, she threw the can of soda to the graveyard of trash on the car floor. "Anyway, I'm gonna get even with her for taking my eye—in this case, my brother Zeke."

Livid ire turned Annie's face a bright red. "She *did not* take your brother! Make me understand how you can *possibly* believe that my daughter *killed* your brother?" Annie raged. "You're the one who tried to kill her!"

"And I'm pissed I didn't finish the job. That bitch will get it, trust me." She pulled the keys from her pocket. "But then again *Annie*," Rubi Lee said as she started the engine, "us two would never be spending so much quality time together, just like mother and daughter, right?" She flicked her eyes to the rear view mirror.

Annie met her gaze with smoldering hatred. "*Never*," she hissed.

Rubi Lee let the car idle as she watched Daisy exit the mall and retrieve her keys from her purse. Pointing them at the vehicle, Rubi Lee heard Daisy's Jeep respond with a rapid *Beep! Beep!* followed by the engine starting. Breathing heavily like a hungry carnivore of the wild, Rubi Lee fixated on Daisy, who favored her left side as she limped to the car door. *Good girl. Now get in the fucking car*, Rubi Lee thought. She rolled down the window. The cool air caressed her warm face and neck.

Rubi Lee and Annie watched Daisy slide into the

driver's seat, start up her car, and exit. Rubi Lee counted to five, put the car in drive, and pursued her prey.

* * *

Up ahead, Daisy came to a near stop. "Great, just what I need, a traffic jam." She hit the button for the AM station for a traffic update. Hearing there was a back-up on the same route she exited the city, she decided to take a more scenic, less congested route back to the office. *I'll shoot Wesley a text that I may be a little late*, she thought and reached for her phone while idling.

As she exited the road and turned onto Independence Way, an ear shattering, heart-stopping buzzing made Daisy jump. *What in the hell was that?* Glancing over her right shoulder at the bag on the passenger seat, she heard it again. "What the hell?" She stared at the bag.

Daisy pulled over, yanked off her seat belt, and dug into the bag. She saw what it was: a small black phone. It buzzed again. Pulling it out, she saw the number read *Unavailable.*

What in the world? It buzzed again. *How did this get in my bag?*

"Uh, hello?" she mumbled.

"Hello! This is the service department. Your vehicle's warranty is about to expire..." The voice was female, yet sounded human, not robotic.

Daisy shook her head. "*What?* Who is this?"

Silence. Then a click.

"Hello? Hello?" Daisy held the phone out and stared at it. An inkling of confusion tinged with an iota of fear stirred in her stomach. *When I get back to the office, I'll figure this out*, she thought. The phone bounced on the passenger seat after Daisy tossed it. She pulled back onto the road.

The phone buzzed again. *What the hell? How in the hell did this get in my bag?* She snatched it from the seat.

"Who is this?"

"Hello *Mrs. Tyson.* Guess—"

The voice was interrupted by another voice—a terrified, familiar voice.

"Daisy! Daisy! Rubi Lee . . . she has me! Please help!" Annie screamed.

"Shut the hell up, you old hag!"

Daisy's stomach dropped. "Oh my God! Mom!" She slammed the brakes with such ferocity the Jeep fishtailed. Car horns blared; two angry drivers swerved around her. Daisy's mind split into two directions: pull over and stay on the phone. *Get to the side of the road safely!*

Daisy looked around, stunned. Rubi Lee was on the other line—and with her, Daisy's mom. She had pulled up in front of a hair salon, where a plump woman was walking out with her equally plump Corgi. At the busy intersection of Independence and Market, a line of cars waited for the green light. A group of people sat around a bright yellow table outside a coffee shop, chatting animatedly. Wispy clouds stretched across the blue sky. The world rotated in a normal way on what was a normal day—but not now.

Flinging open the car door, Daisy jumped out. "You sick, twisted monster! Where are you?"

"Like I'm gonna tell you?" Rubi Lee scoffed.

"I swear, if you hurt my mother—"

"What're you gonna do? You won't find me! *I'm* in

control of everything and everyone—especially you! If you knew how fuckin' stupid you looked marching up and down the road . . ." She cackled.

Daisy stopped with such abruptness that her sore ankle screamed. *She sees me.* Jerking her head from side to side, her eyes bounced around her surroundings. Spinning like a top on the sidewalk, Daisy roared, "Where are you? Show yourself, you scared piece of chicken shit!"

Clink! Clink! The coffee drinkers twelve feet away lowered the expensive lattes onto their saucers and scowled disapprovingly at Daisy.

"Chicken? I wasn't chicken when I bumped into you in the mall, was I? You're lucky I didn't bash your fuckin' head in back there! And I wasn't chicken when I beat the shit out of you in the hotel bathroom last year, was I?" The cackle again. "You'll get that and much worse when I get even with you for killing Zeke."

Daisy stopped moving, paralyzed by Rubi Lee's words. The world around her spun like a Tilt-a-Whirl. The cars, trees, and road spun around her, suffocating her.

Pacing back and forth on the side of the road, hair tossing wildly in the wind, Daisy was unaware of the honking cars that whizzed by. Frustration, fear, and anger hit Daisy in relentless waves. *Please God, help me! I've replayed what I'd say to her over and over. Don't let her sense any fear! Daisy Tyson, you're stronger than that—your mother needs you!*

Marching on the side of the busy road, unaware of anything except keeping Rubi Lee on the phone, Daisy leaped out of her skin when a huge construction truck laid on the horn. Like a grenade, the phone flew out of her hand—and shot four feet ahead of her, into the lane. Fifty feet to her left, the construction truck hurtled down the road toward it.

"Shit!" Her lifeline to her mother had only seconds before being destroyed. There was no other option—she had to get it. Taking a chance, she lunged forward, into the lane.

The angry grinding of the gears downshifting filled her ears. Grabbing the phone, Daisy leaped away from the truck just as the driver yanked the vehicle into the opposite lane—into the path of a packed commuter bus. Blasts of the truck horn and the screaming of brakes from both vehicles reverberated up and down Independence Way.

Daisy's hair slapped against her face from the blast of wind generated by the truck. Grit and sand filled her nose and eyes. Standing on the side of the road next to her Jeep, she clutched at her chest, her heart hammering through her clothing. *Oh God! We all could be dead!* She looked at the terrified commuters who stared at her, many with glaring eyes. Only fifteen feet separated the two stopped vehicles.

Embarrassed, she limped back to the safety of her car. She fell into the seat and panted, "Rubi Lee?" *Please God, let her still be on the phone!* After all that, she couldn't imagine the line being disconnected. "Rubi Lee! Are you there?" Seconds dragged before she got a response.

"Yeah! What in the hell was all that?" Rubi Lee barked.

Daisy almost cried out in relief. "I dropped the phone." Panting and scrabbling for her purse, she clawed through it for her phone and speed dialed Nick. She needed his help. In her left hand, she held the black phone at arm's length.

"Hi Daiz! What's—" Nick started.

She turned her head away from her left hand and whispered, "Nick, listen! Rubi Lee called me on a burner phone! You need to record the conversation!"

"What're you talking about?"

"Trust me!" she hissed. "Record it!" She dropped her own phone on the seat. "Rubi Lee! I'm here! Don't hang up!" Pulling the phone from her ear, she frantically searched for the speaker icon. *Thank God!* She hit the button and Rubi Lee's high-pitched voice filled the Jeep.

"Say hi to Mommy!" A shuffling sound filled Daisy's car until she heard her mother.

"Daisy! Oh Daisy!" Annie wailed.

Any air in the Jeep was sucked away by an invisible vacuum. Daisy tried to draw even breaths. She gasped, "Mom! Mom! Where are—"

"Sorry bitch, that's all you get."

CHAPTER 24

"No! Rubi Lee, don't hang up!" A loud clattering then crunching sound filled Daisy's ear. "Shit!" Daisy yelled. "Nick! Are you still there?"

"Yes! We have a huge problem here. We need to call the cops! I'll meet you at home within an hour."

"Absolutely *do not* call the cops. Just get home and I'll explain everything."

Forty-five minutes later, Nick rushed into the house and found a pale, swollen-eyed Daisy folded into the plush couch in the living room. He sat and kissed her.

"How in God's name did she call you?"

Daisy sighed and rose from the couch. Pacing around the room, she told Nick her theory of Rubi Lee sliding the phone into her bag. "Today at lunch, I ran out to get some shopping done at the mall. Someone bumped into me—now I know it was Rubi Lee—and she dropped that phone, a burner phone, into my bag." She shuffled back to the couch and sank into it.

Nick processed what she said. "Oh man. She had *the balls* to knock into you?" He let out a low whistle.

"Yep."

"Not only is she sick, she's brazen—and smart."

"Unfortunately, you're correct."

"Seriously?"

"What I deduced is that she's blaming me for her brother's death. She kind of said that. Plus, what else would she mean?" Twirling her hair, she continued, "And now she has my mom captive!" Tears pricked her eyes. "Nick, *she has my mother.*"

They sat for a while in front of their fireplace. Watching the flames dance, Daisy held a pillow close to her and poured her heart out. "I can barely focus at work. I'm so tired, angry, and frustrated. I *fell asleep* in a meeting this morning. And now this happens." A sob escaped her.

Nick sat back and studied his wife carefully, holding a box of tissues for her. Puffy bags hung under her eyes. Her usually full, rosy cheeks were pale and dry. She picked at her nails, yanking off a hang nail.

"You did? What did Wesley do?"

"Well, after I told him what's going on with Mom, he told me to take a few days off, to take care of my mental health. Thank God."

* * *

Each morning after Nick left for the office, Daisy fell onto a kitchen chair, drank black coffee, and googled Rubi Lee Dixon. When those searches did not yield much, she left messages for Sheriff Roth. After she wasted three mornings unearthing nothing that brought her any closer to her mother or Rubi Lee, the flood of frustration broke her.

She slammed her laptop shut, flung open the French doors to the patio, and ran out into the brisk morning. She screamed. And screamed. And screamed. She fell onto a lounge chair and pummeled the pillow with her fists until it was flattened. *I can't live like this anymore. I need to call Jaida. I need to hear her voice.* She lay on the lounge chair, eyes closed. The noises of being outdoors—birds, squirrel chatter, a barking dog—centered her. Breathing in the cool crisp air, Daisy returned to the warm house.

Please pick up, please pick up, Daisy willed. On the fourth ring, Jaida's melodious, calming voice answered.

"I was just thinking about you," Jaida said.

"I'm so glad you answered. I have some serious crap to tell you." Daisy enlightened Jaida about everything that had transpired in the last two days.

"She's crafty and desperate. Criminals like her always believe they are one step ahead of the law. Soon, she will falter," Jaida told her. "Win and I have been to Shunk and will continue to look for her. We *will* find her, Daiz."

"I'm going crazy, Jaida. I can't work, eat, sleep—which is want Rubi Lee wants."

"You're not wrong, but don't play her game. Go to work, try to stick to your routine. Don't let her win."

Daisy sighed. "You're right. I won't let her win."

* * *

On the day of her return, an intern dropped by her desk. "Delivery for Mrs. Tyson! Looks like you got some fan mail." He handed her a stack of envelopes.

"Thanks Todd." Daisy flipped through and saw mostly advertisements, several letters, and one large manila envelope. She opened the letters from viewers who liked her stories. It put a smile on her face. *It's always nice to get positive feedback*, she thought and picked up the manila envelope. She saw it was from southeast Pennsylvania. Without a thought she opened it and pulled out the contents. It was a picture.

"Oh no! NO!" She screamed and dropped it just as Wesley breezed by her office.

"Are you all right? What happened?" He rushed in.

Daisy rocked in her chair, hands over her face.

Wesley saw the picture on the floor and picked it up. "Oh my God! What is this?" He gaped at the bruised and scratched face of Annie. Matted hair stuck to her head. One of her eyes had been blackened.

Daisy shook her head in disbelief. She cast terrified eyes up at her boss. "It's my mom! That monster is hurting her!" Cries filled her office.

Wesley stood awkwardly, rubbing his almost-bald head. "Daisy, I'm calling the police."

"No, no! We're working with a sheriff up in Shunk. I know exactly who has her."

Wesley knitted his thin brows and replied, "If you don't want me to call, I'll honor your request as your friend. Please, if there is anything I can do, just ask."

"Thanks. I may need some more time off to find her."

He gave her shoulder a squeeze and walked out. Daisy picked up the picture and looked at it. A note sat in the bottom of the envelope. She reached in, unfolded it, and read: *We will meet eventually. I'll be in touch soon.*

Daisy fell back in her chair. She clasped her hands on her desk and closed her swollen eyes. *Please God, please let me find Mom before it's too late. Please*, she prayed.

Carefully, she returned the items to the envelope and placed it in her bag.

She called Nick after she steadied herself. "Hi Nick, when are you going to be home?"

"Hey beautiful! I've got a light afternoon, so regular time."

"Do you think you could come home earlier?"

Nick detected a certain undertone in her voice—the one when she needed to tell him something. He feared it was about her mother. He did not want to engage over the phone.

"Sure. I can be home in an hour."

"Great, see you soon, love you."

Nick chewed the inside of his cheek during his ride home. He barely kept to the speed limit as his anxiety grew. *It has to be her mom. Oh shit. But she would've told me if Annie was found*, he pondered as he dodged around slow drivers.

He threw open the door and called out to her. "Daiz?"

"I'm up here!" Her voice floated down the staircase. Nick took the steps two at a time and entered their bedroom where Daisy laid under the quilt with her head on her pillow, Gussie by her side. He sat down near her head and rubbed her back.

"Are you all right? Daiz, what is it? You have bad news, don't you?"

She rolled over on her side. "I feel sick, and yes it's something about Mom." She inhaled abruptly. "I got a picture of her in the mail. Her face was all bloody and she looked horrible!" She began to cry.

"A picture? Where is it? Let me see."

"Over there. And there's a note." She gestured to her bag on the floor.

Nick pulled out the envelope and slid out the picture and note. His jaw hung open. "Holy shit. You're right—this is awful."

"Read the note."

Nick opened the note and read it to himself. Anger flashed over his face.

"You know how crazy and dangerous Rubi Lee is, right? That proof was in that horrible picture!" Her voice rose in intensity.

Nick sat down next to her and pulled her to him. "Daisy, the bright side is that your mom is alive—personally I believe that's the case. We'll figure this out. We have done this before and together we can do it again." He whispered into her ear, "The most important thing is for you to feel better. I think we're about to board the crazy train for a long ride."

"I feel bad because you're so busy at work. I'm the one who needs to get on the train, not you. We need to get back up to Shunk and leave no stone, rock, whatever, unturned."

"Yes, we do. We need to stay in contact with Sheriff Roth and I will continue to stay in touch with Winston and Jaida."

"I know we will. The stress is getting to me. I talked to Jaida who said for me to stay in my routine. Rubi Lee wants me to fold in, quit and give up. That won't happen."

"No, it will not especially with me to help." Nick kissed her head. "Can I get you something to eat?"

"I'm sorry but I just don't feel hungry. Thanks for offering though. I think I'll pop this." Daisy reached over to her nightstand, opened the drawer, and pulled out a bottle of sleeping pills. "Will you get me some water, please?"

Within ten minutes, Daisy was sound asleep.

* * *

The next morning Daisy was up early and felt refreshed. Gussie padded down the steps to the kitchen, meowing loudly.

"Okay girl, I know you're hungry." Daisy poured vittles into Gussie's bowl and made breakfast for herself and Nick.

"Good morning. Coffee?" Her voice was chipper.

Nick hugged her from behind. "Yes please. Feeling better this morning, I see." He released her and slid two slices of bread into the toaster.

"Yes. A good night's sleep cleared my head. It also made me realize we are stuck in a waiting game until Rubi Lee contacts me. I hate that she has all the control."

The aroma of cinnamon toast wafted from the toaster. Nick took the slices out and slathered them in butter. "I hear you. Think of it this way: That monster has no idea what *we* are doing to hunt *her* down. She has no idea that we've enlisted the help of Jaida and Winston."

Daisy chewed the inside of her cheek. "You're right. But that doesn't guarantee she isn't going to continue to hurt Mom in the meantime—or worse." She sighed and looked out the window. "I've always been able to solve problems . . . and now? I can't. It's making my stomach ache."

"Fair enough. " Nick rose and put his plate in the dishwasher. "Like I said, we have Winston and Jaida helping. They're trained professionals and they'll find her. I know it." He finished his coffee. "You finished?" He gestured to her cup.

Daisy tilted her cup. "Nope, one more sip. Yes, and given the fact she *followed and called* me, I know she will keep Mom alive. It's all part of her twisted mission of getting even with me."

"But remember, you did nothing." Nick crunched on the last of his toast. "But you're smart to think like she is."

Daisy tucked her hair behind her ears. "Rubi Lee is sick. I have *no choice* but to think like her. We're dealing with a deranged woman whose thoughts I have to adopt as my own." Swallowing the last of her coffee, she added, "And when you and I return to Shunk, and with the help of Roth, Jaida, and Winston, we will hunt her down like the animal she is—and between all of us and her, only one will be left standing."

CHAPTER 25

In the hotel bathroom, Rubi Lee sat on the toilet seat and scrutinized the three different wigs she'd placed on the bathroom counter.

I think I'll go with the red one. I'm sure Bump will love it, she thought and texted him that he needed to help her with something. Like a slimy chameleon, Rubi Lee altered her appearance. Always an edgy, goth dresser, she forced herself to choose a conservative, lackluster outfit for her trip to Philadelphia.

"What about this?" She tugged on an auburn, shoulder-skimming wig, navy pants, and a gray turtleneck sweater. "Well?" she asked Annie again, assessing her reflection in the hotel room mirror.

Annie ignored her.

"Well?" Rubi Lee kicked the bed Annie sat upon.

Annie stared at her. "What am I supposed to say?"

"That I look normal and no one, especially your daughter, will think I stand out."

"There's *nothing* normal about you," Annie hissed.

"You got that right!" Rubi Lee responded from the bathroom where she quickly applied makeup and reappeared. One last check in the mirror and she was ready. "Thanks for telling me your spawn of Satan rides the train. That makes my job that much easier."

Annie could not believe Rubi Lee's transformation. "What're you going to do?" Annie whispered. She feared the answer.

"Oh, you'll see. Be a good girl now. Enjoy your game shows." Rubi Lee stuffed the bandana back in Annie's mouth, patted her on the head, and left.

In the car, she texted Bump, who waited in the diner lot across the street. His heart rate sped up every time he thought about Rubi Lee. Never having had a "real" girlfriend, Bump had fallen hard for Rubi Lee. Morning, noon, and night, she was all he thought about. Rubi Lee made him feel wanted and important. And she was a very willing—and dominant—sexual partner. She left him exhausted and craving more after their sweaty, twisted encounters. He envisioned their next rendezvous in her bed, her skinny, pale body under his. *I can't wait . . .* His fantasy was interrupted by a text.

On my way . . . be ready!

He replied, *I AM. I'm ready to help w/whatever u need . . .*

Rubi Lee pulled in and flashed her lights. Bump exited his vehicle and tottered over. "Ready?" she asked.

Bump pulled on his seatbelt and threw a glance at Rubi Lee. He did a double-take. "Keep that wig on when we get naked later."

You pathetic, vile pig . . . you have no idea, she thought before she replied. "Oh, just you wait, my Bump. This wig will be the *only* thing I'm wearing." She ran her tongue over her glistening red lips.

"Careful girl, or big Bump here may not be able to wait until later!" he replied.

"Behave," Rubi Lee purred and started the car.

On the way to Live5 News Studio, Bump bopped his head to the pop song playing on the radio. "Where are we going?"

"We're going to surprise a friend of mine. We need to go to her office first to make sure we see her leave. I know she takes the train, so I thought it'd be more fun to surprise her at the station!" Rubi Lee lied.

"Oh good. Is she as pretty as you?" Bump reached over and caressed Rubi Lee's thigh.

"No one is, Bump." Rubi Lee smiled at him.

"You know it. I feel like a little kid getting ready for my birthday party!" He giggled and turned his attention to the outside. Brown skeletal trees dotted the landscape. Dead leaves lay on the cold earth. *Maybe Tanya will want to go somewhere warm when we get our money.* He glanced over at her, a lovesick smile on his face. *I can't believe that I get to spend the rest of my life with this woman.*

* * *

Within an hour, they saw Daisy exit the building and hustle down the dark stairway to the station. "There she is, Bump!" She pointed. "I'll sneak onto the train and text you when we get close to where she'll get off, okay?"

"Wow, she's tall!" Bump glanced at Daisy. "See you soon!" He sighed and smiled as he watched Rubi Lee exit the car and follow Daisy down the darkened, crowded steps to the cement platform.

Rubi Lee stood about ten feet behind and observed Daisy laugh and joke with other commuters as if they had their own private club. *I can't stand you.* Rubi Lee's lips curled into a tight, mean line. When Daisy turned, her train pass, which was looped around her neck, flashed the number 3—the Fort Wayne station.

Rubi Lee texted: *Bump, she will get off at the Fort Wayne train station... I'll text you when there's two minutes left.*

K.

A bright light from the outbound train bounced off the wall and a terrible screech of brakes filled the underground station. The commuters stood ready to board as the train crept closer. Rubi Lee's skin burned. She dug her nails into the palms of her hands. *It would be so easy to just give her a shove right onto the tracks*, she thought as the silver car came to a stop and its doors squealed open. Daisy boarded; Rubi Lee followed. Rubi Lee sat four rows behind Daisy and watched.

* * *

The gentle side-to-side rocking of the train sent Daisy into a brief, needed nap. Dancing in front of her closed eyes were crystal clear images of burner phones, Rubi Lee's evil face, and her mother running through thick woods, screaming for Daisy to help her.

"Mom!" Daisy yelped and snorted as she woke. Her jaw ached from clenching back tears. *If that wasn't a premonition, I don't know what is.* Crystal clear in her mind was a decision: She decided to go to Sullivan County. *I know Rubi Lee has her there.*

* * *

Rubi Lee sent Bump a text that the train would arrive in two minutes at Daisy's stop. She also told him that he should follow Daisy to her car and wait near it. *But don't say anything—remember it's a surprise!*

Okay.

Exactly two minutes later, the train arrived. Daisy stood, gathered her things, and deboarded. Rubi Lee lingered ten feet behind. Goosebumps of exhilaration popped up on her arms. *This is the best game ever*, she thought as she trailed Daisy. She texted Bump that they were leaving the train.

Okay, I'm in the parking lot . . . what kind of car does she drive?

A Jeep, red.

* * *

Bump wandered around the parking lot until he saw a bright, cherry red Jeep parked right in front of the station.

That's it, he thought and jumped at the screech of the brakes of an in-bound train on the other side. He took a seat on the empty wooden bench and waited. A bright light lit up the tracks as an outbound train arrived. The doors slid open and out poured the commuters. Among them, he saw the tall redhead. He watched Daisy stride to her car. *That's Tanya's friend!* He did a double-take. Squinting, he got a flash of Daisy's face when it was illuminated under a lamp. *Wait, I know her! She came to the station!* Bump saw Daisy and smiled broadly. *Tanya is so nice to surprise her! I didn't know they knew each other! Maybe it's a birthday surprise.*

The wind had kicked up. Paper and Styrofoam cups bounced and swirled through the vacant parking lot. Strands of Daisy's hair blew across her face as she walked across the empty lot.

Bump stood from the bench and caught eyes with Tanya, who slithered toward the red Jeep from the opposite side. A quick index finger to her lips told him to be quiet, but to move toward Daisy. *She's really gonna surprise her! I love surprises!* Getting restless, Bump walked toward the Jeep, parallel to Daisy. He heard Daisy's clicking heels on the cement parking lot.

* * *

Daisy brushed her hair from her face and pulled her keys from her bag. *Beep! Beep!* The Jeep honked back. Opening the back door, Daisy slid her bag onto the backseat and yawned. *Man I'm tired, what a long day*, she thought and slammed the back door shut. *A cold beer will taste so good.* She turned to open the driver's side door and screamed.

Bump stood a few feet behind her. "I'm sorry, I didn't mean to scare you," he said.

"Who are—" She began but never finished.

Bump watched, his eyes growing wide, as Tanya crept up from behind, tire iron in her palm. *Woosh!* Through the cold night air, she struck the side of Daisy's head. At Bump's feet, Daisy lay like a sack of flour.

Bump gasped audibly. Instinctively, he backed away

and looked at the crumpled body. His lower lip hung open like a gasping fish. He turned and stared at Tanya.

"Don't just stand there gaping! Pick her up!" Rubi Lee barked at Bump.

"Tanya, what's going on? I thought you said—"

"Shut up! Pick her up, put her in the Jeep, and follow me. I'll explain at the hotel." Rubi Lee rooted through Daisy's bag and found her keys and phone. Tossing the keys to Bump, she ordered him, "Hurry the fuck up."

"But Tanya, she may . . . "

I was afraid he'd get soft. Time to change tactics. Rubi Lee squeezed her eyes shut. Speaking in a plaintive, terrified tone, she continued. "Trust me, Bump, she's evil! She hurt me real bad, *real bad.* Please Bump, if you love me, you'll help me!"

Licking his lips and scratching his head, Bump gazed at Rubi Lee. "If you say so. I don't want *anyone* ever hurting you, Tanya. I'll help you!" He bent down, scooped up an unconscious Daisy, and put her in the backseat. "I'll follow you."

"Thanks Bump. I love you." Rubi Lee felt bile stir in her throat.

Before starting the engine, Bump realized his feet did not reach the pedals. He glanced in the back seat at Daisy and commented, "Man, she's a big one!" and wrenched the seat forward several inches.

"I'll see you at the hotel in ten minutes!" Rubi Lee walked off.

Bump steered the Jeep into a spot right in front of their hotel room. Rubi Lee stood by the window and met him when he pulled in. She stamped out her cigarette, opened the car door, and shook Daisy awake. She ordered Bump to keep watch in the parking lot.

Daisy stirred. Rubi Lee made sure Bump was out of ear shot before bending down and hissing in Daisy's face. "I've dreamed of this moment for so long, and now it's here."

Daisy's eyes fluttered open. Something grayish-silver waved in front of her face. She blinked several times and realized it was a knife. Daisy whimpered as Rubi Lee leaned down, her face inches from Daisy, and the two locked eyes. Rubi Lee parted her lips... Daisy gagged at the warm wetness of Rubi Lee's tongue running down her cheek.

"Yum. The taste of fear. I love it." She rested Timmy against Daisy's cheek. "Timmy likes you." She called Bump to come help her. "Once you get her in the room, I'll tell you what's going on. But put these on her first." She threw Bump a pair of handcuffs.

He stared at them, then cast a questioning look at Rubi Lee.

"Please Bump," Rubi Lee said. "Get her into the room."

Bump snapped to and grabbed Daisy from behind. She moaned in pain when he pulled her by her cuffed hands. Pain shot up her arms when he pressed Daisy against the wall outside the hotel.

Daisy quickly turned her head away from this vile assault. "Get offa me, you pig!" Daisy roared and tried to stomp on his foot.

"What the *fuck* are you doing?" Rubi Lee screamed at him. "Get her in there and cuff her to the old lady!"

He jerked Daisy into the room and saw Annie on the bed. "Who's that?" He asked Rubi Lee, pointing his chin at Annie.

"Oh my God! *Mom!*" Daisy screamed. Daisy broke out of his grip and looked around. Her heart stopped at the sight of the lifeless lump on the bed.

Bump's face screwed up in confusion. "'*Mom*'? What's going on here, Tanya?"

Rubi Lee froze at Bump's question. *Fuck! He called me Tanya! Get him outta here before this all goes to shit!* "Bump, you wait outside; keep watch. After I take care of these two," she said, shooting daggers at Annie and Daisy, "I'll tell you everything. Just go outside."

He glanced at the three women, his face a mask of confusion, and opened the door. Rubi Lee followed him.

* * *

Daisy leaned over and threw her arm around her mother. Her tears mingled with her mother's. "Mom! You're alive! I prayed so hard!" she whispered.

"I know honey. Oh Daisy! My Daisy! I'm so happy to see you!" She looked at the knot popped out from Daisy's head. "Oh my, your head!" She lovingly caressed the egg-sized lump.

Daisy shimmied off the bed to kneel on the floor, face to face with her mother. Annie dropped her voice to a whisper. Tears welled in her eyes. "Daisy, I'm so glad you're here. You won't believe what I've been through. We have to beat her."

Daisy stroked her mother's soft cheek. "I know Mom, but she's really smart. And she's crazy. And she sucked Bump into this whole thing. I want you to tell me everything. But first we have to figure out an escape."

"I know, sweetheart. I don't know how that will happen, but we're together now."

"Oh Mom, I thought she killed you!" Daisy studied her mother's face. A small, nasty scar zigzagged over her right eyebrow. Her eyes looked sunken, and more lines surrounded her mouth and eyes.

Annie gently wiped her daughter's tears and told her everything. Her cadence was slow and soothing as she told how Rubi Lee trapped her into captivity. About the brutal murder of Joyce and burying her body in the woods. About how Rubi Lee planned her revenge on Daisy. About the mental and physical anguish suffered at the hands of a madwoman. "What kept me alive is *you*," she whispered and kissed her daughter. "We can beat her."

Daisy sat, absorbing this side of her mother—the resilient, determined, and tough side. One she did not see often. One she knew would help them escape.

"Where's Nick?" Annie asked abruptly.

So caught up in the moment, Daisy realized he did not know what happened. She turned her tear-stained face to the popcorn ceiling. "Oh no! He thinks I'm on my way home! He has no idea what's going on! What're we going to do? I can't call him!"

"First, we're going to stay calm. And we will—"

Their conversation stopped with the sound of a key being inserted into the door.

"Time to move our little party," Rubi Lee ordered, walking through the door alone. "But first, we're gonna text your hubby." Daisy's phone sat in her hand. "Tell me what to text and we'll send it together—how fun!" She squatted next to Daisy, who recoiled at Rubi Lee's sour breath.

Daisy thought quickly. "Um, send something like this." She dictated a text telling Nick she was late and loved him.

"Done. Get up."

Daisy stayed idle. The only thing moving was her pounding heart. She had one hand free. The fleeting thought of punching her crossed her mind. *But that would be disastrous and futile.*

"Get up!" She kicked Daisy's foot. "Next time, it'll be Timmy!" Rubi Lee flaunted her knife, sliding the blade against Daisy's cheek.

"Now, turn around." She cuffed them and jammed the bandanas in their mouths. Before exiting, Rubi Lee made sure the parking lot was deserted. She opened the back door and shoved them in.

From the backseat, Daisy gazed at her Jeep parked adjacent to Rubi Lee's car. She saw a figure in the driver's seat. *Is that Bump?* She leaned closer to the window, her eyes glued on him. Seconds later the figure slumped over; blood oozed from a gash on his forehead. His face pressed grotesquely against the window; dead eyes stared at Daisy. She gasped in horror. *Oh my God! She killed him! In my car!*

Annie turned to see what startled her daughter. She was sorry she had.

Rubi Lee reveled in their reactions. She opened the driver's door. "Didn't need him anymore. I'll be right back." She went back inside the hotel room and jogged back out to Daisy's Jeep. From her backpack, she took something and tossed it into the vehicle.

She drove the three of them to a lot across the street.

Daisy could tell Rubi Lee was fumbling with something in her lap. "In five . . . four . . . three . . . two . . . one!" She rubbed her hands like an excited child about to open a birthday present.

BOOM! The explosion rocked the car the three sat in.

The Jeep exploded in a blazing fireball. Glass pieces shot like wild stray bullets. Black smoke plumed into the night. Flames raced along the gasoline-soaked sidewalk and raced up the door of their room.

Rubi Lee turned around to a cowering Daisy and Annie. "Beautiful night, isn't it?"

* * *

At home, Nick poured a glass of wine and settled himself at the kitchen counter. He combed through a stack of paperwork and half listened to the Live5 News broadcast humming in the background. His phone danced on the counter. Glancing, he saw it was a text from Daisy.

Hi, im working late on a breaking story and wont be home til after dinner. dont wait up for me . . . lve ya.

Nick read the message over the rim of the wine glass. He paused. *Lve ya? Daisy would never send a message that poorly written, and she never says "lve ya."* He shot back a reply, asking if she was okay.

The background sound of sirens on the television caught his ear. Wesley Hines, Daisy's colleague, spoke. "For more information, we will go to the scene of the car fire with correspondent Juan Pizzaro. What can you tell us, Juan?"

"Thanks Wesley. Apparently a car, specifically an SUV,

exploded here, outside the Red Caboose Motor Lodge. As you can see, flames spread through the inn, destroying some rooms. Luckily, the inn was *not* full and there have been no injuries. No one knows exactly how the SUV—which looks like a Jeep Grand Cherokee—exploded. We just received word that there *is* a body in the driver's seat. Again, Wesley, we do not know the cause of the explosion."

Nick paid more attention when he heard the type of vehicle. *Daisy has a Grand Cherokee*, he thought. He zoomed in with his phone and snapped picture of the partially singed license plate. His heart stopped dead when he enlarged the picture; five digits were still visible. *Oh my God, that's Daisy's Jeep!* Blood pounded in his ears. His mouth was dry. *I have to get there!*

CHAPTER 26

Like a bat out of hell, Nick drove to the Red Caboose Motor Lodge. His mind reeled as fast as the car tires sped on the black road. At a stoplight, he pulled out his phone and read the message again. His gut was right: Something was terribly wrong, but his heart did not want to listen. Daisy would never be at a hotel without him. He commanded his car to call Winston. *He'll know what to do*, Nick thought as the phone rang and rang. "Come on Win! Please answer!" It went to voicemail.

He drove on until his emotions overcame him. He exited to the side of the road and undid his seatbelt just in time before he threw up the wine and crackers mixing in his stomach. Hugging the cold aluminum guard rail, he cried. *What if that's Daisy in the car?* Flashbacks of his life with her raced to the forefront of his mind: games of HORSE, playing golf, their accidental meeting after years apart, when he proposed, their first kiss.

When he arrived, fire engines and police cars cluttered the parking lot. The car fire was extinguished. Firefighters were coiling up their hoses. Nick sprinted to one of the police officers.

"Officer, I'm Nick Tyson. I think that's my wife's car!" Nick pointed to the charred skeletal Jeep.

"Can I see some ID, sir?" she asked.

Nick fumbled in his wallet for his license. He showed it to her. She looked at him and handed it back. "Thank you sir."

Nick stepped away.

"Sir, I need you to stay here. This is a potential crime scene."

"My wife drives a Jeep like that! Please!"

"Okay. Stay calm. I'll get Detective Siler." She called over her shoulder to a fit, blond woman dressed in jeans, a black T-shirt, and sneakers. A red baseball hat completed the ensemble.

Siler asked Nick what made him think it was Daisy's car.

"I saw the car—well, Jeep—on the news earlier tonight. I'm terrified it's my wife's car. Five digits of that license plate match this!" Nick showed her his phone. "And I understand that there was . . ." He choked up. "A . . . a body in the front seat." Nick made a move to the burned-out car.

Detective Siler gently grabbed hold of his arm and said, "I'll be right back. Stay right here. This is my job." She walked toward the burned-out vehicle and consulted with the medical examiner who was inspecting the charred body.

Nick watched the ME gesticulate with gloved hands as he talked to Siler. Again, he felt his stomach flip like a fish out of water when he saw their grim expressions. "No, no please! Please don't tell me it's a female! Please!" He pleaded as she approached him.

"Mr. Tyson, how tall is your wife?" Siler asked.

"How *tall*?" Nick's head spun. "Tall, like five ten. *Why*?"

"In the vehicle, the front seat was moved up very close to the steering wheel. This indicates that a person of a short stature would have been driving the vehicle."

Nick scowled at her.

She continued, "This means that either your wife drives her car with her knees bent at a severe, almost impossible angle, or someone else drove her car and moved the seat up."

"Daisy extends her legs as much as she can."

Siler's phone rang. She answered it. "Okay. Yes. I'm with him now. I'll tell him." She hung up and delivered the news. "That was the ME. That makes sense about the car being driven by someone else. Turns out, the body is that of a male."

"Oh, thank God!" Nick's legs almost buckled with relief.

"Which begs the question, Mr. Tyson, and forgive me, but why is your wife's car here?"

Nick dropped his head into his hands. "I . . . I don't know. I got a text message from her phone, but I *know* she didn't write it."

"How do you know she didn't write it?"

"Because Daisy doesn't text like this!" He held out his phone. Detective Siler took a picture of the message and wrote down Nick's phone number.

"Detective, trust me—she does not write like this. But I know who wrote it: Rubi Lee Dixon."

"Please enlighten me about how you know this."

He patiently and concisely explained the events that befell him and Daisy since the night in the garage at the park.

"Quite a story." She cocked an eyebrow at him.

"It's no *story*, Detective. It is the truth. You need to get the hell out there and *find my wife*. Understand? And if you need further assistance, I will call my friend, Winston Wang of the FBI."

This stopped Siler in her tracks. "We'll put out a trace on your phone and try to track down Daisy's phone."

Nick watched her consult with two other officers. Panic swept over him when all three faces turned his way. Looks of doubt and scrutiny were imprinted on their faces. *Jesus Christ. They think I had something to do with this.* Just as he was about to say something, his phone rang. "Win! Thank God!" Nick filled him in.

Winston exhaled. "This is bad. I won't sugarcoat it. Don't worry. I'll get Daisy's phone traced a whole lot quicker than the local police. Hang tight, man. I'll call you right back."

Winston called back within five minutes and relayed that Daisy's phone sent a message from the same address as the inn. "Nick, did you or anyone else search the grounds there?"

"Oh shit! I've been so scattered it didn't dawn on me to search! I'll call you back."

Nick hustled to the reception desk—far from the fire—where the manager and his staff were being interviewed by the local police. He slipped around the desk and flipped through the logbook. Not one of the five names in the book were familiar to him.

"Hey! Can I help you?" the manager barked at Nick.

All heads turned Nick's way.

"Um, I need to . . ."

"Why don't you step out here and keep your hands in sight," an officer ordered.

Nick obeyed. He explained who he was and why he was there.

Detective Siler sauntered into the lobby and asked what was going on. She turned to Nick. "Mr. Tyson, I think you should go home and let us do our job. I promise you'll be the first to know when we find something. And if Daisy contacts you, please call me." She handed Nick her card.

As frustrating as the situation was, Nick obliged and left. He knew they were right. On the drive home he kept thinking about the odd text message he knew Daisy did not send. He called Winston back and told him about the dead-end at the hotel.

"Don't worry, Nick. We'll get to the bottom of this. Do your best to stay calm. I'll call you when I know something."

* * *

At home, Nick chugged the glass of wine he poured earlier. The deep claret liquid burned his stomach. He fell onto the stool and dropped his head into his hands.

"DAISY! WHERE ARE YOU!" he screamed. *The cops must have missed something. I can't just sit here*, he thought. His skin crawled at the deathly silence of the kitchen.

The bottle of wine was to his left. As he poured another glass, the lightning bolt exploded in his head. *She took the train! The train station! They must have video cameras.* He ran out the door and drove to the station.

He explained the situation to the stationmaster, who gave Nick access to the videos. His heart galloped in his chest when he saw, at exactly 7:42 p.m., Daisy deboard the train. His voice caught in his throat. His eyes misted over. He touched the image of his gorgeous wife, clad in jeans and a sweater. Her red curls bobbed against her shoulders as she walked to her car, head buried in her phone.

A few seconds later, a squat man in a police uniform crossed the screen, following her. Nick leaned closer. *Wait, that looks like Bump!* That thought evaporated when another figure—a woman—entered the frame. Based on the short stature, waifish physique, and purposeful walk, it could only be one person. The wig did nothing to hide her identity.

CHAPTER 27

Nick's eyes popped at the screen. "Holy shit! Rubi Lee! Oh fuck!"

"Excuse me Mr. Tyson, is everything okay?" The stationmaster waddled in. "I heard yelling."

Nick apologized for the profanity. "I gotta go! Thanks for letting me see the videos and for your kindness." Nick patted the old man's arm and sprinted to his car.

He called Winston and filled him in on what he saw on the surveillance video.

"Oh man. All right, I'll call Jaida and we'll get back to you asap. Keep the faith. We'll get that crazy woman, trust me," Winston promised him.

Exhausted, Nick flopped down on the sofa in the living room. He cranked up the volume on his phone and placed it on his chest. Gussie jumped up on the couch and nestled in by his side. He stroked the purring feline's head, grateful for the companionship.

"Gussie, I'm so worried! I'm going nuts! And I'm so *damn* tired." He yawned broadly.

Within an hour, he was fast asleep. In his deep dream, Hoot appeared dressed in his khakis, white shirt, and blue hat. His warm blue eyes glimmered. *"Nicholas! Get up, son! You're gonna be late for the club championships! Your girl is waitin' on ya!"*

Nick's legs flailed. Daisy's smiling, freckled face beamed as she waved to him from the first tee. As he ran to her, she reached out her hand. His hand was inches from hers when she evaporated in a mist.

"NO! NO! Daisy!" His screaming woke him. He shot up, struggling to breathe. Gussie meowed indignantly. He blinked and rubbed his bleary eyes. *Oh my God. I can't take this anymore*, he admitted to himself. He felt like a rat trapped in a twisted, horrible one-way-in and no-way-out labyrinth. Sweating, Nick peeled off his shirt and sat in the dark.

Bong! Bong! The clock on the mantle struck twice. *It's only two in the morning?* Wearily, he ran a hand over his face and rose from the couch for a glass of water. Mid-sip, his phone jingled. *Must be Win*, he assumed. "Please tell me you have good news, Win!"

"Wrong person, asshole. It's me."

Jolted wide awake, he yelled, "You crazy bitch! What have you done with Daisy? If you hurt her, I swear I'll *kill* you."

"Ha ha! You think I'm gonna answer that? Fat chance!"

"You won't get away with this. The FBI and cops are on to you! And they will hunt you down like the animal you are!"

"Oh, I doubt that. I've been one step ahead of you *morons* the whole time. Oh, and by the way, for threatening me, I'm going to take it out on her mother when I hang up."

Sweat beaded on his head. *She has them both!* "Wait! I'm sorry. What do you want? Please, I'll do anything to get them back safely."

"Sorry fuck face, not in the plan. I'll be in touch." *Click.*

Looking down, Nick saw his heart palpitating beneath his ribcage. His phone jingled again. "I'm going to find you and kill you!" he screamed.

"Whoa buddy! It's me, Win!"

Nick puffed out his cheeks. "Sorry man. Thank God it's you!" He enlightened Winston to every detail of spotting Rubi Lee on the video and her phone call.

"I'm working on tracing Daisy's phone. We've made some headway, but Nick, your best bet is to stay home. If she calls again, record the conversation. I need to go."

* * *

Rubi Lee sped south on Interstate 95; her petrified prisoners sat in stone silence in the back. She veered from the highway and entered the Philadelphia Navy Yard. The enormous lot was empty and dark. She killed the lights and glided the car to a spot facing the Delaware River. From the glove compartment, she took a pack of cigarettes and lit up.

"Don't go anywhere. Not that you can!" Rubi Lee snickered and got out. Annie and Daisy, handcuffed to one another, watched Rubi Lee flick her cigarette butt into the murky, expansive river.

Daisy took advantage of their moment alone. She faced her mother. "Mom, Nick's not gonna let anything bad happen to us. I know he called Winston and Jaida. We can—"

"What're you talking about?" Rubi Lee's tone sliced deeply in the silence.

Daisy turned to her. "That you *will not* get away with this."

Rubi Lee sighed and cocked her head to one side.

"Wanna bet? Watch me. For starters, this is how." She held up Daisy's phone. "Be right back." The car door hung open like the mouth of a corpse. Daisy and her mother, helpless, heard the hydraulic squeal of a trash truck dumping stuffed cans. The scrape of metal-on-metal tore through the darkness.

Perfect, Rubi Lee thought and approached the driver. "Are you going to the dump soon?"

"Right after we finish over there." He pointed toward a neighborhood.

From the car, Daisy and Annie watched Rubi Lee tauntingly wave the phone in the air before hurling it onto the odious pile of waste to be crushed. She grinned when the truck pulled away. *Trace that, fuckers.* She laughed and returned to the car.

Daisy leaned over and whispered to her mother, "Oh Mom, Nick may never find us now!" As they watched from the car.

"Hush Daisy. Your husband is tenacious, strong and he *loves* you. We have to be strong for him and for each other."

Rubi Lee opened the door and slid in. "Time to head home, ladies!" she chirped and started the engine.

*   *   *

Unable to fall back asleep, Nick sat on the couch, Gussie on his lap, the blue glow of the television alive. But he ignored the show. He checked his phone every five seconds. *Come on Win! Call damnit!* He slapped the phone back on the table next to a framed picture from their wedding. Nick picked it up and rose slowly from the couch. Tracing his finger along Daisy's face, he then clutched the picture to his chest and gazed out the window at the cold, cruel night. *Where is she? I know she's out there somewhere, but where? I know they're alive. She's a fighter! Please help us find them before it's . . .* He would not let himself finish the thought. Staring out into the night, he heard his phone.

"Good news. We picked up Daisy's phone and it's on the move," Win said. "I alerted the Philly police and I'm en route too. The cops are following the pings from the cell towers. I'll call you back."

A few minutes later Win called back with disconcerting news. "The pings ended at the entrance to the Sanitation Convenience Center in Philly."

Nick did not want to accept what this might mean. "Oh Jesus, Win."

"Hey, don't go all doom and gloom. We're going to suit up and dig in. Come down if it makes you feel better. I'll give the guard a heads up."

Within minutes Nick was on the scene. He joined Win and several officers who, over the noise of trucks dumping their putrid contents, questioned him about the events of the evening. "Please, just find her," Nick begged.

Feeling helpless, he wrung his hands as the team— clad head to toe in yellow hazmat suits—entered the dump and worked through piles of every imaginable kind of trash. Two officers used a mobile metal detector and scanned for Daisy's phone. *Please God, let them find her phone*, he prayed and paced along the fence of the dump. He did not allow himself to entertain the thought of them finding something else.

A thin, brilliant orange line of a new dawn cracked the dark sky. Exhausted, the team of searchers halted after finding nothing relevant.

Peeling off his gloves, Winston approached Nick. The look of raw dismay on his friend's face hit Winston in his core. "I'm sorry we couldn't have been more helpful. On the bright side"—he squeezed Nick's shoulder—"we know she isn't here."

"I know she's alive Win, I *know* it!" Nick's voice cracked; his eyes shined with tears.

Winston had never seen Nick so desperate, so afraid. "I do too. For now, I think it best you go home and wait. Keep in mind, Rubi Lee is playing a game of cat and mouse. And we're the cat, got it?"

"Honestly Win, I'm *out of my* mind."

"I know you are. Remember, I'm with you all the way and we will prevail."

An officer brought them coffee. Winston took a cup before Nick waved him off.

"Go home and get a hot shower. Rubi Lee has been one step ahead and soon she will make a mistake."

* * *

Steam swirled into the ceiling, fogging the glass shower doors. But the scalding water did nothing to rid the vile residue of the dump cloaking Nick. He closed his eyes as the water pounded over his body. Flashbacks of his life with Daisy, back to when they were fourteen, filled his mind. *What if she's gone? We just started our life together!*

What will I do without her? The bathroom swirled around him. Dizziness and nausea hit him in ferocious waves. He struggled to breathe.

He lunged across the bathroom in one urgent stride to the toilet. Bent over, he retched and threw up. He dropped to his knees and finally crumpled to the floor. The tiles cooled his face. He curled himself into the fetal position. His sobs echoed throughout the dark, still house.

Aimlessly, he wandered the house, Gussie at his side. Food made him nauseous. Sleep was out of the question.

Winston was very patient with Nick, who called him hourly. "Hey, maybe you should try working? It may distract you. I'm sure you have lots to do."

Finally, his living hell came to an end when the call came. The number was unfamiliar and, following Winston's directions, he frantically searched for his work phone to record it. But he was not quick enough. The phone went dead. *Oh Shit! What have I done? Please call back!* He looked around and saw his work phone on the counter.

His phone rang again, and he hit record on his work phone. He scribbled the unfamiliar number on a corner of newspaper.

"Hello! Hello! I'm here!"

"Next time your phone rings, you better answer it by two rings. Got it?" Rubi Lee said.

"Yes, yes. I'm sorry. Tell me what you want."

"Well, *Nicholas*, I *want* to kill your precious Daisy, but Mommy Dearest has to go first."

Nick fought to keep his breathing level. He did not want her to know she had the upper hand. For now.

"Hold on. Hold on. We can work something out. I will give you *anything* you want. Just please, please, don't kill them!"

"You'll give me *anything*?" Rubi Lee liked the sound of that.

"God yes!"

"Hm, let me think. I got it! Since I like pretty things, I want you to gather all your wife's favorite jewelry and put it in a small bag. You will deliver it to me when I say so. I want that stuff as partial payment for my brother's murder and in exchange for your wife. Maybe."

Nick knew better than to try to negotiate. "Fine. I'll do it, tell me where to meet you."

"I'll be in touch soon. Meanwhile, tell your FBI and cop friends to *back off.* Or else."

Nick hit stop on his work phone and called Winston.

CHAPTER 28

After another relentlessly sleepless night, Nick stood in the kitchen, velvet jewelry bag in hand. His mind raced all night, which brought on another debilitating panic attack. Coffee did nothing to ease his fatigue. But the jingle of his phone did.

"Good boy, you answered right away. Do you have what I want?" Rubi Lee said.

Nick looked down at the bag and sighed. "Yes."

"What are you bringing me?"

Nick carefully shook out the contents of the bag. "Um, a gold necklace, a pair of diamond earrings, a gold ring with a red stone, and two gold bracelets with sapphires in them."

"*Lovely*. Put the stuff into a duffel bag and drive to the park."

"Park? What park? Fairmount Park?"

"No. Valley Forge Park."

"All right. Where?"

"Park near that stupid arch. Three o'clock—no earlier, no later. I'll call again."

Nick called Winston and relayed Rubi Lee's directive. Winston said they would stake out the area of the park located near the arch.

"Arch?" Winston asked.

"Yes. The National Memorial Arch. It's past a group of recreated cabins."

"Right. We'll find it."

They discussed the possibility of using fake jewels. Nick rejected that idea because he was afraid Rubi Lee may discover they were not real. And that would be deadly for Daisy and Annie.

"Nick, we will be surrounding the park. No one will get by us. We're heading there now."

"Thanks man. See you soon."

Nick sped to the park. The sun shone brilliantly and as he drove toward the spot, sadness overwhelmed him. He glanced longingly at happy couples strolling hand-in-hand, families enjoying a picnic, and bikers zipping around the six-mile loop around the park. *Daisy and I should be out here enjoying this day. I can't believe this is happening.* He parked by the side of the arch. He left the duffle bag in the car.

He tried not to twist an ankle when he hustled up the crooked stone pathway to the arch. Looking around, he saw two wedding parties waiting to have pictures taken. His heart lurched. Visions of his and Daisy's wedding punctured his thoughts. He felt himself sliding into a dark place. *Come on Nick, clear your head.* On the other side of the arch, two groomsmen pointed at him—and not in a subtle way. They approached him like two little kids seeing their favorite athlete.

"Um, excuse me sir. Aren't you the guy who works at city hall?"

Nick paused before he answered. A distraction was the last thing he needed. "Ah yeah. I work in the mayor's office." He looked over their heads and saw no one except for the bridal parties. Sweat stained his shirt.

"Cool! I've seen your picture in the paper!" The shorter groomsman grinned. "You may be mayor someday! Can we get a pic?"

"Ah, yeah. But make it quick fellas."

Nick stood in the middle of the two men. It occurred to him to ask if they had seen other people. "Hey fellas, did you happen to see anyone else around here? Three women, one has red curly hair?"

"Sorry, no," one replied. "Can we get one more pic with the whole wedding party?"

"Ah yeah, I guess," Nick said.

Amid twenty-plus laughing people, Nick stood while the photographer snapped myriad pictures. He glanced over at his car and saw the door was open. "Oh God no!" he yelled and sprinted downhill to the car. The duffel was gone. "No! Fuck! You *idiot*!" He pounded the door with his fist.

His phone rang. "Where's the bag?" he snapped.

"Oh, it's safe and sound with me. God, you're so dumb. You *actually* thought those wedding people knew who you are?" Rubi Lee cackled. "Dumb, dumb, dumb."

Frantically he raced around the arch looking in all directions. "Where are you?" he screamed. Startled tourists stared at him.

"Far away from you. Thanks for the jewels. Oh, and your FBI pals? So easy to dodge those dumbass fools." *Click.*

"Son of a bitch!" His hand shook as he dialed Winston. "Win! I fucked up! I was in such a hurry, I forgot to lock the car and she took the bag! How could I be so *fucking* dumb? God!" He kicked the car tire. "Where are you guys?"

"Don't beat yourself up. We'll get her," Win responded. "We are passing what looks like a chapel."

Jaida chimed in, "Yeah, the sign says Washington Memorial Chapel; we're on Route 23—it's on the left. Where are you?"

"Near the Memorial Arch. It's at the intersection of Gulph and Outerline Drive. You should be able to see it from where you are."

Winston tapped the brakes. He and Jaida turned to their right. "Wow," Win uttered as they absorbed the breathtaking view of acres of green rolling hills, fields, and the reds and oranges of fall foliage. A mile away, the arch sat perched on a hill. It rose six stories into the bright blue sky. *That's one awesome, dignified arch*, Win thought. "Okay. I see it. Stay there. Jaida and I will be there in a few."

Winston and Jaida crawled up the one-way road stuck behind a pack of brightly clad bicyclists, and brown trolleys loaded with tourists. Winston exhaled loudly. "One-way road—not good when you're in a hurry."

"I know." Jaida tapped the side window with her long nails. She turned attention to the countless park enthusiasts enjoying the bright warmer-than-usual day. Strollers, dogs, joggers, and bird watchers ambled down the wide black path that ran parallel to log cabins.

"What do you think those cabins are for?" Win asked.

Jaida put the window down. An earthy, leafy aroma wafted into the car. She inhaled deeply. "Since

Washington spent the winter of 1777 here, my guess is that they're replicas of the cabins those poor soldiers slept in."

Win looked at her out of the corner of his eye. "Aren't you the history buff."

Jaida nodded. "Look, there he is."

Winston pulled around the arch where they saw Nick pacing.

"Nick!" Winston yelled.

Nick jogged down the hill to the full parking lot. "We have to find them!"

"We will. One of my guys saw a bridesmaid take a green duffel from your car when your back was turned. She got on a bus, which my guys are following."

"That's all well and good, but if Rubi Lee was actually here, how come your guys didn't see her?" he yelled.

Win reached out to his friend. Taking ahold of his forearm he replied, "First of all, try to stay calm. And secondly, she may not have even been here by the time we all arrived. Chances are, she's *been* gone."

Jaida added, "Give the fact that a bridesmaid took it, I'm sure Rubi Lee bribed them. Remember, she's cunning."

"I'm freaking out! Do you *not* get it, guys? Rubi Lee has Daisy and Annie! She could kill them! And I can't do a *fucking* thing to help! And now, she has the jewels and who knows what the hell else this crazy bitch is gonna do!"

Jaida's phone rang. "Campbell here." She threw Win a look and walked off.

Winston's heart ached for his friend. Quietly, he replied, "Nick, I love Daisy too. I want nothing more than her and Annie's safe return—not to mention putting Rubi

Lee behind bars. But you *have to* trust me and my team. When we see where the bus stops, my guys will go in and we will question every single person. They're highly trained professionals and they know what they're doing."

"I know all that intellectually. Emotionally though, it's a whole different story."

"I understand. On another note, it may take some time for my team to search the van containing the bridal party, let alone interview them all."

"Speaking of bridal party," Jaida said, returning to the car, "the buses pulled into a casino not too far from here. I ordered our teams to interview everyone on the buses. Win, you should stay with Nick. I'll get an agent to pick me up here and go to the casino."

"Okay. Did they say how many busses pulled in?"

"Four, all fully loaded too. This could take a while." Jaida dialed an agent.

* * *

Rubi Lee parked toward the back of the casino lot. Before she got out, she pulled on the auburn wig and told them to stay quiet. Daisy and Annie sat in the back of the car and watched gamblers of all ages excitedly walk into Valley Forge Casino. Four shuttle buses pulled up and its passengers, dressed in wedding garb, exited.

Annie sighed. "It reminds me of your wedding. You were a beautiful bride. I was so proud of you, and I know your father was too." Her voice cracked.

"Mom, don't cry. We're going to get out of this. I know it." Daisy kissed her on the cheek.

Daisy watched with mounting trepidation the interaction between a bridesmaid and Rubi Lee. Rubi Lee pointed to the ground around the bridesmaid's feet. Daisy scowled when the bridesmaid lifted the bottom of her flowing dress to extract a small duffle bag from between her sneakers and hand it to Rubi Lee.

"*What the hell?*" Daisy said aloud.

"What?" asked Annie.

"That!" Daisy pointed to the bridesmaid who handed Rubi Lee the green bag. Rubi Lee pressed something into the woman's hand, who smiled broadly.

"What just happened? You stole from that girl!"

"No, I didn't. She got paid, thanks to you and your husband." Starting the engine, Rubi Lee exited the parking lot as the team of agents drove in from the opposite side. Throwing a glance in the rear view mirror at the SUVs, Rubi Lee laughed out loud, "Ha ha, morons! Ya missed me!"

Annie and Daisy turned in the seat and saw the SUV doors open. Based on the morose, monochromatic style of dress, they knew those people were agents.

Annie gasped then screamed. "No! No! Help us! We're right here! *Please!*" Her face fell with the last strangled word.

Daisy's stomach seized at the plaintive sound of her mother's voice. Squeezing her mother's freezing hand, she whispered, "Mom, it's okay, we'll get out of this."

* * *

Rubi Lee threw a protective hand over the green duffel bag. She licked her lips in anticipation of what lay inside. *I need to see it now, not later*, she thought and flipped on the right turn signal and came to a stop at a rest center.

The lot was scattered with various vehicles. Choosing a spot far from the rest center's cameras, Rubi Lee parked and turned off the engine.

"What are you doing?" Daisy asked. "And what's in the bag?"

"You'll see." Rubi Lee unzipped the bag and pulled out the necklace and admired it. The other pieces followed. The ring and earrings were last. "Wow! I did well with this stuff!"

Stunned, Daisy yelled, "Hey! That's *my* jewelry!"

"Not anymore. They're *all mine* now! You have no need for them."

Annie slid her hand onto Daisy's knee, giving it a tap. Daisy glanced at her mother who gave a subtle shake of her head.

Rubi Lee put the diamond earrings on and turned her head side to side, admiring them in the rear view mirror. She saw Daisy's expression and gave a smirk, then blew a kiss at Daisy's reflection. Daisy spat at Rubi Lee.

CHAPTER 29

After Jaida departed, Nick and Winston went to a local restaurant, Christopher's, to discuss their next steps. "This whole thing sucks, and I'm sorry as hell for you."

"Tell me about it," Nick replied and fell into the wooden chair. "What're you drinking?"

"A tasty pilsner. I ordered you two," Win replied. "I figured you needed it."

"Thanks."

Their server plunked down two beers in front of Nick. Seconds later, one glass stood empty.

"Thirsty?" Winston laughed.

"More like losing my mind."

Winston could feel Nick's knee was bouncing up and down at a wild rate. He also noticed that Nick shifted in his seat like a bored child at church. He could not help himself. "You're gonna knock over your beer with that knee!"

Nick shot daggers at him.

Winston held up his hands. "Okay, okay. On the way up here, Jaida and I discussed the strategy we are going to utilize to capture Rubi Lee and save your family. We are narrowing in on her location. I'm not at liberty to discuss the details since this is of a sensitive nature."

"Seriously? Come on, Win."

"Look, what I *can* tell you is that you will most likely be involved. You're going to be needed as bait. Criminals like her expect that. And my team will work with you. No more." Win sipped his beer.

"I've been thinking a lot about this. Rubi Lee has been one step ahead of us the entire time," Nick commented. "What I want to know is how."

"She's had since last December to plan her revenge. And she's treacherously intelligent."

"I'm thinking she had inside help, or got info somehow? Do you think she coaxed someone into helping her? Maybe someone in law enforcement?" Nick surmised.

Winston drank his beer. He cocked his head to the side and pushed his horn-rimmed glasses up his small nose. "Roth?"

Nick gazed out the window. "No, no way. He's been in touch with us. Why would he throw it away to help a criminal?"

"True. He may be lazy, but he's loyal. What about that dufus deputy?"

"Bump? He's a moron and he would be of no use to her."

Winston sat up. "Exactly! She's the type who exploits the weak link—in this case it's Bump."

"But why would she put herself in a precarious position? He's in law enforcement. That seems really stupid."

"People like Rubi Lee don't see it that way. They know they need an inside source, so they bribe and use people. Promises of money, drugs, or sex, whatever are the chosen tools of coercion. I've profiled people like her, and they know how to prey on the weak." Winston peered at Nick over his glass. "And when a perp like her is finished with their puppet..."

Ice ran through Nick's veins. He ran his hands through his hair and exhaled loudly. "Christ, we're dealing with a real psycho."

"Yup, and one hell-bent on revenge. She's quite dangerous too. I've alerted people in the bureau about her and what she's capable of."

"How do we—"

Winston's phone rang. "Hold on, Jaida. I'm putting you on speakerphone. Nick's here too."

"Hey Jaida," Nick said. "I hope you have something for us."

"Do I ever. Get this: After interviewing the bridal party, we got a hit. Apparently, Rubi Lee bribed some of the groomsmen to distract Nick by taking pictures. And she also bribed a bridesmaid—from a different wedding party—to watch Nick and grab the duffel bag when you weren't looking."

Nick and Winston stared at each other over the phone.

"Did anyone see the car? Or get a description?"

"Both. One of the witnesses said a skinny woman in a white medical coat got out of a beaten-up sedan. The same witness, a groomsman, caught a glimpse of the name on the ID badge of the woman. So I ran it through and got a hit."

"And?" Nick fiddled with his coaster.

"Turns out the name was that of a young woman named Tanya Holston. She left Louisiana months ago to start a job in Sullivan County as a health care worker. She drove a—"

"Wait! Did you say Tanya Holston?" Winston interrupted. He turned to Nick and said, "Her name was on a list of new residents, the one Roth gave us!"

"I was hoping you'd pick up on that. Let me finish." Jaida filled them in about the real Tanya Holston. "Apparently, Tanya's father said he got a few texts from her, but nothing over the past few months. Consumed with worry, he contacted Roth's department more than once and told them about Tanya."

"Holy crap. This just keeps getting better and better!" Winston exclaimed.

Jaida continued, "I know, and not in a good way. To me, it's clear that Rubi Lee has been impersonating Tanya. *For months.*"

"Which means," Winston began, "she—"

"Killed Tanya!" Nick finished. "And stole her identity. Oh God. And now she has Daisy and Annie." He banged on the window and swore under his breath.

Jaida informed them she sent a picture of the real Tanya to the sheriff's department. "But I have heard nothing back from them. If need be, I'll raise holy hell about this."

Nick shredded his napkin into a pile. "Hold on a second." He finished his beer. "If Rubi Lee killed Tanya, that means she's somewhere in Sullivan County! And probably has been *this whole time!*"

"And most likely, she's responsible for the explosion at the Red Caboose Motor Lodge. Who else would it be?" Winston said.

"Along with that, I'd bet a million bucks this sicko also blew up the Black LaSalle and the garage at Margaux Ford Park!" Nick finished.

"Yep," Jaida replied. "I gotta go. I'll send a picture of Tanya."

Deliberately, Winston lay his phone on the table. He shifted his eyes to Nick who stared glassy eyed at the bright, busy avenue outside. He placed his hand over his friend's. "Nick, we can *and will* beat her. However, it's gonna take our A game. We are going to do this together."

Slowly, Nick met Winston's eyes. "How, Win? *How*?"

"I'll converse with my team, and we will—" He was interrupted by a saxophone riff blasting from his phone. "It's from Jaida."

Nick observed his friend study whatever it was Jaida sent.

"Wow." Winston pushed his glasses up.

"What?"

Silently, Winston turned his phone to Nick, whose jaw fell open. Staring at him from the phone was a woman in her late twenties or early thirties. Nick studied her short, black hair, small dark eyes and sharp, elfin features. "Oh my God," he whispered. "This isn't good, Win. I can't believe how much this woman resembles Rubi Lee."

"I know. It's uncanny."

"Jaida's right. No doubt Rubi Lee has taken on Tanya's identity and life."

Winston stood and nodded. "And we've been looking for Rubi Lee when we should have been looking for Tanya. We're going to the Red Caboose Motor Lodge." He threw a wad of cash on the table.

Nick called the Red Caboose Motor Lodge and spoke to the manager. "Please provide all video footage from the last ten days," Nick requested. "Thank you."

"Well?" Winston asked.

"Everything will be ready when we arrive," he told Winston.

* * *

In the cramped office Nick and Winston scanned through hours of video. Nothing jumped out at them. The manager hovered over them like a helicopter parent.

"Rather than hang over us, go get the guest book, okay?" Winston asked.

The manager smirked and disappeared. He returned, book in hand.

"This would have been helpful from the start," Winston scolded him.

"My bad, sorry," he replied and backpedaled to the take-out container on the counter.

Nick ran his finger over the page. Scrawled in child-like print was *Tanya Holston.* "There it is—Tanya Holston." His shoulders slumped. "No other names though."

"Hey, can you tell us what room this woman was in?" Winston walked with the book in hand back to the manager.

"Ah yes, yes. Please hold on." He found the room number. "Understand though, the fire destroyed it and many more rooms. She was in room 106. But like I said, fire destroyed it."

"Was she alone?" Winston asked.

"I'm sorry sir. I don't know. I was not working that night."

Nick shot a scalding look at the manager. "Of course you weren't."

After staring into the black hole that was once room 106, they walked to Winston's car. "Win, we know Rubi Lee is using Tanya's identification. Wouldn't it make sense that she's living in the house that Tanya was *supposed* to be living in?"

"Yes."

"Do you think Rubi Lee is headed back there now?"

"I'd say so. I'll call Sheriff Roth and get him to go to the house. He's closer anyway."

Sheriff Roth answered and agreed to Winston's request. "And Sheriff, this woman is really dangerous."

"Thank you, Agent Wang. I'll be in touch soon. I'll head over now."

"Thank you, sir. We're headed back to the Tyson house."

At Nick and Daisy's house, they waited for any message from the sheriff. Nick fed a hungry Gussie while Winston ordered pizza. Within the hour, Roth called back.

"Hey fellas. Hate to be the bearer of no news, but the house was dark. Not a soul around."

Nick pounded the counter. "Shit!"

"Thanks, Sheriff. Talk in the morning." Winston hit end call.

* * *

In the den, Nick slouched in a chair and Winston curled on a couch. Sleep had overcome them and neither heard the battering of the rain on the windows or Nick's phone.

Gussie's meowing finally woke Nick. He rubbed his stiff neck and rose from the chair. It was one o'clock in the morning. Winston snored loudly.

Light from Nick's phone broke through the darkness. He noticed a message from eleven thirty. *Crap.* He listened to the familiar and infuriated voice of Rubi Lee.

"Where the hell are you? You don't seem to understand that not answering this call will be costly to one of my captives—or maybe both. I'm gonna force you to decide who gets punished. Call this number, 800-555-0101, and leave a name: Daisy or Annie. You better get me an answer by ten o'clock tomorrow morning."

He shook his friend's shoulder. "Win! Win, wake up! I got a message from Rubi Lee."

Winston sighed heavily and sat up. He wiped his face with his hands trying to wake up and make sense of what Nick said.

"Did you say you got a message? What did she say?" He fumbled on the table for his glasses.

Nick replayed the message for Winston. "This is *not* good. One of them may suffer somehow."

Nick had a major decision to make, one he could not stomach. "I can't put my wife or mother-in-law in harm's way. But she's forcing my hand here. What am I going to do, man?"

Winston emitted an enormous yawn. "Put on some coffee. We're not gonna sleep any more tonight."

Nick hauled himself from the chair and hustled into the kitchen. He found a bag of coffee, tore it open, and upended it into the coffee maker. The water gurgled for a few minutes until the rich aroma of French Roast permeated the kitchen.

Over two pots of high-octane coffee they discussed all aspects of the situation.

"Win, you heard her. I'm terrified she's going to kill them both. She's making me choose the fate of my wife and mother-in-law." Nick's voice was barely above a whisper.

Win glanced at the coffee cup in Nick's hand. It was clenched so tightly Nick's fingers were white.

"I know. I heard her. And the friend in me will be honest with you. There is a chance—a very small one, in my opinion—the unthinkable happens." He swigged his coffee and continued, "The agent in me says that won't happen. Reason being is that she is enjoying this twisted chess match too much."

"What do you mean?" Nick stared at his friend.

"In my experience with people like Rubi Lee, they thrive on being in control and try to maintain that control as long as possible. She knows she has to keep them alive to get you. Eventually though, they do make a mistake."

Nick puffed out his cheeks and released an exasperated breath. "So I need to play her game and give her what she wants, right?"

"For now yes. But since she keeps calling you, it's clear she wants to continue communicating. So you're going to be the one who will wrest control away from her and buy more time."

Nick stood and glanced out the kitchen window. "How? She may be crazy, but she's not dumb."

"I know." He finished his coffee and placed the mug in the sink. "I need to make a call."

Winston called the bureau to have a trace put on the phone number Rubi Lee told Nick to call—even though they both knew the number would be untraceable.

Nick paced the kitchen and stopped in front of the microwave. 6:07 a.m. glowed from the microwave's clock. "I only have three hours and fifty-three minutes until I have to call that psycho. What're we gonna do? We've gotten *nowhere*."

"We're going back to Shunk."

* * *

As the car drank in gallons of gas, Rubi Lee caressed the blade of her knife lovingly. She thought of the ultimatum she gave Nick. *Who is he going to pick? I'm sure it will be the old hag. And a thin scar running down Daisy's perfect cheek would be the icing on the cake.*

Turning around, she glared at her two sleeping captives. Harming them at any time was an option. *But that would put an end to this game with her dipshit husband*, Rubi Lee thought. *It's too damn fun terrorizing him to end it. Plus, I'll never get caught!*

Rubi Lee's elated mood was short-lived when she saw there was a message waiting on the phone she ordered Nick to call. Stepping out of the car, she put the phone to her ear and listened.

"We are getting closer and closer to finding you. You will not win this battle, Rubi Lee. Or shall I say *Tanya*." It was Nick's voice.

Bastard! Who the fuck does he think he is? She let loose a crude stream of obscenities that woke Daisy and Annie.

"What's going on?" Daisy demanded when Rubi Lee threw herself back in the car.

"Shut up! I need to think."

Daisy and her mother shrunk into the back seat. Huddled together, they dared not disturb her.

Rubi Lee pounded the steering wheel. Her voice dripped with venom when she finally spoke. "Your husband thinks he's so damn smart. He has *no idea* who he's dealing with."

Daisy glanced at her mother who nodded slightly. "You may think that, but you're so far off base. I wouldn't be surprised if he was right around the corner waiting for you!"

Rubi Lee whirled around and plunged Timmy into the seat, inches from Daisy's thigh. Daisy and Annie stared wide-eyed and pressed themselves into the seats. Silence enveloped the car.

Her eyes sprung back and forth between Daisy and Annie. "Yeah, I thought so." Rubi Lee started the car and left the gas station. Several hours later, she turned onto Pinetree Way, she kept her eyes peeled for Sheriff Roth. *I wonder if he's at work*, she wondered and dialed the station. The woman who answered told her it was Sheriff Roth's day off and asked if she could be of help.

"No, no." Rubi Lee hung up. She remembered Bump telling her where Roth lived. *Watch out Sheriff, here I come!*

"Where are we? Why are we stopping here?" Annie asked, looking at the unfamiliar house as they drove up.

"Me and Timmy are gonna pay Sheriff Roth a little visit." From the glove compartment, she took the two damp bandanas and stuffed them into their mouths. From the trunk, she pulled twine and tied Annie's right ankle to Daisy's left.

"Be back soon. Be good!" She laughed. One last tug on the handcuffs and Rubi Lee disappeared down the rocky driveway to the low-slung ranch house.

Scouting for any other car and seeing none, she slid Timmy into her back pocket and slunk to the front door. Heart pounding, she entered. A carpeted living room to her left was empty. The dining room was still. She stopped and listened for any noise; the silence calmed her nerves.

Recalling her fleeting days as a dancer, she padded noiselessly through the kitchen across the white linoleum floor. Large bay windows opened out to a visual feast: lush grass, mature trees, and a river. Rubi Lee slithered through the screen door to the deck, her eyes leveled on the dark water skimming around rocks. There, in the middle of the meandering river, stood Sheriff Roth, waist deep in the water, fishing pole in hand, waders on. On silent feet, she scurried down to the river's edge and dodged behind a tree.

Rubi Lee sized him up. She could see his white earbuds. *Good, he won't hear shit*, she thought. Roth snapped the line back over his shoulder and released it. After being airborne for several seconds, the hook landed with a gentle *plunk* on the water.

Rubi Lee crept close enough to hear him humming. She crept closer. *I need to make this quick*, she thought and reached for her knife, but thought better of it. *I can't risk losing Timmy*, she decided and scoured her surroundings. Several feet from her hiding spot, she spotted a long wooden canoe paddle.

Paddle raised, sweat pouring down her back, she stepped over rocks into the cool water. Roth stood about ten yards from her. She could hear him still humming along with whatever song was playing. She waded closer, hands gripping the paddle. Roth bent down to undo his line. He turned his face up to see Rubi Lee swing the paddle at his head. It hit Roth square in the temple, and a deep angry gash sliced his graying hair.

He dropped into the river like a bag of rocks.

She nudged him with her foot; there was no movement. *Good, he's out of the way.* She basked in her victory and the blistering rush of adrenaline.

Rubi Lee dragged the lifeless, burly man by the armpits toward the rocky shore as far as her energy let her. Lungs on fire, she finally dropped him, half submerged in the river, and collapsed on her knees and sucked in fresh air.

* * *

In the car, Annie and Daisy worked to untie their legs. Despite the chill in the car, perspiration glistened on their foreheads. Struggling to untie the twine, Daisy kicked the car seat in frustration. Daisy and her mother struggled to stay calm. Their throats felt like sandpaper.

After what seemed like hours, Rubi Lee, soaking wet and bloodied, came around the corner of the house. Looking like a ragged warrior, she marched back up the driveway.

She yanked open the door. Her eyes were wild. Water and blood stained her shirt. "Well ladies, I just landed me a huge, dead fish!" She cackled and pushed aside a wayward hair from her glistening eyes. "Now get out!"

CHAPTER 30

Inside Roth's house, Rubi Lee pulled the bandanas from their aching mouths. Daisy and her mother sucked in lungfuls of air.

"Don't even think about screaming. No one will hear you—especially the sheriff!" She laughed and shoved them into his office where she ordered Annie to sit down in Roth's desk chair and shackled her to it. "You"—she gestured at Daisy with Timmy—"sit there." She nodded at the floor, near an old radiator.

Daisy did not move. She sliced her eyes to Rubi Lee. Taking a step toward Rubi Lee, she stopped when her mother cried out.

"Daisy, stop! Listen to her. Sit down, please."

"You have three seconds," Rubi Lee threatened.

Daisy lowered herself to the wooden floor. The boards creaked under her weight.

"That's a good girl." Rubi Lee cuffed her to the radiator and turned her attention to the computer and other equipment on the desk.

"Let's see what's happening in the police department." She fiddled with the walkie-talkie and exclaimed, "Come to Mama! I can hear everything and read everything—thanks to Bump. He told me exactly how to log on to the sheriff's computer." She turned up the volume of the walkie-talkie and listened to police chatter.

A woman's voice filled the room. "Sheriff? I know it's your day off sir, but we just got a call from the FBI. They want to send a team out to meet with you after you call in. Please call in when you get this. I'll try your cell. Thank you, sir."

Rubi Lee froze. *FBI? Oh crap!* "Not gonna happen, assholes!" Rubi Lee shrilled at the walkie-talkie. "You jackasses have no idea how far ahead of you I am!" For several stilted minutes, they listened to ongoing police chatter. From the corner of the room, BeBop music sang over the crackling of the walkie-talkie. All three women turned to see a cell phone on a side table. It was Roth's.

"Pity he can't answer it," Rubi Lee commented.

Daisy swiveled her head to where Rubi Lee stood. She paled when the weight of Rubi Lee's words sunk in. "What did you do to him?" Daisy yelled.

"What do you care? It's not like he's gonna be able to *save* you."

Alarm bells screamed in her head. Daisy glanced at Annie whose face was ghost white. "What did you *do*?" She leaned forward and shouted, "Where is he?"

Ignoring the question, Rubi Lee replied, "Time for a change of scene!" She squatted down, uncuffed Daisy from the radiator, and pulled her up. Slapping the cuffs back on, Rubi Lee whispered in her ear, "Now the fun *really* begins."

Knife in hand, she marched Daisy onto the sprawling cedar deck. A glass-topped table surrounded by six leaf-covered white chairs sat in the center of the deck. The wind kicked up and swirled twigs across the deck. A large, covered grill was pushed up against the side of the house.

Rubi Lee snatched a chair and said to Daisy, "Sit your bitch ass down until I come back for you."

If my hands were free, I'd squeeze every ounce of evil life out of you! Daisy thought. As she lowered herself into the chair, she cast her eyes up to Rubi Lee and gasped. Instead of human eyes, dark pits of hell gazed back set over a twisted, diabolical smirk.

After tying Daisy's feet together, Rubi Lee took her phone from her pocket and propped it up on the railing directly across from Daisy. She hit the video button, winked at Daisy, and announced, "Be right back!"

Okay, I have the women where I want them—for now at least. After Nick sees this video, he'll race to save them and fall right into my hands. Killing him will close the circle! Rubi Lee thought.

Daisy squirmed in the chair, trying to free herself. The cuffs and rope dug into her skin the more she twisted in the chair.

"Damnit!" she screamed. *Come on! You were a high school and college volleyball player! You're strong! Dig deep!*

The slam of the screen door made Daisy startle. She stopped moving. "What're you doing? Show me what you're doing!"

Rubi Lee sauntered back onto the deck and stood behind Daisy. "Before Mommy goes for a swim, I need to make sure you have a great view of the river!"

Daisy heard a *slap slap slap* directly behind her. *What is that?* Shifting onto one side, she leaned back and craned her head to see what it was.

Rubi Lee clamped her hand down on Daisy's head and twisted it to face forward. "If you're smart, you won't move."

Every nerve in Daisy's body burned. She stole a quick glance at her hands; they shook in her lap. Daisy recoiled and gasped when she felt the insides of Rubi Lee's forearms brush the top of her head.

"I *said* don't move."

Daisy's heart pounded through her shirt. "What—"

"Shut up." Rubi Lee lowered the cold leather strap in front of Daisy's unblinking eyes. Daisy caught a whiff of the earthy smell. She felt it lay on her collarbone where it pulsated in unison with her throbbing heart. A flush of heat ran up her neck and tingled her scalp.

Rubi Lee took the two ends of the strap. "Now, sit still." She tugged on the strap and smiled when Daisy retched. Tying the ends together through the slits in the chair, she remarked, "You have the perfect angle to watch!" She stepped toward the house but stopped. "How could I forget this?" Waltzing around to face Daisy, she waved the sour bandana in front of Daisy's unblinking eyes.

"No! No! Please don't! Please! I won't scream!" Daisy tried to whip her head from side to side, but the leather strap impeded her movement. The tautness forced her chin to point to the sky.

Rubi Lee grasped Daisy's chin and shoved the sour bandana back into her mouth. "Don't go anywhere!" Rubi Lee cackled.

Daisy heard the door scrape again and Rubi Lee reappeared with an exhausted, sagging Annie in her clutches. "Time for Mommy's swim!"

Daisy watched helplessly as Rubi Lee dragged her mother down the steps toward the river. A panicked scream, lodged in her stomach, wound its way up her throat and exploded into the damp rag. Every muscle in her chest constricted and tightened with her muffled screams.

Screaming and straining forward until the veins bulged on her scalp, Daisy twisted her wrists in the cold metal cuffs. She banged her feet on the deck, praying someone would hear her. No one did. Eyes closed, she rocked back and forth like a trapped animal.

Unaware of the blood dripping from her raw wrists and seeping into the deck planks, Daisy regained her resolve. *Don't give up! Don't lose hope! They know you're here! Nick will not let us die!*

Annie's head bobbed like a doll as Rubi Lee dragged her toward the river. Waist deep in the water, Rubi Lee yelled to Daisy, "Watch this, Daisy!" With one hand on the back of her head, she pushed Annie's face into the water, completely submerging it. And she did it again and again.

Eyes bulging out of her head, Daisy could not her pull eyes from the violent scene unfolding in front other. Her mother's gasps and coughs carried over the wind and settled into Daisy's soul. Rubi Lee laughed with gleeful delight. *Jesus Christ! I feel like I'm in a movie! Stop! Please God, make her stop!* She thrashed in the chair, almost toppling over. The swooshing and splashing of a screaming Annie being dunked over and over made Daisy almost vomit.

I have to do something before she drowns Mom! I have to try to stop her! Turning to her right, she noticed she sat within three feet of the glass-top table. *I know this may not stop her, but I have to try!*

Squeezing her thighs and glutes tightly, Daisy hopped

the chair toward the table. *Please God, let her hear the chair thumping!* Four hops over, she lifted her feet to the table. *Fuck!* Inches short, she inhaled deeply, bit into the rag, and pushed hard off the deck. Pain shot through her gimp ankle. Ripples of angst shot through her cheeks as she ground her teeth into the bandana. *At least I'm closer.*

Hair whipping wildly in the wind, sweat popping on her brow, Daisy screamed into the bandana and flung her feet at the table. They connected. The table toppled over with a bang.

The glass tabletop cracked. Daisy kicked it again and again. Shards and flecks of glass shattered like a broken icicle. Panting profusely, Daisy looked out at the river and saw Rubi Lee staring in her direction. *Oh thank God! She heard it! Please let her stop hurting Mom!*

She closed her eyes and sent up a silent prayer for help. Daisy opened her eyes and saw Rubi Lee had dragged her mother onto the riverbank. Near an aluminum canoe, Rubi Lee threw Annie to the cold, wet ground like a soggy sock puppet. Daisy squinted into the distance. *Mom! Please move! You have to move!* Daisy did not take her eyes from her mother. From her tilted angle, Daisy saw her mother's hand move. *Thank God!* Short puffs of breath escaped from her nose. *Breathe deeply, Daisy.* Inhaling deeply, Daisy felt her heart race less forcefully. *Try to calm down. You need to stay alive!*

Stomping up the deck stairs and gaping at the shattered glass, Rubi Lee laughed. "What in the hell did you think you were gonna do? *Stab* me?" She bent down and snatched a sharp piece of glass. She sauntered over to Daisy, waving the glistening piece.

Daisy gasped when Rubi Lee brought the makeshift weapon close to her face.

"I wonder if I could just slice the bandana right off your hideous face?" Hovering the shard under Daisy's ear, Rubi Lee pulled at the bandana out and poked it with the glass. "Nah, that'll take too long."

Daisy jumped when she heard the splintering of the shard on the deck. "Now, look into the camera and beg like the dog you are for Mommy's life!"

Rubi Lee stood in front of Daisy and yanked out the gag.

Pulling in lungfuls of air, Daisy struggled to breathe and beg at the same time. "Please! Please don't drown her in the river! You've hurt her enough. She's innocent! Please just stop!" Daisy pleaded into the camera.

Rubi Lee stood behind her and stared into the phone. "Now we play by *my* rules, Nick. Answer the fuckin' phone when it rings and call off the FBI!" She stopped recording, saved it, and dashed into the office where she downloaded it onto Roth's computer.

Heart in her throat, Daisy strained to look through the railings at her mother who lay like a rock by the canoe. "Mama!" she screamed. "Please move again!" Daisy saw her mother feebly wave her hand.

Rubi Lee returned and leaned right into Daisy's face. Daisy twisted away as far as the constricting strap allowed. "You can't escape me now, can you?"

Daisy's scalp crawled as Rubi Lee ran her hands through her hair. With her thumbs, she stroked Daisy's forehead and ran and finger over her mouth.

"Pretty girls like you never know what it's like to be

like me—ugly. But I can take that away in one slash." She jerked her head back. "It must be nice to have all this hair."

Daisy thrashed in the chair, twisting away from her, until Rubi Lee grabbed a handful of her hair and yanked Daisy's head to the right.

"Hmm, looks like you have some split ends. We can't allow a *famous* reporter to have split ends now, can we?"

Head tilted at an abnormal angle, Daisy's neck muscles felt as though they were going to snap. She felt more tugging accompanied with a sound she could not identify. Daisy tasted the fear that wrapped around her like a sheet.

"*No! Stop! Stop!*" She screamed as she identified the sound: A knife hacking through her hair. The tug and pull felt as if her scalp was peeling away.

"There! No more split ends!" Rubi Lee stood in front of her, a wide grin on her pale face, a fistful of red curls blowing like yarn in the wind.

Exhausted, Daisy said nothing. She studied the tiny, dirty woman standing in front of her. The wind blew scraggly pieces of hair across Rubi Lee's shimmering forehead. Dried blood mixed with dark river mud caked the sleeves of her light blue sweatshirt. Her torn jeans were damp and filthy. *Pathetic woman*, Daisy thought. *I have one last card to play. It's now or never.*

Inhaling deeply and speaking in a soft tone, Daisy began. "Rubi Lee, you don't need to do this. If you murder all of us, you'll be looking over your shoulder forever. Do you really want to live like that? In constant fear of being caught? Always on the run?"

For a split second, Daisy saw a flicker of light pass through the black eyes. Rubi Lee shifted her stance.

I know I'm taking a chance, but I have to say this. Daisy continued, "Do you *really* believe Zeke would be happy that you killed us? Do you think that's what he'd want?"

A thick tension lay between the two women. Nature's glorious sounds filled the air: the rustling of leaves, the shrill honk of Canada geese flying south, the rushing water of the river.

Rubi Lee pounced at Daisy, knife in hand. "How dare you tell me what my brother would want!" She pulled Daisy's head back so her pulsating throat faced the sky. Rubi Lee delicately lay her blade on Daisy's neck. She leaned in, centimeters from her mouth. "How does this feel?" With her papery cheek pressed to Daisy's, she hissed, "I will win and *you will lose!*"

She stood up and began to walk away. "By the way, I just sent your video off to your husband. I'll give him some viewing time before I call him. I'm sure he'll be glad to hear from us." She laughed and left Daisy on the porch.

Daisy watched Rubi Lee chain Annie to a rusty, moss-covered tractor. "You can't leave her there! It's getting cold and she'll freeze."

"Whether she stays out here or not depends on your precious Nick." Rubi Lee pulled the door shut and vanished into the house.

Daisy was not sure how long she sat outside. Her only clock was the setting of the sun behind a thick row of pine trees. "Mom, are you okay? What're we going to do?" she yelled in vain.

The slam of the door behind her was the only response Daisy heard.

"Brr, it's cold out here." Rubi Lee positioned herself

behind Daisy and began to rub Daisy's arms.

"What're you doing?" Daisy whispered.

"Just getting a feel for your fear." Slowly, Rubi Lee moved to her neck. Her grip tightened, causing Daisy to gasp.

"Reminds me of the night you killed my brother: cold and dark." She squeezed until Daisy flinched.

"Alex killed him," Daisy coughed out.

Rubi Lee released her grip and threw the glass of water she was drinking into her face.

"If you hadn't interfered, Alex would not have shot him. *You*, you bitch, *you* forced her to kill Zeke."

Water dripped from Daisy's chin and plopped onto her pants. She knew that trying to change Rubi Lee's mind about her lack of guilt in Zeke's death was pointless.

You failed earlier at that, she thought. *She's consumed with killing us; nothing may stop her. The only thing I can do is try to buy time. Keep her talking.*

"What about Victor? Isn't he the one to blame for all of this? He's the one who ran the smuggling ring!" Daisy said.

Venom shot from Rubi Lee's eyes. "Victor tried to *help* us! He hired me and Zeke! He tried to give us a better life!"

"What? As *criminals*?" Daisy countered.

"It was a lot better than hacking up chickens like before! Me and Zeke *liked* working for Victor! He paid us good money! But because of you, he's dead too!" Rubi Lee paced the deck. "You took my life and Zeke's life! You took away any future me and Zeke could've had! You took away any hope me and Zeke had of being normal!" She spat out this last sentence.

Oh no, this is spiraling out of control. I have to fix this!

Shift the focus! Maybe if I tell her she can come out of this with me and Nick, she'll let Mom go.

Daisy stared up at wild-eyed Rubi Lee. "Rubi Lee, please help my mother. You can have me and Nick. But please, please don't let her freeze. I ... I promise you. I'll get Nick here if you promise to let my mom go." Daisy looked at her mother, who had rolled over. "Even if she wanted to, she can't hurt you. You know how weak she is!"

Rubi Lee smiled at Daisy. She thought Daisy's offer over. "I like when you beg. I'll think about it."

CHAPTER 31

The normal three-hour ride to Sullivan County was shortened with Winston behind the wheel. Clear morning sun streamed through the SUV's sunroof and warmed Nick's face. For most of the ride, he was quiet. He gnawed on his thumbnail as he watched the trees whiz by.

Winston turned into the police station and Nick asked, "What do you think Rubi Lee is going to say after she hears that message?"

Nick spat out the thumbnail and flipped his hand over to see how much time he had before calling Rubi Lee—fifteen minutes. "Not sure, but I know she'll go nuts. I hope I did not push her over the edge."

"If she does get pushed to that edge, that'll be beneficial for us."

Nick turned. "*How*, Win? This whole thing sucks! I hate it!" He pounded the dashboard with his fist.

Winston let him vent. "When criminals like Rubi Lee feel cornered, they make mistakes. Trust me, she'll make one."

"I sure hope so. I wonder if I just gave Daisy and her mom a death sentence."

* * *

Inside the cramped station a deputy slouched at a desk, unaware of anything but his phone.

"Excuse me," Nick said.

The deputy's ears were deafened by earbuds. Eyes closed, he riffed on an imaginary drum set.

Nick banged his hand on the desk. "Excuse me!"

The deputy jumped and tilted his boyish face upward. A flush of red filled his cheeks. "Oh sorry! I didn't hear you. Can I help you?" He came to his feet.

"My name is Nick Tyson, and this is Special Agent Winston Wang. Is Sheriff Roth here?"

"I'm sorry, he's not."

Nick glared at him. "Of course he's not here."

Winston asked him how many on-duty officers were available.

"Um, just me, and it's only my second day here," Sam, the new deputy, replied. He sensed Nick was about to explode. "But I can make some calls?" he stammered.

Winston declined his offer. "Never mind. But if the sheriff calls in, have him call me ASAP." He gave Sam a card and thanked him.

They stepped back out into the sunshine. Winston called Jaida, who told him she was in Philly and would be in Sullivan County soon.

"Did you find anything on the Holston girl?"

"Sorry, nothing new on Holston, but get this." Winston could hear the click-clack of computer keys. "Here we go. The burned body from the hotel has been identified from dental records. His name's Chuck Willis—the deputy from

Sullivan County, also known as Bump," Jaida replied.

"I see. If I were a betting guy, I'd say Rubi Lee is responsible for his demise. Nick and I nailed that one."

"I'm sure she was using Bump. She's a manipulator," Jaida agreed.

"Thanks Jaida. I gotta go. See you when you get here."

"What did she say?" Nick inquired.

"Looks like our girl has been on a murder spree, including the burned body of Deputy Bump. So, I think your theory of her having an inside source was right on. Why else would Bump be at that hotel if he *wasn't* helping Rubi Lee? Now we know how she's been one step ahead of us." Winston pulled out and headed to the Holston house.

* * *

No one answered the front door. They looked in the windows to see things seemed ordinary.

"Come on. Let's go out back," Nick suggested.

Around the corner of the split-level house was an unkempt yard choked with tall weeds. A few discarded tools lay near bundles of rusted chicken wire.

Nick eyed the back of the house. The sight of the closed shutters gave Nick pause. *That's not right*, he thought as he approached the windows. He yanked at one of the shutters. Nothing. He tugged hard with both hands on the other one. It groaned and creaked until it finally relented. Sharp nails protruded from it.

"Win!" He called over his shoulder. "Check this out. These shutters were *nailed* shut."

Winston ran over and inspected the shiny nails. "No

rust means they're relatively new. Someone, Rubi Lee, wanted to hide something or *someone*."

"We need to get inside this house now!"

"I agree, but we need a search warrant. I'll get it expedited. Remember though, it could be a few hours. Meanwhile, we wait for Rubi Lee to call you back."

Nick could not sit by and wait. "I'm gonna call the local real estate agency to see what they know about this property." He disappeared for a few minutes and returned ashen faced.

"The rental agreement on this house is in Tanya's name. Which tells me Rubi Lee is definitely impersonating her and that is how she's been moving about without any trace."

Nick was alarmed at the raw frustration and aggravation on Win's face. Saying nothing, they trudged back to the car.

Nick shifted in his seat, head resting on the window. Looking forward, he questioned Winston, "How're we going to find them?"

"To start, I will have agents canvass the town of Shunk and all of Sullivan County. Now that we have a recent picture of Tanya, we can paper the town with flyers. There *must be* someone who saw something or someone that sent up a red flag. Often, people are not aware they have witnessed something crucial to finding a missing person. Secondly, if there are any leads, we will follow up on them. Third, we can involve the media . . ." Winston paused. "However, involving them may be risky."

Nick knew why. "Media involvement could be the icing on the cake—not in a good way."

"And we still haven't heard from Roth or that bonehead Sam," Winston added. "We're in a waiting game now. Sorry."

Tense silence filled the car. The muscles in Nick's shoulders seized into taut knots.

"I gotta get outta here!" He flung open the car door and stomped down the driveway to the road.

"Hey, where are you going?" Winston called out to him.

"I can't sit around with my thumb up my ass! I know she's here somewhere and I'm going to find her!" Nick yelled.

"Hey Nick, stop! You can't just walk the roads! This is a big area."

"Damn it! I can't *sit and wait* when Daisy is in trouble. She's my *wife*!"

Winston jogged down the driveway. "Nick, I understand how upset you are. We *will* find her. You need to trust me, just like that night in the garage." He seized Nick's arm and turned him around. He gazed at Nick's darkened face. "If you go looking for them, it could be a costly mistake."

Nick exploded. "Get the *fuck* off me! I don't care about you or waiting or making a mistake!" He broke away from Winston.

Winston stood and watched his friend walk away. "You know that's what she wants," he called and Nick stopped. "She *wants* you to make a mistake! She wants you to come after her! You screw up? Daisy, Annie, and even you are dead. If that happens, she wins, and you lose!"

Suddenly Nick felt the ground fall away. His heart raced. Sweat drenched his trembling body. He collapsed onto all fours.

Winston's heart broke. He stood his ground. *He looks like a marionette puppet whose strings were tangled by a careless puppeteer*, Winston thought. *He's one stubborn SOB, but I gotta make him see the light.* Winston had to drive home the point. "Did you hear me! *She wins and you lose!*" He yelled louder, "Is *that* what you want? Daisy and Annie dead? Can you live with that? We need to stay the course and not screw up!"

"I'm sorry Win. This is killing me. I'm exhausted. I don't know what to do!" A strangled sob escaped his throat.

Winston knelt and put his arm around Nick. "We're going to get her, and I feel it's going to be very soon. Hang in there. I'm going to be with you every step of the way." Winston helped Nick up from the ground.

"Rubi Lee isn't going to win anything except a long jail term." Nick's phone rang. The 800 number lit up the screen. "It's her."

"Stay calm, Nick. Listen and don't speak."

He answered and put Rubi Lee on speakerphone.

"Seems you're not as dumb as I thought. I got your fuckin' message, but you *really* should check your email. Talk soon."

The video would not download on either of their phones. "Damnit! Won't load! We need to get to a computer fast!" Nick said. "Let's go back to the police station!"

En route, Winston alerted several agents. "You need to get here ASAP!" He punched the gas.

* * *

Sam was busy playing video games. "You're back. Can I help you guys?"

"Get out of the way," Winston ordered.

Sam slinked away like a scolded puppy and waited in the break room. Nick sat down and logged on to his personal email account. One new email was waiting. With trembling fingers and a thudding heart, Nick opened the email and the attached video.

He gasped sharply at what he saw. "Oh Daisy!" With a trembling finger, he reached out and traced her contorted, begging face. Nick rewound it and watched again. Then again and again. Awkwardly, Winston patted his tense back while the video of Daisy pleading for her mother's life ran.

"Nick, stop. We've seen enough. Email it to me so I can send it to Jaida."

"Winston, I know Daisy. She is sending us a message. I don't want to watch it again any more than you do. But I know her and she's trying to help."

Winston knew Nick had a point. "Good thinking. Let's play it again and see." He walked to the hallway and called to the agents, "Hey gang. Everyone in here. We need more eyes."

"Right there! She said, 'Don't drown her in the river.' They're somewhere near or at the river!"

"Go get Sam!" Winston commanded an agent.

"Yes sir."

Sheepishly, Sam ducked into the room. "You need something, sir?"

"You are not in trouble. What river is this?" Winston pointed at the computer screen.

Sam recoiled at what he saw. "Oh, um that's Muncy River; it runs through the whole county. Most of the area is rocky with foot trails."

"Does this deck or landscape look familiar?" Winston asked.

Sam's young eyes grew as large as dinner plates. "Oh God, this is awful! I don't recognize any of that. But I know it's Muncy River." He turned away from the computer.

"Thank you. You are dismissed," Winston told him. His phone vibrated in his pocket. Jaida's voice floated into the room.

"Hey Win."

"Hi Jaida, any news on the warrant?"

"Not yet. Waiting on McIntire to get back to me."

"I'm going to email you a highly disturbing video. If you could use GPS to narrow down the exact location where it was filmed, we'll find Daisy and her mother."

"Okay. Is it really that bad?"

"Yes. Brace yourself."

"Thanks. I'll be in touch."

Winston gathered his agents and instructed them to gear up to canvass the area in which the river flowed. "Be careful. We're dealing with an extremely intelligent, dangerous perp."

He turned to Sam. "Get me a map of the area, please."

CHAPTER 32

Against every fiber in his soul, Nick forced himself to watch the video again to try and pinpoint a location. Winston and his team had pinned the map to the wall. They discussed possible entry points to the river. Chatter stopped when Nick's phone rang. He put it on speakerphone.

"How'd ya like that video?" She laughed.

"You're a horrible excuse for a human being."

An annoyed sigh. "Do you love your wife?"

Why is she asking that? Play along, Nick. He glanced at Winston and mouthed, "What?"

Winston gave Nick the *keep going* sign.

"More than anything. Why?"

Nick heard the muffled handing over of the phone.

"Hello?" a shaky voice said.

Nick's heart skipped. "Daisy! Daisy!"

Hearing her husband's voice, Daisy sat straighter and mustered up her resolve. "Oh Nick, please help! She's gonna kill us!" *I know he's nearby! I feel it in my gut.*

"No! I'll find you! Daisy, where are you?"

Muffled sounds filled the air.

"Sorry Nick. That's all ya get."

"Are they okay?" He did not know what else to ask. *This frustration is killing me! My family needs me and I can't help them!*

He looked to Winston, who circled his pointer finger in the air. He mouthed, "Keep her talking!" Seeing his friend's anger and frustration, Nick knew he needed to do more. He lifted the console and rummaged for paper and a pen.

"Seems she's cold. Poor baby. And your mother-in-law? She's part of this too."

"What do you mean? She's innocent!"

"No one is *innocent*! I'm going to slowly and carefully take everything away from you so that you know how it feels."

Nick stared at the phone and then at Winston. Winston put up his pointer finger and scribbled on a piece of paper.

"Are you there?" Rubi Lee barked.

"Yeah, yeah!" Nick yelled. "I'm here! I'm not gonna hang up!"

Winston snapped his fingers at Nick. He cut his eyes to Winston who held up a note scribbled on a receipt: *Tell her you're sorry and you'll give her freedom . . . BEG. That's what she wants.*

Nick's eyes flew over the words. *Is he serious? She's never gonna believe me! People like her aren't normal!*

"I'm getting impatient, and you don't want that!" Rubi Lee's voice was shrill.

Winston snapped his fingers again and pointed at the note.

Nick sighed deeply. "I'm here." He read the note again and blew out the breath he was holding. Rubbing his face, he reasoned with himself, *What if she knows I'm lying and that I'll never give her freedom? But she is also taking a risk by maybe believing me. At this point, I don't have a choice.*

Clutching his churning stomach, Nick spoke to Rubi Lee. "Okay, okay. I'm sorry, Rubi Lee, for your brother. I'm sorry for everything. Please, please just let them go and in exchange, you'll be free to go."

A pregnant pause and then, "How do I know I can trust you?"

Nick cut his eyes to Winston. "Because I will come alone. No cops. No FBI. I swear."

Winston nodded.

"I'll think about it. I'll be in touch." The phone went dead.

*   *   *

Winston and his team turned their attention back to the map. "Here's the county and over here is the river. It winds through this thickly wooded area. Pinetree Way is here and runs east by the river and then dead ends at this spot." He pointed down. "About one hundred yards from *that* spot"—he squinted and leaned in—"is what looks like a waterfall. Therefore, I doubt any houses would be built on that terrain."

"Do you think we can work our way east through the woods from the west side of the river?" an agent asked.

"I'm not sure," Winston said, eyes locked on the map. "There is a road over here." He pointed. "But I'm not sure how long to get to the river—I would assume longer than shorter. The terrain is challenging as well. I *like* the idea, but we need more information."

"We could get a chopper to fly over and take aerial photos. May even be able to see the houses," the agent suggested. "Or a drone?"

"Great idea. Make the call."

"Hold on, Win. A drone or chopper? Rubi Lee will get suspicious, right? We need to contain her."

Winston ordered a halt on the chopper. Ideas were tossed around by the agents.

Another agent chimed in, "How about one of us visits a local realtor to get a street map? Chances are it'll have all the houses listed." She glanced around. "Right guys?"

"I like it. You two head there and report back." Winston pointed at two agents, who departed.

Winston and the agents hatched a plan in which they would dress in hunting gear and work in pairs. They would park on the road opposite of the river then work their way to the edge.

"Each twosome will have audio capabilities. We don't know if Rubi Lee knows it's hunting season. If she does, then seeing hunters should not raise her suspicions."

"But what if she *doesn't* know?" Bewilderment was thick in Nick's voice. "What if she freaks out and kills Daisy when she sees another person?"

"Rest assured Nick, my agents will make sure they are dressed appropriately—rifles included—as hunters." Winston felt Nick's agitation. "Trust me, Nick."

"I *do* trust you, Win. But this crushing feeling of helplessness is killing me." He exhaled and ran a hand through his hair. "What do you want me to do?"

"I know you're going to disagree, but I think you need to stay here. I don't need or want you getting hurt; this is what we do."

Nick shot Winston a fiery glare. "No way! You *know* I

can't stay here. If our roles were reversed, you'd say the same thing."

Winston regarded his friend. "Touché." He placed a hand on Nick's shoulder and squeezed. "Know this, though: You will listen to everything I tell you and follow my directions. Running wild into the woods will not happen. Lastly, this ain't no walk in the park. The terrain is hilly, rocky and you'll run out of gas. Don't say you weren't warned."

They dressed in camouflage hunting gear, orange vests, and boots. All earpieces and sleeve microphones were tested to ensure clear communication. Winston ordered Sam to drive them in his pickup to the dirt road where the woods started. "Sam, I also need you to use the walkie-talkie to tell Sheriff that the seasonal hunting licenses have arrived. Got it?"

"Yes sir. But may I ask why?"

"Just do it, okay?" Winston ordered before embarking into the woods.

* * *

Under thickening slate clouds, Nick and Winston set out into the unfamiliar, beautiful terrain. Thick towering pines spread in all directions. Their heady spicy aroma perfumed the brisk November day. Bursts of red and orange leaves from sugar maples poked through the greenness of the pines.

Winston and Nick slung their backpacks over their dark hunting jackets. Glancing out into the wilderness, Winston whistled. "It's so beautiful out here. Knowing there's a crazy woman out there threatening to do harm to your family just does not fit in with what we see before us."

Captivated by the beauty of Mother Nature, Nick took in the stunning vista. *I did not think of it that way.* "I know. But they need us. Ready?" Nick tugged on the straps of the weighty backpack.

"Yep. Let's roll!"

Navigating the uneven landscape was made even more difficult by numerous various-sized rocks jutting from the ground like broken molars.

Close to an hour passed until a deep ache throbbed in Nick's back under the heavy backpack. He willed himself to ignore the pain. Winston plowed ahead, leaving Nick breathless.

"Win, I have to rest," he said into his sleeve. "My back's killing me."

"Okay, I'm just ahead of you. I'll wait for you to catch up."

Man, I'm in crappy shape, he thought as he pushed deeper into the woods to where Winston waited. A noise to his left startled him. He whipped his head to the side just in time to see the flash of orange from a red fox. *Holy shit!*

Twenty yards away through the woods, he saw Winston scanning the area with his binoculars. Huffing and puffing, Nick approached him. "Man am I tired. When this is all over, I'm getting my fat ass back in shape."

"I told you this was tough terrain. The woods only get thicker as we go. Because of that we're going to take longer than I calculated." Winston frowned as he stared into the impenetrable woods.

"Why did you tell Sam to make an announcement

about hunting licenses?" Nick asked.

"Knowing how Rubi Lee used Bump, I'm sure she is somehow listening to chatter. Therefore, if she happens to see one of us creeping around the woods, she'll assume it's a hunter."

"Smart guy."

The tangible silence surrounded them. Winston pointed to his right. "Nick, this river will lead us to them. Let's go." Slowly, they hiked up the side of a steep rise strewn with enormous boulders. Dizziness hit Nick when he glanced down below at the rushing river. *Eyes forward, eyes forward*, he reminded himself.

Nick wheezed climbing up the sharp side of the face. *I can't wait to climb down; at least I'll be able to breathe*, he thought, reaching the top. "Win, I need a rest!" He called to his friend.

Winston turned and nodded. A large boulder served as a much-needed seat.

"You doin' okay up here?" Winston asked, pointing to his head.

"Yeah, yeah I am." Nick looked at the view below them. Acres of pine trees, maples, and other trees spread before them.

Winston rose and pulled his friend up. "You ready to finish this?" Winston turned away and studied how to scale the rocks.

"I am. And . . . Win?"

Something in Nick's tone made Winston turn around. "Yeah?"

"I could not rescue Daisy without your help. Thanks man."

"You know it. It's my job!" Winston smiled and resumed his march.

As they were slowly descending the steep face, an acute pain shot through Nick's left knee. Nick grimaced and fought to keep his balance. "Ouch! Damnit that hurt!"

"What's wrong?" Winston called over his shoulder.

"My knee—the one I screwed up playing pick-up basketball last year—is killing me."

"Oh yeah, that game where I kicked your ass! Sorry, but you're gonna have to deal with it!"

"Nothing's gonna stop me from getting to Daisy and Annie."

"You're right," Winston agreed. "Now, when we get to the . . . oh shit! No!" Winston's foot slipped on the sheer face of rock. His feet went out from underneath him and he thudded onto his back. Grasping at anything to stop from sliding off the side of the sheer, slippery face, he screamed at Nick for help.

"Nick! Help! Help me!" Winston's cries turned Nick's stomach.

"Win!" Nick yelled. "Hold on! I'm coming!" Nick fought to keep his balance on his throbbing knee.

"Hurry! I can't stop myself from sliding! Oh shit! No!"

Winston's panicked screams mixed with the scraping of his backpack on the rock face propelled Nick forward. But he was too late.

Nick watched in horror as his friend went tumbling like a rag doll off the exposed faces of the jagged boulders.

For a split second, Nick froze. He felt removed from the situation, as if he was sitting in a movie theater and someone stopped the movie halfway through. Scrabbling over on all fours, he was unaware of the burning pain in his knee.

"Win! Win!" He screamed to a motionless Winston who lay at the bottom . . . *Oh shit! Please answer! Please!*

Nick slid down the sheer face and hobbled to his friend. "Oh God, Win! Are you all right?" He crouched next to his friend. "Win! Please, God!" *Please let him be alive.* Placing two shaking fingers to his friend's warm neck, he cried out when he felt nothing.

"Come on man! I can't do this without you! I don't know what I'm doing!" He leaned his cheek to Winston's mouth and nose. He felt something but was unsure if it was the breeze or breath from Winston.

He laid his head onto the left side of Winston's bony chest. *Please let me hear a heartbeat!*

He felt and heard a faint rasp and saw Winston's chest rise slightly. He kept his head there to be positive Winston was alive. After hearing a continuous heartbeat and labored breathing, Nick sat up. Relief flooded through every pore of his shaking body.

"Thank God! You're alive!"

Winston opened his eyes. He moaned, "My . . . ankle . . . "

"Don't talk man, save your energy. Stay still." Nick checked for bodily injuries. Based on the gruesome angle of Winston's ankle, he knew it was broken.

"I think my ankle is busted." He grimaced. "And my shoulder feels pretty fucked up. Call for help."

Nick obeyed and almost cried with relief when an agent replied they were not far.

"Nick," Winston panted, "you need to . . . to continue

down to the river. You . . . she's waiting. You . . . must save Daisy." He screwed up his face. "Holy shit my shoulder hurts!"

Nick stared at his friend. "Are you nuts? I can't leave you here. Alone."

Winston's steely eyes bore into Nick's. "Nick, yes you can . . . and you will. You don't have a choice. And . . . and neither does your family." He placed his hand on Nick's forearm. "The woman . . . you love needs you."

Nick's emotions swirled like a cyclone. "Win . . ."

Winston's dark eyes flashed angrily. "Look, you survived a shootout last year. You are going to save your wife. Go."

Guilt about leaving his best friend flamed inside Nick, but his love for Daisy extinguished that fire. "You're right. I'm gonna save Daisy and put an end to Rubi Lee Dixon." Awkwardly, he bent down and hugged his friend. "I'll see you soon, amigo."

Nick spoke into his sleeve, informing the team where they were. Through his earpiece came a clear response: "Yes sir! We are about a tenth of a mile east."

"Win, they're on their way. Wish me luck." Nick squeezed his friend's hand and patted his chest. "You'll be fine."

"I know. Now go."

Stepping gingerly over rocks, he reentered the woods. The swooshing of the river grew louder and more pronounced. Soon he came upon the brackish water; it flowed with determined intensity. Turning upriver, his gaze landed on a spot where he could see a house. Through his binoculars, he saw young kids running in their yard with a dog. Down the bank he went, binoculars aimed at the houses. *Come on! She's got to be here somewhere!* Finally, he landed upon a large and powerful waterfall. The sight was ominously, captivatingly beautiful: water slithered like wet fingers around rocks and thundered down into a frothy basin roughly thirty feet below.

His phone vibrated in his pocket. He exhaled, "Rubi Lee."

"I'm waiting for you. I will soon finish the job if you don't show up soon."

I can't wait to wrap my hands around this woman's skinny neck and watch her eyes bulge as I crush her throat! Nick counted to three before answering. "We have a deal. If you don't hold your end of the bargain, you're going away for a very long time. Do you want that or do you want freedom?"

"You better be here before sundown or we're moving and then you'll never find us!"

I hate this woman! I just wanna kill her! Marching along the river, he felt his anger churn like the river. The words shot from his mouth. "You bitch! We know you killed Tanya and took her identity! You can't hide anymore. I'm gonna find you!" Nick yelled. "You thought you were one step ahead; you're so wrong."

A long pause filled his ear followed by a hollow, hoarse voice. "Nick, please do as she says. I think she may have killed Mom, tethered to a tractor by the river—I can't see her moving anymore—and now she has a knife to my neck. Nick, I love you."

"Now do you believe I mean business?" She heard Daisy scream in the background.

No! You have to stop her, Nick! "Is there another way?"

"You will surrender to me. Then I'll have all of you."

Nick thought about her demand, and the consequences of him surrendering to Rubi Lee. He saw no other way out. Over the roar of the falls, he yelled, "Fine. Tell me where you are, and I'll come surrender!"

"Good boy. But do you *really* expect me to tell you where I am? I'm not stupid. I'll call you soon."

"Son of a bitch!" he cried into the wilderness. *She wants to play this game? Fine. She'll never be able to dream how sorry she's gonna be!*

He circled around the waterfall and found the fourth house, a ranch house sitting on an unkempt property. Raising the binoculars, he saw the windows on the back of the house were boarded up. *Looks like something Rubi Lee would hide out in. Think clearly. You need to cross the river safely and get close to the house*, he decided. Based on the flow of the water, he knew he must cross downriver past the basin where the current was slower. He informed Winston and the agents he was on the opposite side of the river.

He jogged down the tree-lined riverbank to the base of the waterfall. Nick crossed through the basin toward the shuttered house. He no longer felt the gush of cold water. Every nerve in his body was electrified. His heart clobbered against his ribcage.

On light feet, he approached the house. He pressed his ear against the cold, damp siding. No sound. Taking refuge under the wooden deck, he stood still, praying to hear something. Damp silence answered him. At the front of the house, he peered in through a window. Ghostly shapes filled the rooms. "What the hell?" He squinted and saw old sheets thrown over the furniture. Glancing at the front door, he shook his head. *I know no one is here.* But he knocked anyway.

Defeated, he slid down the side of the wall to a sitting position. Tears ran down his face. He leaned his head back, eyes closed. The telltale *thump thump thump* of his heart signaled a potential panic attack. He breathed heavily while gently pressing the base of his hands against his eyes. *Please God, no. Not now.*

After a few minutes, his technique worked, and his mind was clear. He knew where he had to go. *Oh Daisy, you are so smart. That's why I love you!* He tapped his earpiece and relayed a message to the agents.

"A tractor! We need to get to the property with a tractor out back! It's gotta be near the riverbank! I'm off course! I'm heading back upstream to the other houses. I know they're in one of them!"

CHAPTER 33

The tractor, I have to find that damn tractor. Nick marched upstream. To his right, he saw lights flicking on inside warm houses. Drained and cold from searching, he came to the last house on the river. Sheriff Roth's house.

The sun had set, and the cool evening air dragged the temperature down five degrees. Chills ran up his spine. He made sure his coat was zipped and buttoned tight against the elements. As he trudged through the mud, his mind wandered to what Daisy said about her mother being left out in the cold.

He loved Annie. The first time he met her was when he was twelve years old during his first visit to Cab Station, Virginia, where his grandparents lived. Annie and her husband, Jackson, were guests at one of his grandparents' famous summer parties. Her interest in everything he did made him feel important and confident. Nick shook his head. *And who knew that I would end up being her son-in-law*, he mused.

He trudged on. Night creatures battled each other with their own symphony of sounds. It was a fleeting slice of peace in an otherwise chaotic environment.

The binoculars thudded against his pulsating chest when he stumbled over a branch lying on the bank. Nick assumed it may take most of the night to find Daisy. He stayed close to the water's edge to take advantage of the cover of brush and trees. Long-dead branches stuck out at odd angles. He ducked under them, slogging through thick clumps of stale, musty leaves. Gaining footing, he lifted the binoculars and saw it: the tractor. "Yes!" He lunged forward.

Suddenly, a hand reached out from a clump of brush on the bank. It grabbed his jacket sleeve, causing Nick to stumble backward and fall into the water. Terror ripped through him. He shot up out of the water and tore his sleeve from the hand. He plunged headlong toward the hand.

"You're dead!" Nick bellowed.

"Stop, please stop. Help me." A tired voice floated up from the ground.

Nick stopped short. It was a male's voice. Peering in through the bushes, he saw a figure lying on their side.

"Who are you?" Darkness and debris obscured facial features.

Labored breathing before he answered, "Sheriff Roth. I need help."

"Sheriff! It's Nick Tyson. What the hell happened to you?" Nick helped haul him to his feet. Blood caked the side of his head.

He rubbed his head. "I . . . I don't know for sure. I was fishing and the next thing I knew I woke up on the bank. My head was bloody, and I think I have a concussion." He panted heavily. "And my ankle hurts like a son of a bitch." He looked around, trying to orient himself. "Seems the current carried me down here. I'm frozen and . . . I . . . need help."

Nick put his arm around Roth's waist and helped him

to a storage shed Nick spied on an adjacent property. Shuffling slowly, he carefully steered him toward a woodpile under the overhang of the roof. Gingerly, he lowered the exhausted man to the ground and collapsed next to him.

Nick tapped his earpiece but got no response. The river water had rendered it inoperable. "Shit!" Same with his sleeved microphone.

"What's . . . what's . . . wrong?" Roth sat, eyes closed, head resting against the woodpile.

"What's *wrong*? Besides trying to rescue my wife and mother-in-law from a crazed woman? The earpiece I was using to stay in touch with the FBI is dead."

Roth said nothing at first. Sluggishly, he rolled his head toward Nick. "I'm sorry . . . what . . . what did you . . . say?"

"My wife Daisy and mother-in-law Annie. Don't you remember our conversation? I told you they've been kidnapped. And I'm pretty sure they're right near here."

Roth grunted. "Kidnapped?" Nick barely heard him. Roth's eyelids fluttered.

"Yea, by a crazy woman—Rubi Lee Dixon. We believe she killed the real Tanya Holston and has been impersonating her for months! And I'm sure she's the one who beat the crap outta you."

Glassy eyed, Roth stared off into the distance. "I need . . . help. My head! God it hurts. Please, please . . . get me help."

"I will, I promise. I know FBI agents are crawling around the woods. Where are we? I need to tell them our location." Alarm bells rang inside Nick.

Roth opened his eyes. Squinting, he tried to peer through the dark.

"Come on Sheriff, try. I saw a tractor in a backyard. Is it yours?"

"Yeah, I have one."

"Then we're at your neighbors, the house to the right. What's their name?" Nick pushed aside the hysteria he felt.

"Oh, the, Doyles. Tell the agents the Doyles."

"Thank you, Sheriff."

"You should try to get some rest while you can." He pointed at Nick's ear. "And maybe that earpiece and microphone will dry out. They make really durable ones these days."

With all his might, Nick attempted to battle the lurking fatigue. Eventually, it slammed him in waves. Every muscle felt like cement. He laid back and sighed. Eyes closed, he soon fell into a fitful sleep. Dreams of Daisy and him as kids biking around Cab Station, rafting on Martin's Creek, and playing golf with Hoot played like a movie in his mind.

* * *

Morning crept in with a cool mist stretching over the land. The crackling of the earpiece made Nick jump. He snorted awake, rubbed his face, and tapped his earpiece and spoke into the microphone. Roth still slept. *Oh shit! I fell asleep!*

"I'm here!" Nick spoke.

"You're alive! Christ, what the hell happened?" an agent asked Nick.

"I found Sheriff Roth—he's pretty beaten up. You need to get him." Nick gave them his location. "Where are you guys?"

"At the station. We rescued Winston and brought him back here. We tried to locate you, but we couldn't find you."

"You need to rescue the sheriff. I don't want to leave him here alone, but I have no choice. Daisy and her mother are at Roth's house. I need to finish this once and for all."

"We're on the way."

"You gonna be okay?" Nick asked the sheriff a minute later. "Agents are coming to get you."

"I'll be fine. You go do what you need to do." His color was still pallid, but his voice sounded more alive.

Nick patted him on the shoulder. He stood up and stretched his sore legs and arms like a gymnast. The chill of the overnight air still hung in his stiff muscles and bones.

Plip plop, plip plop, he heard from behind. Nick held out his hands where raindrops trickled down the lines of his palms. *Of course it's raining*, he thought as he wandered to the edge of the river. Inhaling the chilly morning air, he waded in and instantly regretted it. Before his feet turned to chunks of ice, he skittered from the river. *I need another plan*, he decided. *I need to hike up to—*

His thought process was interrupted by the buzzing of his phone. He patted at the breast pockets of his coat and pulled it from the plastic bag. His hands shivered so badly the phone nearly bounced from his hand into the river.

A voice in the not-so-far distance spouted unintelligible words. *What did that person say? Is this the same person on the phone? I need to get closer! The reception sucks!* His feet squished in his wet shoes when he scrambled up the bank. Squatting behind a fat clump of pines, he peered through the binoculars and saw a teenager on a phone, pacing on a deck.

The phone buzzed again. He tried to answer it with one hand and hold the binoculars, but hit end call instead. "Shit! Shit! Call back!"

He looked through the binoculars again. The wind whipped over the deck so fiercely it blew the baseball hat off the person's head.

Holy shit! That's not a kid—that's Rubi Lee! Nick stared through the binoculars at her. *Daisy's gotta be somewhere in or near that house!*

* * *

"Looks like your jackass hubby has given up on you," Rubi Lee barked at Daisy. "He didn't answer the phone when I called. He's too stupid to listen." She marched over and yanked Daisy out of the chair by the back of her sheared head. Daisy bit the inside of her lip, hoping to stave off the pain emanating from her scalp.

I'll be damned if I'm gonna let her see me in pain. Daisy could not see where she was going. Rubi Lee edged her forward. Suddenly, Daisy felt herself spun around and pushed against the railing. A splinter lodged in her stomach. Daisy stared down—at least ten feet—at the ground. Wooziness swept through her. Heights were not her friend. Sweat popped out on her neck.

"I should push you over this rail and hope you break your fucking neck!" By the shrill, crazed tone, Daisy knew that Rubi Lee was rapidly becoming unhinged.

That will be her demise, Daisy thought, *good.* Focusing

on her breathing, Daisy ventured a gaze toward the river. She saw a tractor with her mother's limp arm fettered to it with a three-foot chain. Casting her eyes to the right, Daisy saw Annie laying under a tilted canoe.

"Time to head down to the water!"

Rubi Lee ordered Daisy to sit down while she flipped over the canoe. Annie lay still in the grass, raindrops falling all around them. She dragged it by the stern to the water's edge where it scraped over rocks into the frigid river. It bobbed like a toy boat; churning waters knocked at its sides. Rubi Lee took hold of the bowline and demanded Daisy to get in.

Daisy gaped at her mother who lay on her side, eyes shut. A whimper escaped from her throat. *She's alive! I know it! Please wake up, Mom!* Daisy willed. Annie's eyes fluttered open. She cast them first at Rubi Lee whose back was turned. She then winked at Daisy—she was okay.

Thank you God! Daisy obeyed and sat on the damp metal seat of the boat. Rubi Lee tied her feet together and then gagged her. Daisy moaned in protest, but it was futile.

"Have a nice trip." Rubi Lee cast off the boat from the bank with her foot. It slowly floated backward into the middle of the river. Soon, the current had it in its clutches and pushed it down the river halfway from the bank, but not before it came to a jerking halt. Daisy turned and saw that Rubi Lee tied the bowline to a tree that was leaning into the river.

Rain pelted the river and soaked her. The clouds grew into a dark menacing ball above. Shivering in the cold, soaking rain, Daisy turned her face to the sky. The angry gray clouds swirled menacingly above. *That's how I feel right now.*

* * *

"Hello," Nick said and peered through the bushes. Fifty yards from his hiding spot, Rubi Lee stood directly in his line of vision. *There she is. I wish I could run out there, tackle her, and make her pay for what she's done!*

"You decided to answer this time."

"I didn't hear your call before." He watched Rubi Lee through binoculars.

"Whatever, asshole. Daisy is stranded in the middle of the river in a tiny canoe. Looks like a heavy storm is coming, which means the river will rise and the current will be fast and strong. Too strong for a simple rope tied to a tree to hold the boat still. Oh, too bad if she goes over the falls."

Nick quickly swept the binoculars to the river. His mouth fell open at what he saw. In a dented canoe Daisy—with uneven hair—sat shivering, bound and gagged. *Oh Daisy! Stay strong! I'm coming for you!* "Wait! What did you do? We have a bargain!"

"Did you idiots really think I was gonna stick around to find out if you were lying or not?"

Careful what you say. She does not need to suspect you're as close as you are. "Rubi Lee, I don't know how to make you believe me. But if I give up then you'll let her go?"

"Um, no. No, Nick. I've never trusted anyone but Zeke. I don't believe you and I'm sick of waiting for your sorry ass.

She will feel either the pain of my knife or plummet over the falls—while you get to watch. Sorry not sorry."

Nick doubled over when his stomach seized and twisted. *I won't let her beat us.* "You bitch."

Rubi Lee clicked her tongue. "Now Nicholas, here's a little lesson. Revenge makes you do crazy things, crazy. I've planned on getting even with you fucks *for a year!*" Her voice shrilled an octave higher. "You destroyed any chance me and Zeke had at normal life! We did nothing to you!"

She's lost it. There's nothing rational about her thinking! I've got to get there! Tread carefully. "Rubi Lee, we can—"

"Shut up! Choose how your bitch dies: waterfall or knife. You make the choice."

Nick turned his eyes to the sky for an answer. Rain bounced from his face and dribbled down his coat. Seeing nothing but endless, wrathful storm clouds, he responded between clenched teeth. "Neither. You won't have the chance."

CHAPTER 34

He put the phone back in the plastic bag and slipped it into his coat pocket. The rain hammered Nick's back and shoulders. Soggy mud squished under his shoes. *Please let me able to see something through this damn rain*, he thought and lifted the binoculars. Through the watery lens, he saw the house and deck—but no people. Sweeping them left, he froze. *Oh my God, it's Annie!* She was lying on the ground in the weeds.

"Come on, move! Please move, Annie!" He waited ten seconds and saw no movement. *Focus, Nick! Keep moving, you can't stop.*

Daisy resembled a sad, wet lump. She slumped in the canoe, mouth gagged, hands tied behind her back. The current grew in strength. He could see the rope starting to strain against the power of the water. *You need to make a decision—and now*, Nick told himself. "Hang on Daiz, I'm coming," he whispered. *But how?* Several options ran through his mind.

He guessed the canoe sloshed in about ten feet of water in the speedy current. If he plunged into the river and waded to the canoe, he would have to fight a strong current to try to find a safe place for the craft. *If I pull the boat onto shore, Rubi Lee will see the whole thing and the plan will fail.* He could set the boat free and try to prevent it from crashing over the falls. He disregarded that option. *The riverbank is soaked. My feet would plunge into the muck—not gonna work.*

Gusty winds swirled around him, blowing leaves and small branches into the churning river. He watched helpless branches float away when his plan dawned on him. He glanced at his watch and saw how long it took him to get to his current location: a little over twenty minutes.

Please forgive me Daisy! But this is the only way to get to you quickly! Glimpsing once more at his battered wife, he turned downriver—away from Daisy—and hustled about a tenth of a mile to the base of the waterfall. He looked up at the rain-swollen river as it thundered thirty feet below into the basin which had doubled in size. *I gotta cross this river in one piece.* Scrutinizing the flow, he spotted a shallow section and waded in.

"Holy fuck this is cold!" Adrenaline hurtled him forward. Despite the frigid water, sweat trickled down his face as he forged on. *I have to get up stream as far as possible to save them.* From his vantage point he could see Daisy struggling to keep her balance as the current tossed and pushed the canoe. *Come on Daiz! Stay strong!*

He stopped momentarily to catch his breath. When he tilted his head back to stretch his tight neck, he saw a large branch jutting out over the river. An idea came to light. *Perfect! I can use that to wade through the water.* Fueled by a fresh resolve, he trudged over to it, reached up, and pulled with every ounce of strength he had. It cracked off into Nick's hands. Gripping the branch like a wooden flotation device, he kicked furiously toward the middle of the river. Eye level with the water, he silently begged the current, *Come on current! Carry me down to Daisy!* Water slopped into his mouth and shot up his nose. He knew he needed to pass Daisy on the far side to keep the canoe between him and the house.

A cramp in his hamstring caused him to stop for a split second. *You've had worse! Suck it up!* He continued to propel himself downstream to his wife.

With only his head above water, he neared the canoe. His heart raced out of control when he saw Daisy fighting to stay balanced. Holding onto the branch for all he was worth, he aimed it at the bow. The forceful current was like an underwater vacuum sucking him in the opposite direction, away from the canoe. *Kick! Kick! Come on!* Kicking and sputtering, Nick felt all his muscles strain as he steered the branch to the bow. *Bang!* Bullseye.

The jolt jarred Daisy and rocked the canoe. Startled, she glanced around. Seeing nothing, she strained forward to see what caused the boat to move.

Through the pelting rain, Nick called in a hushed voice. "Daisy, Daisy it's me. Down here!"

Her eyes popped out of her head. She moaned through the wet gag.

"Shh!" Hidden by the branch, he grasped the side of the canoe, careful not to rock it.

"Oh Daisy!" he cried when he saw his wife's lovely, fatigued eyes. Reddish purple bags puffed underneath them. Dirt smeared across her left cheek. A chunk of her red curls was gone; the rest of her hair lay plastered on her shivering shoulders.

Her heart galloped in her chest. A small moan escaped her throat. She longed to reach down and stroke his stubbled face. Hold him close.

"It's gonna be okay." His voice was carried downstream.

She leaned closer as he continued.

"But you need to slowly turn your back to me. Keep your arms behind your back so I can free you. Rubi Lee won't be able to see through the rain from this distance. And just keep sitting that same way."

She followed his directions.

"I have a plan." He took a deep breath. The rain made it hard for Daisy to hear clearly. "I'll distract her, and when I do, that's when you grab the rope and pull the boat to shore. We have one shot of doing this." He wiped his hand on the side of the canoe. "Let's make it work."

Daisy blinked. Labored puffs of air made her heart gallop.

"Okay. After I float away, count to fifty and begin to pull yourself back in. I love you, Daisy."

Tears and rain mingled in her eyes. Still as a statue she sat; no longer could she feel the relentless rain. She sent up a silent prayer to her father to help them, then she began to count.

* * *

From the kitchen, Rubi Lee squinted through the rain-streaked window. "Freakin' weather. I can't see shit!" She walked outside to the deck to check on Daisy.

"What the hell?" She noticed the large branch that seemed stuck to the side of the craft. She frowned, chewed the inside of her cheek. *That looks very strange. But that river is really moving.* She saw that Daisy had not moved, but she wanted to be sure.

Wrapping her arms around her, she started down the deck steps and kept her eye on the canoe. Suddenly, the branch freed itself and drifted away from the boat. It continued its trek down the river. *She ain't goin' anywhere*, she thought and returned to the warmth of the kitchen.

On the kitchen table sat Timmy. Rubi Lee picked it up. "So Timmy. Are you ready for—"

She jumped when her phone rang. *What the hell?* She knew it could be only one person. *But he's not supposed to call me! I'm in charge here!*

"Why are you calling me? I guess you're calling to quit. Right, loser?"

"Time for the game to change. I'm telling you what is going to happen," Nick ordered.

Rubi Lee listened closely. *Is that rain I hear?* She leaped up from the table and hustled to the sink. *Oh shit, is he here?*

Yanking the kitchen curtains aside, she peered outside and saw nothing. Running to the front of the house, she flung open the front door—nothing but rain and mud. She returned to the kitchen and stepped back out onto the deck. "You're full of shit!"

"Actually Rubi Lee, I'm not. In fact, that red top you're wearing? Not your color."

"*What the fuck?*" Like a blender on full speed, Rubi Lee's head swiveled in all directions, searching for Nick. "Show yourself, you wuss!" *I do hear rain! He's here!* Irate and crazed, she cursed Nick. Around the house she raced, looking out every window. "I'm gonna find you!"

"Good luck with that! See you soon, you piece of shit."

* * *

Daisy spit the gag from her mouth, mustered all her strength, and began to haul the canoe through the choppy water. Her hands slipped on the rope. The wind blew leaves and dead twigs into her face. *Go! Go! Come on, Daisy!*

Hand over hand, she pulled until she felt as if the tendons in her forearms would snap. The canoe pitched left and right as small, vicious whitecaps knocked at its sides.

Ribcage heaving, arms on fire, Daisy continued. *Come on, Daisy! Pull!* Feet firmly planted, weight equally distributed, she closed in on the last feet between her and land.

Rubi Lee tore through the house to the deck and saw Daisy pulling on the rope, coming close to shore.

"Oh no you don't!" she screamed through the rain and wind. The phone thudded to the ground.

CHAPTER 35

Like a locomotive, Rubi Lee charged from the deck toward the bank, slipping on the wet ground. "Noooo!" Rubi Lee shrilled like a banshee. "You're *fucking* dead now!"

Annie, lying on her side, soaked to the bone, shifted her head at the screech and saw Rubi Lee slip sliding down the yard toward her. *I must do something.* She squirmed closer to the path Rubi Lee cut. *Please let her run in my direction,* she prayed. Footsteps drew nearer. Annie heard loud panting. Timing was everything. She prayed and stuck her foot out just in time.

Thwack! Rubi Lee flew to the ground like a duck blown from the sky.

Daisy heard a scream. Whirling around, she saw Rubi Lee rising from the ground, cursing at her mother. Wind blew sheets of rain into her face. She was only feet from the muddy riverbank. Daisy stood, wobbling in the hull.

"Don't even *think* about getting out of that boat! If you do, she's dead!" She pushed the knife's blade against Annie's throat.

Daisy sank back down. She looked at the sodden, pathetic Rubi Lee. Rain plastered her hair down against her ashen face. The knife shook in her hand.

"Let her go, Rubi Lee! This is between you and me!" she yelled; her voice carried on the wind.

Rubi Lee cocked her head and yelled, "You're right!" She tossed Annie to the ground, stuck Timmy in a pants pocket, and hurtled through the rain. Ten feet stood between Rubi Lee and Daisy. Then five feet, three.

Suddenly, Nick charged out from his hiding place and knocked Rubi Lee backward onto the muddy riverbank. "You're done!" He pulled her up and put her in a headlock.

Knowing she was no physical match for him, Rubi Lee extended her arms out in a conciliatory position.

"It's over, Rubi Lee. Time to let it go and surrender."

"Over? Never!" She reached down with her right hand. Out came her knife. She swung wildly and plunged the knife into Nick's right thigh. He roared in pain. Blood oozed from his leg. He released Rubi Lee and grasped his thigh.

Wasting no time, Rubi Lee lurched forward and buried the blade in his side. Nick collapsed to the ground. Blood from his wounds mingled with the rain and formed a red rivulet.

"Nick!" Daisy screamed out.

Rubi Lee turned and saw the canoe was close to landing. Bloody knife held high, she leaped at Daisy. They hit the bottom of the canoe in a screaming tangle of arms and legs. Daisy reared up and clutched Rubi Lee by the throat. Squeezing with tired hands, Daisy locked eyes with her nemesis.

"You are *done!*" Daisy screamed and squeezed tightly. She relished how Rubi Lee slapped at her arms, eyes bulging. A violent wave crashed into the canoe and propelled it back into the roiling river. Water sloshed over the edges, causing Daisy's foot to shoot out from underneath her. Unbalanced, she twisted to her right and lost the advantage when she fell on the side of the canoe, jolting her ribs.

Rubi Lee slammed her elbow into Daisy's shoulder and raised Timmy above Daisy's head.

On her back, Daisy let loose a powerful kick and landed it squarely on Rubi Lee's raised arm. The blow knocked Timmy out of Rubi Lee's hand. The knife flew through the wind and rain, flipping blade over handle until it plunged into the water.

"No! Timmy!" A panicked Rubi Lee scrabbled to the side of the canoe. Peering over, she howled, "*Timmy!* Come back!" Rubi Lee frantically pawed in the freezing water, staring as the blade spun below on the surface. Suddenly, Zeke's face appeared as Timmy sank to a watery grave.

Time screeched to a halt.

"Your turn, you monster!" Daisy hauled off and kicked Rubi Lee in the face. Rubi Lee's head snapped back; blood shot from her nose and splattered her face. Punching, wrestling, trying to survive, neither woman was aware of the rapidly approaching, raging waterfalls.

Nick lay on the ground, eyes squeezed shut against the white-hot pain shooting through his thigh and side. He rolled onto his opposite side to see the canoe. All he could see were arms and legs flailing. On the shore lay the rope line, coiled like a wet snake. *Oh my God! They're gonna crash over the falls!* Frantically, he searched for something to help get the boat back.

Strength waning, he crawled to the slowly unfurling coil. He threw a glance out to the river and saw the other end of the rope was still tied to the bow.

The pain radiating in his side and leg was unbearable,

but the thought of losing Daisy was greater. Blood continued to leach from his wounds. Numbness and weakness began their slow assault into his body. He reached out and gripped the end of the rope. The line was taut but slippery in his soaked hands. With all his might, he tried to halt the pull of the current on the canoe—but Mother Nature was too powerful. The engorged river would not yield.

Crippling fatigue enveloped him. He had to make a snap decision. *I will die before I let the love of my life die.*

Slowly, he looped the rope around his arm and allowed the force of the current to pull him like a leaf into the water, down river. The ice-cold water dulled his pain. Ahead he saw the canoe with the two combatants' arms and legs thrashing.

He knew if he made it to shore, he could tie the rope around a tree.

Nick knew trying to kick with a shredded leg was most likely useless. *Nick, try! Do it!* He bit through his lip at the pain when he tried to kick. He threw his head back and screamed into the storm.

He spun like a leaf in the whirling river. It turned and directed him toward a large boulder. Nick felt a surge of hope. *If I could get over there and brace myself against it*, he thought, *I can help Daisy.*

Breathing rapidly, he dog-paddled cross current to the rock. As the water became shallower, the riverbed scraped at his feet. Grasping at the rock, he braced himself with his good leg and with waning strength, held on to Daisy's lifeline.

In the canoe, the battle raged on. Daisy and Rubi Lee's screams and curses sliced through the wind. The rope snapped tautly, forcefully, knocking the women off balance, out of the boat—and over the falls.

"NO! Daisy! No!" Terror flooded him. His shoulders felt pried from their sockets. Every muscle shrieked. The rope slid through his trembling, cramped hands and the canoe plunged into a watery grave into the basin.

He dog-paddled through swirling water to the side of the waterfall. Exhausted, he hoisted his head and shoulders onto a flat rock. He was too exhausted to heave his entire body up. Water he'd ingested sloshed in his stomach. He peered over the edge of the waterfall. The glint of the canoe's hull stared back. It was trapped on a fallen tree.

It was if someone hit pause on a tape recorder. Just seconds earlier, the air was thick with screams; all Nick heard now was the rumble of the falls.

Unblinking, he gazed left and right. Brown water surrounded him, carrying debris away from him to be pushed over the falls.

"Daisy! Daisy! Answer me please! Please!"

Only the deafening crash of water responded. The stone on which he lay chilled him to the core. His sobs tore through the wind. Blood and tears dribbled into the river. Fatigue won.

* * *

Caught in a hammock of thick intertwined branches, Daisy lay. Her eyes fluttered open. She stared at the fierce, cruel sky. Rain pelted her face. Her ribs throbbed; she tasted blood. *Where am I?* The thundering of the falls and the stale, muddy taste of the river brought it all back. *The canoe . . . Rubi Lee . . . falling.*

Slowly, Daisy untangled herself and fell into the mud. She landed hard on her wrist; sharp pain shot through her arm.

She managed to get on her knees. Throbbing pain radiated in her wrist. *It's broken*, she thought, cradling it to her chest. Staring up at the falls, she could not believe she survived. *Oh God, did Rubi Lee?*

Glancing around, she got a grisly answer. Several feet off the ground to her left, Rubi Lee hung from a splintered pine tree.

Daisy's brain did not absorb at first. She just stared at the limp body balancing on a branch. The severed, sharp edge of the broken tree had pierced Rubi Lee through the middle of her back. Her head dangled backward, her arms outstretched. Blood seeped from her fatal wound.

Daisy pushed herself up with one arm, and cradling her wrist, stumbled to the macabre sight.

Her head looks like a dangling piñata, Daisy thought limping toward her. The blood trickling from the corner of her thin mouth was the only visible movement. Still, Daisy needed to be sure. She grabbed a stick and poked her.

"He . . . help . . . help me . . . please," Rubi Lee gurgled.

Emotions of every kind—anger, hatred, pity—surged through Daisy. A quick evaluation of her injuries, coupled with flowing blood, Daisy knew Rubi Lee's time on earth would soon be over.

Daisy leaned in close to Rubi Lee's face and said, "Enjoy your time in Hell."

"Please . . ." Rubi Lee's eyes rolled back in her head.

Daisy spat at the dead woman.

Turning away from the corpse, Daisy ran in search of her husband.

* * *

Nick lay still to conserve whatever energy he had left—until he was roused by the scream. He looked up and saw Daisy. "Daisy! Daisy! Up here!" He waved from the top of the falls.

The feeble wave caught her eye. "Nick!" Daisy scrambled to him as fast as her beaten body allowed.

"Oh God! Nick!" She squatted next to him. Tenderly, she lifted his head. Fear clenched her heart at the sheet-whiteness of his face. His beautiful, full mouth was turning blue.

He slowly opened his eyes and smiled. "You're here. I knew you'd find me. Please don't leave me. Please."

A sob caught in her throat. "I'm not going anywhere. Help will be here soon."

He grimaced in pain. "Ah, my leg and my side. She . . . she stabbed me."

"She's dead. Don't talk." She cradled his head.

In the distance Daisy heard the barking of dogs. *Thank God!* She screamed, "Over here! We're over here!"

She glanced down at her husband's face. His eyes were closed. He looked angelic, peaceful. "Nick, wake up! Help is here! Wake up!" She gently tapped his chilled cheek. "Stay with us!"

He opened his glassy eyes and peered at her.

"Stay with me!" Fear engulfed her, listening to his shallow breathing.

"Daisy. I'll...always...love you," he gurgled as he reached out his hand. His eyes rolled back.

"Nick! Stay with me!" She wailed. "I can't live without you!"

His head lolled to the side.

"No! No! Help me! Help me please!" Daisy's screams tore through the trees. "Nick!"

German shepherds strained toward them through the rain. Their handlers called, "We found them! Get down here!"

Within minutes FBI agents descended on them. They found a crumpled Daisy, sobbing on her husband's chest.

"Daisy! Daisy!" The voice was familiar.

Her head snapped up. "Jaida! Oh God! Help us!"

Jaida knelt and threw her arms around Daisy. "I'm here! We're going to help you and Nick." Jaida called out to an agent. "He's in bad shape. Tell the chopper our location, ASAP!" She placed two fingers onto Nick's neck. "He has a slight pulse. Daisy, we need to keep him in the cold water. It will stop the bleeding. We are going to airlift you both out."

The sound of the chopper drowned out the falls. The water swirled in white eddies; leaves and sticks blew around from the power of the chopper. A black basket slowly descended from the chopper, manned with an EMT. Several agents gently loaded Nick into the basket.

Daisy broke away from Jaida and clutched Nick's head and kissed him on the mouth. "I love you. You're going to be okay!" At Jaida's signal, the basket rose from the ground.

Wind whipped and the harsh, bitter rain did not let up.

Daisy did not feel the elements; she only felt the metal sides of the basket holding Nick. Arms extended to the sky, she sobbed watching her beloved being hoisted skyward— through rain and wind—in a swinging, twisting basket. *Will he be alive when I get there?* The Air Medical Service Personnel carefully lifted Nick into the chopper and gave a thumbs up.

Daisy gasped with a sudden realization. "Mom! What about my mom?!" Daisy yelled to Jaida.

"We found her and we're taking her to the same hospital. She'll be okay," Jaida yelled back over the pounding of the helicopter rotors.

"Oh Jaida. I don't know what to do! Nick could die! My whole world is shattered!"

Jaida struggled to keep it together. *Don't cry! Your friend needs you to be strong!* Jaida thought. Squeezing her tightly, Jaida promised her, "I will be with you later. I promise. For now, you need to go with Nick."

Jaida secured her friend into the basket and gave the signal. Right before the basket ascended into the sky, she cradled Daisy's face and touched her forehead to hers.

"Daisy, you're going to be okay. I'll come to the hospital. Everything will be okay."

Jaida waved the signal and Daisy was lifted to the helicopter. Inside, the EMT had hooked Nick to a portable ventilator. IVs snaked from his arms. Daisy held his hand and caressed his damp head. The *thup thup thup* sped up as the thick blades sliced through the wind. With a sudden lurch, the chopper tilted forward and flew off into the gray sky like a gigantic metal dragonfly.

CHAPTER 36

Wesley Hines began his newscast with his usual, hearty greeting. "Good evening, Philadelphia and tri-state area. We begin tonight with a story about an attempted burglary at the hallowed Philadelphia Art Museum. Allegedly, a band of burglars shattered a large window on the west side of the museum. We go live with—"

He was interrupted by his co-anchor handing him a folded piece of paper. His dark eyes flicked to the co-anchor, who nodded gravely. Wesley read the note. His handsome angular face suddenly became veiled with shock and sadness. He inhaled deeply before raising his worried eyes to the camera.

He continued, "Pardon me. In a few moments, we will go to Lauren Schade." He cleared his throat and continued. "We just received word that our own Daisy Tyson and her husband, mayoral staff member Nick Tyson, were hospitalized earlier today with life threatening injuries. At this time, we do not know exactly what happened. As we get more information, we will pass it on. We certainly hope their injuries are not serious. Now, we go live to Lauren."

* * *

In Nick's cramped hospital room, four pairs of eyes were glued to the television. "When I called Leo, our van driver, he almost cried! I felt so bad!" Daisy said to Nick, Winston, and Jaida. "I miss those guys so much—even crazy Randy, my cameraman." She clicked off the television. "You guys are great for stopping by. I don't know what we would have done without you."

"We're so sorry all three of you went through that nightmare—*again*. I'll probably burn in Hell for saying this, but I'm *glad* Rubi Lee is dead," Jaida declared.

"We'll never be able to thank you enough. *We* could be dead . . ." Daisy's voice trailed off. She cast a look at Nick and squeezed his hand. Several tears rolled down her cheeks.

"Don't cry, Daiz. We're all fine and Rubi Lee is dead." Jaida jumped from the plastic chair and hugged her friend.

"I know she's dead. It'll take a while to digest all of this," Daisy replied.

Nick steered the conversation elsewhere. "How long do you need to be in that boot?" he asked, pointing at Winston's ankle.

"Doc said six to eight weeks, but I'm hoping for a quick recovery," he replied. "I'll heal up in about two weeks and back to running within three."

"Wait, what now, big boy?" Jaida cast her eyes on Winston. "You are going to follow the doctor's instructions, *verbatim.* I need you all healed up for the big day." Jaida patted Winston on the shoulder.

"Big day?" Daisy asked as she and Nick traded a confused glance.

Jaida raised her left hand and turned the back of it to Daisy and Nick. She wiggled her fingers. Daisy and Nick's eyes were drawn to the ring: two shiny diamonds flanking a deep blue sapphire set in a gold band. The blue of the sapphire leaped against her beautiful mocha skin. "Daisy Tyson, will you be my maid—or is it matron, since you're married—of honor?"

"Oh my God! You're engaged! And yes of course!" Daisy shot from the chair to give Jaida a big hug. Daisy grabbed Jaida's hand. "Win, this is beautiful!"

Nick attempted to sit up to congratulate them but winced. The stitches in his side pulled his tender skin. "I'm so happy for you guys! Sorry I can't hug you!" He reached out to Winston for a handshake. "Congratulations man! I guess we all need to heal up and be one hundred percent. There is going to some major partying going on."

Winston rolled over to Nick's bed. "You got that right, brother!" He grasped Nick's hands with his. "Would you consider being my best man?"

Nick's eyebrows shot up. "Only if you pay me!" Nick joked. "You know it. I'm honored."

"Thanks. Who knows when we'll tie the knot— probably within a year, right Jaida?"

"That's the goal. But we need everyone all better, including Annie," Jaida said.

"Mom's tough. She'll probably heal faster than any of us. She wanted to come visit, but they carted her off to PT," Daisy said. "She sends her love and thanks."

Jaida's phone dinged a reminder. "Hate to end this party, but we need to get going to the airport. Our plane leaves in two hours."

"We'll never be able to express our gratitude for saving all of us," Daisy said.

"You're welcome. But don't sell yourselves short. *You're* the one who battled with Rubi Lee in a freakin' canoe on a raging river!" Jaida said and turned to Nick. "And *you're* the one who waded through a freezing river to help save everyone, as you were bleeding like a pig!"

Silence fell over the room until Daisy quipped, "I should write a book about all this craziness."

They all laughed, and Nick added, "It'd make a hell of a movie too!"

Jaida laughed. "We'll be in touch soon. In the meantime, take care and get better." Jaida and Winston hugged their friends gently. "Love you guys!"

"Love you too," Daisy said, watching Jaida wheel Winston down the hall.

She plopped down on Nick's cramped hospital bed. "I knew they would get married. They're meant for each other," Daisy said. She glanced at Nick, whose eyes were closed.

"Guess your meds knocked you out." She took his hand and settled in for a catnap.

* * *

"Knock! Knock!" said a nurse carrying a bouquet of flowers. "How's everyone feeling?"

Daisy and Nick sat up, still in the clutches of sleep.

"Hi, oh they're beautiful," Daisy commented. "We're feeling pretty good."

"I'm glad. I'll place them up here." The nurse placed

the brilliant bouquet on the institutional dresser.

"Oh, how pretty. Wonder who they're from?" Daisy sat up and rubbed her eyes. She walked to the dresser and plucked the note from the vase.

"They're from Ira and Henderson wishing us a speedy recovery. They said they have two barstools reserved for us at the *new* Black LaSalle."

Nick smiled at Daisy. "Great news. Maybe we should take a weekend away to DC? We could visit those guys and do the tourist thing?"

"Sure." She began to gently pick at the flowers and rearrange them. Nick's low chuckle made her turn around.

"What?" she said when she realized he was staring at her.

"I think you should go back to work. The doctor said the cast will protect your wrist and I know you—you're getting antsy sitting around here."

Daisy thought for a minute, knowing all too well that he was right.

"I don't want to leave you here alone. The doctor said your recovery could take up to two weeks."

"Daisy, I'll be fine. I can get work done here and your mom is my physical therapy partner. You can come visit every night after work."

Daisy stroked his face and batted her eyelashes. "I *do* kinda miss being at work," she confessed.

"I know. So that settles it." He laughed.

* * *

Ten days later, Nick was discharged from the hospital. The doctors were impressed with his progress in physical therapy and his overall recovery. He and Daisy thanked the staff profusely and wished them a Merry Christmas and happy holiday season.

"Ready?" asked the nurse who helped Nick into a wheelchair.

"You have no idea!"

He was wheeled outside into a bitter winter day, to Daisy's new Jeep. "I can't wait to sleep in our bed," he said to Daisy when they pulled out. "I miss your warm body."

"I can't wait to have you back. Gussie misses you too," she laughed. "And I'm sure you're *really* sick of hospital food, aren't you?"

Nick chuckled. "That's an understatement!"

She turned into their driveway and pointed at the living room window. "Look! There's Gussie. She can't wait to welcome you!"

"Ah, home sweet home." A broad, happy smile spread across Nick's face. "Let's go."

Daisy unlocked the back door and helped Nick into the house. Soon, he was settled on the couch. He laid his head back and closed his eyes. *I'm so happy to be here, especially after what we've been through.*

"Before you doze off, I'll head to the store. I think we need to have a celebratory dinner."

"I like it."

* * *

Daisy dropped the grocery bags on the counter. She smiled broadly when she heard Nick's laughter from the other room. Snippets of conversation floated into the kitchen. *It's Winston*, she knew. After putting away the groceries, she poured two glasses of red wine and joined Nick on the couch.

Cheers from a college football game rang out from the television. The fire she built before shopping crackled and popped in the fireplace. Their short, plump Christmas tree twinkled and delicately scented the room with pine.

Nick hung up and took the glass of wine from Daisy. "Cheers!" They took a sip. "Winston sends his love."

"I'm glad. I'm excited for their wedding, even though it isn't until next summer."

"Me too." He took a long sip of wine and placed his glass on the side table. He turned to Daisy. "So, you and I have known each other for what? Like ten or eleven years?"

Daisy cocked her head. "Yup, since the end of sixth grade. That's when you first came down to Cab Station. So like twelve years? Why?"

"Well, before Win called, I was thinking about everything we've been through in the last ten years. Think about it, Daiz. We kind of helped to figure out—when we were *fourteen*—who murdered my Great Uncle Clay. Then we didn't speak to or see each other for like seven years, and then . . ." He yawned.

Daisy continued, "And our paths finally crossed again on the way to Hoot's funeral. Following that, we accidentally got involved in Victor's smuggling ring."

"Yeah, and you got kidnapped by Zeke and Rubi Lee, who almost killed all of us in the garage at the park."

"And to finish the trifecta? Rubi Lee and her murderous, wacko plan of getting even with us." Shaking her head, her curls—in a new asymmetrical haircut to camouflage Rubi Lee's hack job—swung across her shoulders. "Insane," she mumbled and took a deep sip.

They sat back on the couch and watched the orange flames dance. Gussie leaped up on the couch and nestled in between them.

Nick placed his hand over hers and whispered, "I don't know about you, but I've had enough near-misses to last me a lifetime."

Daisy rolled her head to the side and saw he closed his eyes. She shut her eyes and rested her head against his shoulder. "Same here."

The End

Acknowledgments

My Framer: Without your wildly creative mind, this book may still be languishing on my laptop.

My gifted, enthusiastic, and supportive editor, Kristen Hamilton: Thank you for everything. You're right, we do make a great team.

Cheryl and Ed: What would I do without your constructive criticism and knowledge of cars? Your time and feedback are invaluable.

Thank you to my other beta readers.

Police Captain Terrence McGrath, Retired: I loved picking your brain about police procedures. You're a gem. Thank you.

As always, my gratitude to those who inspire me: my family, friends and all my readers. I am truly grateful for all your support, enthusiasm, and help. Happy reading.

About the Author

Holly began her writing career in 2015. Her first book, *A Letter for Hoot*, was published in 2017 and became a finalist for the Indie Book Award by *TopShelf Magazine*. The sequel *Hot Ice, Cold Blood* was named Finalist for Thriller of the Year by Indie Brag, Finalist for the Killer Nashville Silver Falchion Award for Best Thriller, and Finalist for Thriller of the Year by the Independent Author Network. *The Even Game* is the final novel in the Taylor–Tyson: A Decade of Danger trilogy.

Holly lives outside of Philadelphia with her husband John.

To learn more please visit www.hollyspofford.com. You can also follow Holly on Instagram @hssauthor and Facebook @ Holly Spofford Author.

Made in the USA
Columbia, SC
02 April 2022

58414389R00185